---------- ★ ----------

Claire had to move away from the man and step back for the paramedics to take over. She knew that. But she had been trying to find any indication of life and had just seen a flicker of something when the hand touched her shoulder.

She forced herself to back up and watch Jed be swarmed by two T-shirted young men. Like sparks of light, they flitted around him, not moving him yet, checking his pulse, machines flying out of the back of the ambulance.

Another spotlight was aimed on the scene, and suddenly it turned as bright as day. She took another step back and realized she had other work to do. She had to stop focusing on Jed, let the doctors do their work and turn toward the crime scene. Find out what had happened here and who had played a part in it.

She looked down. But the first thing she needed to do was wash all the blood off her hands.

---------- ★ ----------

"Logue does everything right in *Dark Coulee*.... Highly recommended."

—*Mystery News*

"Small-town life is described here with informed sensitivity, and the Wisconsin bluff country is vividly painted by a skillful and smooth writer."

—*Dallas Morning News*

Previously published Worldwide Mystery title by
MARY LOGUE

BLOOD COUNTRY

DARK
COULEE

MARY LOGUE

W⦿RLDWIDE®

TORONTO • NEW YORK • LONDON
AMSTERDAM • PARIS • SYDNEY • HAMBURG
STOCKHOLM • ATHENS • TOKYO • MILAN
MADRID • WARSAW • BUDAPEST • AUCKLAND

To Lee, my good neighbor
and
Peter, my dearest companion

DARK COULEE

A Worldwide Mystery/October 2001

Published by arrangement with Walker Publishing Company, Inc.

ISBN 0-373-26398-8

Acknowledgments

I have set the Claire Watkins mystery series in a part of the country I know and love. There are distinct advantages to this, and, of course, problems. I made up the town of Fort St. Antoine, and I wish that I had made up the country, too. There is a Pepin County in Wisconsin. It is a beautiful place to live and only in the positive ways does it resemble the county in my book.

I have many people to thank. For information on law enforcement: Ray DiPrima of the Minnesota Bureau of Criminal Apprehension. Special thanks to Robbi Bannen, Ted Fisher, Tom and Cindy Hanson, and Kay and Chuck Grossman for advice on various aspects of country life. Thanks to the readers along the way: Mary Anne Collins-Svoboda, Marianne and Jim Mitchell, Christine Andreae and Elizabeth Gunn. I must always thank my two sisters, Robin LaFortune and Dodie Logue, for their love and their wisdom. Special thanks to Steve Stilwell, bookman extraordinaire, for advice and support.

Thanks to Pete Hautman for the many readings, the many talks, the many tips on the fine points of writing. I could not live this life without him.

[Coulee] is derived from the French word *couler* which means "to flow." While "coulee" is used in different contexts in different regions, in the hill country of western Wisconsin and southeastern Minnesota it refers to steep-walled, tributary valleys, with sandy beds that are only intermittently occupied by water flow.

—Cotton Mather and Ruth Hale,
Prairie Border Country

DARK
COULEE

—▸ ◂—

It often starts with cloth: sheets, curtains, scarves. I'm struggling to get out of them, to get into them. That vagueness. I'm not sure where I am. The confusion of fear.

Then I know.

I know he's there, waiting for me. I know there's a gun that will go off. I know, once again, I've walked into my own death.

The material, the cloth, is smothering me. I can't breathe. I can't move. I can't see. I'm paralyzed.

And I know he's in danger too. That's the only thing that gets me to move

But I'm always too late.

I come into the clearing just as it ends. The gun goes off. The sheets drop away. He falls at my feet. A sacrifice. Instead of me.

My death leaves.

But I know it's only a matter of time.

What never leaves, what is always with me, is the fear.

Do you think the cloth is the fear?

Maybe, or the very air I breathe.

ONE

LOVE IS A STRANGE FLOWER that blooms in drought, in despair, even in darkness. As Claire dressed for the street dance, she thought about love and wondered if that was what she was feeling. She had been seeing Rich Haggard for over three months, but it wasn't moving very fast. Their courtship had the feel of a slow, courteous country romance. They saw each other once or twice a week. He would come over for dinner; she would stop by for coffee. They had gone to two movies, even went bowling once. That night they had taken Claire's ten-year-old daughter, Meg, with them. Meg was part of the problem. Actually, Claire didn't see it as a problem. The slowness of their dating suited her fine. Claire didn't want Rich to stay over when Meg was at the house; at least not yet. And Claire couldn't stay at Rich's house because she didn't want to hire a baby-sitter for the whole night. The small town of Fort St. Antoine was gossiping enough about her, a deputy, going out with the pheasant farmer, without giving them more to work with.

That's what made this night special. Meg had gone to stay with Bridget, Claire's sister. Rich would pick her up in fifteen minutes. They hadn't really talked about it, but Claire was pretty sure that they would spend the night together. What a perfect evening for love. Unlike the climate in which she and Rich had met—one of the worst seasons of Claire's entire life.

The late-August air smelled sweet with clover and roses. The moon would be full tonight, and the sun wouldn't set until after eight o'clock. The warm air felt soft against her skin as she walked out the back door and looked up at the bluff. Someone else might find it oppressive to live in the shadow of the bluff, but she loved this three-hundred-foot-tall sloping wall of limestone, covered most of the way up with red cedar, birch, black walnut, and sumac. It lifted out of the field behind her house, and she felt sheltered by it. This whole Mississippi River valley had a warmer, softer feel to it, sitting on the eastern edge of the plains. Claire felt ready to move forward with Rich. He was on the quiet side, but stir into him a little, and you found humor and cleverness. And, she suspected, passion.

It had been a long time since she had slept with anyone. Her husband had died a year and a half ago, and she had only slept with one man once since then. That had been a mistake—one she would never forget. That was one of the reasons why this slowness with Rich felt so comfortable to her. He seemed like a man who could bide his time.

Claire walked back into the house and looked at herself in the mirror by the back door. She had done the best she could with the materials at hand. She laughed. That was her mother's voice coming out in her. Such a practical woman. She missed her. Claire twirled in front of her reflection, and her hair lifted off her neck.

RICH LOOKED DOWN at his cowboy boots, good old shit-kickers that they were, and wondered if he could dance in the things. He wondered if he could dance, period. Would Claire want to dance? He supposed so. And the idea of holding her in his arms, even in a crowd of loud, drunken people, took his breath away. He had wanted to hold her since he had met her. Lately, he'd felt like he was about to explode if he couldn't touch her. On this warm, humid summer night, he wanted his skin to melt into hers. He wanted to kiss her neck, put a hand on the small of her back, and spin her around the world. Hell, maybe he would be able to dance after all.

He had polished his boots, and he thought they looked pretty good. Good old Stewart cowboy boots. Like him, they were well worn but comfortable, but with a little polish, they could shine. He knew that Meg was staying at Bridget's; Claire had let that slip out when they talked earlier. He would invite her to stay the night. That way his car wouldn't be sitting in front of her house come the morning light. He had changed the sheets on the bed, cleaned up the bathroom, even scoured the tub, and bought some rolls for breakfast from Stuart's bakery.

He knew that they had been smart to move so slowly, but it had been damned hard on him. When they had first started going out, he had really been careful with her, after all she'd been through, but he'd found her as resilient as they come. Meg wasn't the spunky little ten-year-old girl she was for no good reason.

Rich looked at the clock. He'd told her he would pick her up at seven. Ten minutes away, and he was ready. He walked out the front door and stretched his arms up to the heavens in the front yard. The moon would rise up full tonight. A real harvest moon, red with the rays of the setting sun. Blood red. It would be a beauty. Tonight, he was sure, would be a night he would never forget.

JED SPITZLER STOOD in the doorway and looked out over his land—ripe, golden heads turned toward the rising sun— forty acres of sunflowers. He had taken a risk, but it had worked out, and this fall he would reap the rewards.

Some of the other farmers had laughed at him while putting their fields in the same old crops: corn, alfalfa, soybeans. But he had wanted to try something different.

He knew he appeared a quiet, conservative man, but there

was a side to him that few people knew about. Better that way.

How had Lola talked him into going to this stupid dance? He'd rather stay home and drink a beer or two and watch TV, but she had made him promise. The older kids were going too. Nora would stay home. He didn't want her shuffling about a dance like that. Who knows the trouble she might get into? At twelve, she was old enough to stay home alone. When he was a kid, his mom had left him and his brother alone when they were eight and four. They made out okay.

People babied their kids so much these days. Didn't sit well with him. He told his children they had to pull their own weight, do their chores, and help around the house.

When he thought of Lola, he realized he was tiring of her. At first she had seemed very agreeable, would do anything for him, but lately she had become more demanding. He had already had a wife once; he didn't need another one.

Nora came to the door. "Whatcha looking at, Dad?"

"The crop."

She spun around and threw her hands out toward the fields, then smiled up at him. "All the sunflowers?"

"Yes. Come here."

She came to him, and he pulled her up against his waist, wrapping an arm around her chest and stroking her golden hair. She was his baby girl, but she was getting bigger every day.

RIDING IN THE TRUCK, Claire felt awkward with Rich. She couldn't seem to think of anything to say. She hadn't told him that she had started seeing a therapist. Every time she opened her mouth to mention it, she could think of no way to lead into it. If she told him about the therapist, she would have to tell him about the panic attacks. She didn't want to scare him away with her fears.

They had turned toward Little Rock. The land rolled in green hillocks around them. The bluffs fell away here, and the river would glimmer, then disappear behind the pine trees. It seemed a different landscape from her place in Fort St. Antoine—more bucolic, more intimate—as the bluffline softened.

"How's work?" Rich asked.

"I like my new job as investigator with the department. It's been a quiet week. We had two drunks in the tank and a hit-and-run driver last night."

"I heard somebody got burglarized down in Nelson."

"That's right. Back door was open. They walked in and took a couple guns and a microwave and a case of beer."

Rich started laughing. "Quite a haul."

"Yeah, probably some kids. Don't like the idea of them getting some rifles, but firearms are easy enough to come by around here. I've never lived in a place before where the kids get out of school for deer-hunting season. Certainly says something about the priorities of their parents."

Rich didn't say anything for a moment, then he said quietly, "Hunting isn't so bad."

"I'm not saying anything against hunting. I think a walk in the woods under any circumstances is probably a good thing. But compared to a week of school? Take the kids out hunting on the weekend. Plus the idea that twelve-year-old boys and girls can be tromping through the woods with guns in their hands, shooting at anything that moves, scares me. Meg doesn't get to go anyplace that week. She can stay at home and read."

"I could take her hunting."

"Are you purposely missing the point of what I'm saying here?"

"Yup." He smiled over at her.

"She would do anything with you. She adores you. It kind of worries me."

Rich slowed down as they approached the town. "Hey, her dad died. Every little kid needs a guy in their lives. I'm not a bad guy. Plus, could be she's glad to see her mom happy again."

Claire blushed and looked down at her lap. "That's gotta be it."

Little Rock was a small town built on the north side of the Chippewa River. It was on the way to nowhere, and there wasn't much in the town: a couple of bars, a gas station, a small grocery store, and a feed store. But once a year, it exploded. The town threw a great street dance, and everyone came from the whole county and beyond. Cars and pickup trucks lined the main street of this 134-person town. The street had been blocked off, so Rich pulled behind the gas station and parked in the weeds. He turned off the truck and put his hand on Claire's shoulder. "You seem a little edgy. Are you trying to pick a fight?"

"Maybe."

"Why?"

"Nervous."

"What you need is a beer."

"A beer might help."

RICH FELT THE EYES on Claire. Other men taking barbed looks at her, wanting to reel her in. She looked gorgeous tonight. Gorgeous was exactly the right word for her. She was wearing a sleeveless cotton shirt that was cut low. Like a fruit that had ripened to perfection, her skin looked lush. Her jeans fit her to a T. Her hair was loose and full around her freckled face, and she was wearing ruby lipstick. As they walked up to the street dance, Rich recognized a few neighbors. He and Claire couldn't go many feet without saying howdy to someone. The strains of the old rock and roll tune "Roll Over, Beethoven" floated down the street from the band at the far end.

About three hundred people of all ages were dancing in the street or watching from the sidewalks. People had brought their own lawn chairs and coolers. The two bars in town—Porky's and the Riverside—were selling all sorts of food from stands outside their establishments: cheese curds, barbecue sandwiches, hot dogs, grilled chicken. Porky's had kegs out in front of the bar, and bartenders were serving the lines of people just as fast as they could. For many people in the area, this was the big summer celebration.

When they got close to it, they could see the street dance was in full swing. "Hank Texaco and the Gas Guzzlers," according to the banner hanging over their heads, were playing, whipping the crowd into a dancing frenzy. The sun had set, and the afterglow lit up the clouds into cotton-candy colors.

Near the stage everyone was dancing: eighty-year-old women with ten-year-old boys, older couples who had been dancing together for forty years, and teenagers who flailed around and danced in clusters.

Rich maneuvered Claire up to one of the kegs in front of Porky's and bought them each a beer. A tall, dark-haired man bumped into Rich, making him slosh some beer on his shirtfront. When he turned to see who it was, Rich recognized Jed Spitzler.

"Sorry," Jed said.

"Hey, Jed."

"Rich. How're your pheasant doing?"

"Getting nice and plump. What're you raising this year?"

"I'm trying my hand at sunflowers."

"Maybe I'll buy some as feed."

"No, these are high quality. They're for human consumption, not animals. I aim at getting top buck a bushel."

Rich introduced him to Claire and noticed that Jed looked her up and down. "Looks like you've got some spunk in you," Jed said, staring at her breasts.

Rich didn't like the tone in his voice, but he figured the guy must be loaded already to talk like that. "Let me buy you another beer," Jed said.

"Forget it. This shirt needed a wash anyway."

Jed laughed, nodded good-bye, and walked off.

When Claire took a swig of beer, she took a healthy swig. Rich could tell she was relaxing. In the truck, she had seemed all wound up tight, and Rich wondered how the night would play out.

CLAIRE WOULD THINK BACK to this moment with Jed Spitzler over the weeks to come. What she would remember about him is that he stood tall and straight. His hair was dark but thinning. And his blue jeans were pressed. She assumed some woman was taking good care of him. She was wrong. She wished she would have noticed him better, but she was focused on Rich. The beer he bought her tasted good. It made her feel giddy.

"Thanks for not telling him that I'm a cop."

"Sure. Why's that?"

"Sometimes I don't feel like being one."

TWO

"I THINK RICH IS perfect for my mom," Meg told Aunt Bridget as she tried to put her leg behind her neck. She wanted to show her aunt how agile she was. One of her friends at school had showed her the trick, and she thought it looked really cool, like a swami or something. But her leg would reach only to her ear.

Aunt Bridget wrinkled her nose at Meg and gave her a lopsided, questioning look. "You do?"

"Uh-huh." Meg stared up at Bridget, who was standing above her in the living room. She said she couldn't sit down because she wasn't hardly able to fold in half comfortably. Over seven months pregnant, she was as big as a beach ball. "Sometimes I think I like Rich better than my mom does."

"You do?"

"After I practice this a few more times, I'll show you again. I think with a little practice I'll be able to get my foot back there, don't you?"

"As far as I'm concerned, you can do anything you set your mind to."

Meg sat down on the couch. "Aunt Bridget, maybe you could lean against the wall. You look so uncomfortable."

"I'm fine. So you like this guy?"

"Rich's the best." Meg thought about it for a second. "Almost as good as my dad, but no one will ever be as good."

"That's the truth."

"Hey, Aunt Bridget, what exactly happens when people sleep together?"

Bridget looked even more uncomfortable, if that were possible. "Meg, sweetie, I think you should talk to your mom about that."

"But she said you would be a good one to talk to, since you're the doctor."

Aunt Bridget rolled her eyes to the ceiling, then tilted to one side and flopped straight out on the couch, her head landing in Meg's lap. "I got an idea. You tell me what you think happens, and then I'll tell you if it's right."

AFTER LISTENING TO a few songs, they decided to join the mob when a slow dance started. Rich put a hand on Claire's shoulder and turned her to face him. Then he took her other hand in his and began to lead her through the mass of spinning dancers. She looked at him, and her eyes widened slightly, like a cat saying hello. She smiled and dipped her head.

He pulled her in closer and stepped as gracefully as he could through the crowd. Just a simple waltz. Bless his mom for teaching him how to do the waltz. Claire seemed to be able to follow him, and he slid his arm onto her back, feeling her skin warm beneath his hand. Now that he was here, now that he was dancing, he wanted to do this for the rest of the night.

The air was the same temperature as his body; to move through it was to flow in a warm current. Claire tucked her head into his neck, and they waltzed together as if they had done it many times before. An odd thought crept into his mind: I could live with this woman the rest of my life. He tightened his hold on her, and she snuggled in closer. When the dance ended, he could feel her breath on his neck.

Then the music notched up as the band played a fast one.

Rich hated to let go of Claire, but everyone was jumping and hopping and they would look silly holding on to each other, so reluctantly they separated and started to dance like everyone else. Claire swung her hair back and laughed with her mouth wide open. The Guzzlers were singing about crazy love, and Rich laughed too. God, it felt good to be in love.

When the next song slowed down, they fell into each other's arms, sweating and laughing. They started in close and somehow got closer. The light had dropped from the sky, and the streetlights only lit up pockets of the dark. He felt Claire's breath on his neck, and this time he turned toward her and bent down and found her lips. They were sweet and salty.

What he felt jolted him. He wanted to eat her up. He felt himself wanting more of her, and he held himself back. He kissed her gently, and her lips blossomed under his. Dancing didn't seem like enough anymore.

Suddenly, there was a rumble in the crowd, a woman's scream. Claire pulled back from his kiss. Rich was sure it was just someone having too much fun, but then they started to hear shouts and people yelling for the music to stop.

Claire, the cop again, moved toward the noise. He followed her through the crowd as the band fell silent. As they got closer, he heard a woman yell, "Help! Get some help!"

CLAIRE COULD SEE instantly that the man was in trouble, even in dim light from the streetlamps. A crowd had gathered around the far side of the stage, behind the loudspeakers. A teenage girl was off to the side, whimpering. An older boy was comforting her.

Claire had pushed through the crowd and now found herself standing right over the man, the farmer. What had Rich called him? Jed something.

She knelt quickly and found a faint pulse in his neck. Blood was smeared across his face from his nose, but that just looked bad. Something else was going on here. This guy was barely breathing. She didn't want to move him until she understood better what had happened to him. She wouldn't let him be moved until the ambulance got here. She needed to be sure one had been called.

Claire grabbed a tall, blond kid who was standing next to her. "Has someone called the ambulance?"

"Got me."

"I do got you, buddy. Could you check on that for me?"

The kid looked at her and curled his lip. "Look. I'm a deputy. I'd appreciate your help. Did you see what happened here?"

"No, I didn't."

One of the band members jumped down off the stage and told Claire, "We called nine-one-one on our cell phone. They said they'd be here in fifteen. Where they coming from? Over by Durand?"

"I sure hope so." Claire felt a hand on her shoulder and half turned to see Rich standing next to her.

She asked Rich, "Could you watch over him for a moment? Keep people away. I need to get some order here."

Then she turned back to the band member. "Did you see what happened here?" He might have been Hank Texaco; she wasn't sure. He had a big thick mustache and long, thin hair pulled back in a ponytail.

"I don't really know. With the lights on us, we can't really see much in the audience. I didn't see anything. Then this woman started screaming, and some other people ran over in this direction."

"Do you know who the woman was?"

"Young, blond hair, I didn't see her very good."

"Could you get them to shine one of those lights over this way?"

"Absolutely." He climbed on the stage and shouted an order. Suddenly a spotlight pointed her way.

Claire took advantage of the light and commanded everyone's attention. "I'm a deputy sheriff. There's been an accident. Please, everyone stand back. We need you to keep out of the way. And is there a doctor or nurse available?"

Rich helped her move people away from the scene. But no doctor or nurse came forward to help. Claire knew she needed to look at Spitzler again.

She kneeled down next to the man again. He looked like he might be dead already—the way his body sank into the ground, the way his eyes were half open but unseeing. She touched his head, and he didn't move. It looked as if someone had punched him. That had probably caused the bloody nose.

With the light from the stage shining on Spitzler, she was able to see the dark pool of blood he was lying in. It stained the side of his shirt, telling her where the wound might be.

Blood, and she had no gloves. Claire was very careful to keep her hands away from it as she checked him over.

As she kept tentatively exploring, she noticed a sticky spot on the side of his ribs. She lifted his shirt and saw the slice. A knife wound. Maybe hit the lungs, possibly even the heart. If it had found that mark, he was gone.

THREE

THE LIGHT FORMED a circle around the two of them. People had all stepped back, afraid to be touched by the spotlight. Rich stood just on the edge of the darkness, watching Claire. She had taken charge of the scene. After clearing an area around Spitzler, she knelt by him, gently checking him over. Lovely white-shouldered woman bending over bloody body of a dark-haired man. The scene looked ancient.

What had happened to Jed Spitzler? And why? The man didn't look good to him.

Rich watched as Claire lifted up Jed's shirt. He was close enough to see the gash in his side, the blood oozing out of it. He touched Claire on the shoulder and asked, "Is there anything you need?"

"Do you have a piece of cloth, something for a pressure bandage?"

He reached in his pocket and pulled out a clean white handkerchief. Claire took it from him, folded it smaller, then pressed it hard into the wound.

She turned her face to him, and he could see how focused she was on what was in front of her. "I don't know if he's still alive. I'm afraid if he doesn't get help soon, he won't make it. Can you watch for the ambulance and direct them here? We don't have any time to lose."

Rich walked through the crowds of people toward the road that led to Durand. The ambulance would be coming from that direction. The street dance had deflated, like a balloon with the air popped out of it. People were huddled together, talking and drinking. No reason to quit drinking.

Once they took Spitzler away, the band might even start up again.

Rich hit the street and walked past the last building in town. Something had been within his grasp, and now it seemed gone. Claire had changed in front of his eyes. Did he really know what he was doing, getting involved with a woman like that? Her work was all-consuming. He raised pheasants, and in the winter he read books and fixed old chairs. She went after killers and handed out speeding tickets. Where would their lives intersect? But he was in love with her. He would have to keep walking forward and see where this road would bring them.

Far up the street he heard the shriek of the siren, pulsing through the night.

CLAIRE HAD TO MOVE AWAY from the man and step back for the paramedics to take over. She knew that. She felt a hand on her shoulder, pulling her away. A sheer plastic glove covered that hand. They would know what to do with him. But she had been trying to find any indication of life and had just seen a flicker of something when the hand touched her shoulder.

She forced herself to back up and watch Jed be swarmed by two T-shirted young men. Like sparks of light, they flitted around him, not moving him yet, checking his pulse, machines flying out of the back of the ambulance.

Another spotlight was aimed on the scene, and suddenly it turned as bright as day. She took another step back and realized she had other work to do. She had to stop focusing on Jed, let the doctors do their work, and turn toward the crime scene. Find out what had happened here and who had played a part in it. If she needed to, she could go to the hospital later, after she had gathered what information she could at the dance.

She looked down. The first thing she needed to do was wash all the blood off her hands.

ON HIS WAY BACK to Claire, Rich ran into his nephew, Eric Duvall. The kid would have walked right by him if Rich hadn't grabbed him by the arm. At first Eric tried to throw him off, then when he saw it was Rich, he smiled. "Hey, Uncle Rich."

"Where you heading?"

"Home. Not much going on here."

Rich had always taken an interest in Eric. His parents let him run a little wild, and Rich tried to encourage him to make something of his life. He thought Eric was smart and should go on to college, but none of his friends were going to. That made it hard for Eric to consider it. All he wanted to do was take engines apart and put them back together. "You need a lift?"

"No, I'm on the bike."

Rich had forgotten that Eric had bought a little dirt bike a few months ago. He had put in a few days helping Rich out with the pheasants to earn some money. "You interested in helping me with the birds this fall?"

Eric's smile cracked his face. "Sure thing."

"Hey, you know what happened to Jed Spitzler?"

"No. I just saw all the commotion."

"Do you know his family?"

"Not well, but I do know his son, Brad. He's a year ahead of me in school. Kinda quiet, keeps to himself. Seems like an okay kid."

"What is he, a senior?"

"Yeah, lucky duck, he's graduating this spring."

"Who else in the family?"

"He's got two younger sisters."

"I remember their mom died, didn't she?"

Eric shrugged. "Yeah. It was a while ago. I think I was about twelve or thirteen. Some kind of farm accident."

CLAIRE STARTED TO look around for Rich. He had been standing next to her when she was kneeling by Spitzler, but then he had gone off to direct the ambulance. She couldn't see him in the crowd, but she figured if she stayed near the stage, he would show up.

The paramedics were sliding Spitzler onto a gurney. He didn't move or react as they rolled him from side to side. She shivered. That was bad. No movement, not even in reaction to pain, was certainly a bad sign.

People were quiet as they watched him being lifted on the sling. Then a scream split the air, high and keening. It was a sound Claire would never forget, a half-animal howl.

Claire turned to see the woman who had made the sound. A dark-haired woman wearing a flowered dress launched herself at the entourage. Her hair flew around her head like it was full of electricity. She looked frantic and all charged up. Probably in her late thirties, although she was dressed like a teenager.

"Jed!" she screamed as she tried to get to him.

A large man with a cowboy hat grabbed her arm, but she shook him loose and reached the side of the gurney. She tried to touch Spitzler, but the paramedic grabbed her and blocked her way. She fought to get near him, and again Claire was struck by the animal intensity of her.

"Let me go with him," she begged. "I'll ride in the ambulance. Please, let me be with him."

The paramedic told her, "We can't do that, ma'am. You'll have to meet us there."

As Spitzler was loaded into the ambulance, the woman stood and watched and shook, her arms wrapped around her body and her hair covering her face. She looked as if she might collapse.

Claire had started to move toward her when the man with a cowboy hat stepped up again and tried to wrap an arm around her shoulders.

The dark-haired woman screamed and pushed him away. "Don't you touch me. How do I know you didn't do this? You've hated him since day one."

The cowboy shook his head and walked away.

Claire walked over to the hysterical woman and asked her, "Can you tell me what happened here?"

The woman looked at Claire as if she were a freak. "What do you want? Just leave me alone."

Claire reached out to touch the woman's arm, but she pulled away.

"I need to find out what happened here. I'm a deputy sheriff. Can you tell me your name?"

"Why'd you want to know that?"

"I need to find out what happened to Jed."

"Yes. I can tell you. But I need to get to the hospital. His kids already left, I think."

Claire kept her voice low and reasonable and stood right in front of the woman. "I'll see if I can get you a ride. But if you'd be good enough to answer a few questions first."

The woman wiped her face and sucked in her tears. "My name is Lola. Lola Anderson."

When Lola lifted her face, Claire saw that she wasn't a bad-looking woman, but her skin was pockmarked, and she was older than thirty, maybe into her forties. "Did you come with Jed tonight?"

"Yeah. We were having a good time. Jed doesn't like to go out so much, but I got him to come tonight."

"So what happened?"

"Can I tell you my suspicions?" Lola brightened.

"Shoot," Claire said.

"I think this is what happened. Jed and I were standing listening to the music and everything, and then he had to go to the bathroom, he said. So he left. I didn't think too much of it, and I stood there by myself. Then I see Leonard, that's my ex-boyfriend, going that same way." She stopped to see if Claire had gathered the significance of this.

Claire nodded at her to keep her talking. "Was Leonard the man who grabbed hold of you a moment ago?"

"Yeah, that's him. You gotta understand, the two of them don't get along. All because of me. I mean, they might not have gotten along anyway. They're both too damned stubborn, but Leonard pretty much just hates Jed because I left him and went with Jed. He's said as much. You can ask other people. It's a well-known fact. So I know that Leonard went over in that same direction. And then I saw him staring down at Jed when the ambulance guys came and everything."

"But that was after he had been assaulted. How do you know he was anywhere near Jed before that?"

"I think you better seriously question him, and you can call me as a witness to his character if you need that, which you probably will if you're going to take him to court. I had to tell you all of this before I went to the hospital, because I've watched a lot of TV shows, and I know how important it is to track everything down at the scene of the crime."

Claire thanked her. She took the woman's name and number, wrote them on a bank slip from her purse. She looked around to see if any other deputies had shown up. What was taking them so long?

Lola's face crumpled as she asked, "I need to get to the hospital. Do you think he's going to die?"

Claire answered truthfully. "He didn't look good to me.

When some other deputies arrive, I can try to arrange a ride.''

"No. I can't wait that long. I've got a friend here.'' Lola ran off, her dress flowing behind her.

AFTER QUESTIONING a number of dancegoers who had seen nothing, Claire finally found an older woman who had been standing near where the attack had taken place—Mrs. Gunderson. She was sitting in a lawn chair with a can of ginger ale in her hands. Her hair was a halo of white curls, and she smiled as Claire questioned her.

A sprightly woman in her late sixties, she told Claire she had taught fifth grade in the local school. "But I'm retired now. I had Jenny in my class. That's Jed Spitzler's daughter. She was such a sweet girl. So smart and full of life. Until the accident. Do you know Jenny?''

"No, I just met Mr. Spitzler for the first time tonight.''

"She was a joy to have in class.'' Her face clouded over. "I haven't seen much of her these last few years.''

"Did you see what happened to Mr. Spitzler?'' Claire asked.

"No, my eyesight just isn't what it used to be. Even with these glasses, I can't make out much. They tell me I have macular degeneration. The middle of your vision goes. I've started to listen to Books on Tape because I can hardly read anymore. I wish I could help you. I didn't even know that was Jenny over there until she screamed.''

Claire didn't remember seeing a young girl near Spitzler. "So the daughter was there?''

"She found him, I think. And her brother. So awful for the both of them. What that family has had to endure.''

Claire thanked her and said she might have to talk to her again.

"Oh, I would enjoy that. Since I'm retired, I seem to

have more time than I know what to do with. You're welcome to stop by my house anytime.''

Claire thanked her. When she turned away from Mrs. Gunderson, she saw that two deputies, Billy Peterson and Steve Walker, had arrived in a patrol car. She went over to tell them what she knew and to have them help her with the questioning.

RICH SAT ON the stage, drinking a beer, and watched Claire work. Jed Spitzler had been taken away. Two more deputies had shown up, but Claire hadn't slowed down at all. She was talking to everyone she could corral, pointing at the spot where Jed had lain, asking them questions, noting things down on slips of paper she pulled from her purse. It was odd to see her working as a deputy in her dancing outfit. He wasn't against women doing anything a man could do, but she just didn't seem to be wearing the right getup for police work. He knew Claire would agree.

This night was shot to hell. He could see that clearly. But there would be other nights. He finished his beer and wondered what he should do with himself. It was nearly midnight—a late night out for him. Might be best just to take himself home. He was sure one of the deputies could drive Claire back. He hated to let go of what he had felt earlier, how she had felt in his arms. He'd sit a while longer and hope she might leave things to her fellow officers, but he doubted it. Just not in her character.

Rich waited until Claire was done talking to the other deputies, then walked over to where she was standing and put an arm on her shoulder. ''I'm wondering what I should do here. Is there anything I can do to help?''

She spun into him and said, ''I'm sorry about this, Rich. Last thing I thought would happen tonight.''

''Well, it is all your fault,'' he teased. She hadn't pulled away from him, and in fact it felt like she was leaning into him more than a little bit. A kiss might not be appropriate for the middle of a police investigation, but it was almost all he could think of. "I had a perfect evening planned."

She looked up at him and said, "I know. But now that I'm investigator, I should probably follow up on this while it's fresh. I'm sorry. I had plans too."

That's what he liked about Claire. She didn't pull away, she didn't back off, she never played coy. She might be slow coming to him, but when she got there, she was there.

"What're you going to do?" he asked.

"Talk to a few more people here. But I also want to talk to his children, and I've heard they went down to the hospital. I'll probably go down to get statements from them. Billy can take me. You don't need to stick around through all this. I don't know how long it will take."

"Billy can bring you home?" Rich hated to walk away from her, but she was doing her job.

"Yeah."

Rich thought about what he wanted to say and then decided to say it. What the hell. "You might ask him to drop you off at my house."

Claire thought for a moment, then nodded. "I could do that. I could tell him I left my car there. But it would probably be pretty late."

"I'll leave the door open."

"Okay. I'll see you later."

He pulled her close for a moment and leaned down and kissed her. She kissed him back, quickly and deeply. He walked away with a spring in his step. The old cowboy boots felt pretty good on his feet. He imagined Claire waking him in the middle of the night. What a pleasant surprise that would be.

FOUR

CLAIRE SMILED TO HERSELF as she watched Rich walk away. He didn't quite swagger, but there was a little back-beat in his walk. She was glad she would get a chance to see Rich later on tonight. She had surprised herself by agreeing to stop by, but now she was glad. That last kiss had been full of promise.

Billy came over to talk, and she asked him if he had found anyone else who saw what had happened.

"Not really."

"I find it surprising that no one saw someone get stabbed at a street dance. Everyone was all crowded together."

"What're you suggesting?" Billy asked.

"I'm not sure. Often people are eager to tell what they saw. Was Jed Spitzler not well liked?"

"Could be. Didn't really know the guy myself."

"You feel like taking me over to the hospital? This guy's kids are over there, and I'd really like to talk to them tonight while it's all still fresh in their minds. Steve can stay here and keep on with the questioning."

"You're the boss," he said.

"No, I'm not. I'm not even here in an official capacity."

He slapped her on the back. "Hey, you are the investi-gator of the Pepin County Sheriff's Department. You are as official as they come. If you weren't here now, we'd prob-ably be hauling your ass out of bed."

She laughed. She liked Billy. Straight brown hair cut des-perately short, lake-water blue eyes that sparkled when he smiled, and a lanky body. He was just out of the academy,

and had chosen to work for a small sheriff's office because
he had grown up in this area. Also, he was one of the deputies who liked her. He did not appear to feel threatened by
her, and in fact he went out of his way to let her know how
much he appreciated her help on anything. She found him
completely charming in how open he was to most everything.

A month ago, Chief Deputy Sheriff Stewart Swanson had
assigned her to be chief investigator for the department.
This had caused a commotion, since a couple of other deputies had more seniority, but Swanson had explained that
Claire had more experience and ended his announcement
by commenting that Claire had worked on more murder
cases in a year than all of them combined had ever worked
on. It had the effect of shutting complaints up short-term,
but Claire had felt the resentment from the others. For her
the appointment, because it meant she always worked the
day shift, was a godsend. She could be at home every night
with Meg.

As Claire and Billy were walking toward his patrol car,
a balding man with a big mustache walked up and tapped
Billy on the shoulder. When Billy turned, the man asked,
"What have we got here, son?"

"Pit, how you doing?"

Billy knew Little Rock better than she did. He lived out
this way. "This is Claire Watkins. She's a deputy too. She
was here when it happened, she can tell you more than I
can." Billy introduced her to the mayor, a man by the name
of Pit Snyder.

She wondered how he got the name Pit but figured she'd
ask later. There was nothing fierce about Pit, a short man
with a soft fuzz covering the front of his head. Claire felt
the urge to pet him.

"Jed Spitzler was stabbed. They took him off to the hospital, but between you and me, he looks bad. I'm not sure he's going to make it,'' Claire told him.

"I don't like to hear this. It'll give the town a bad name. Can't believe something like this could happen here at our annual street dance.''

"Do you know Jed?''

Pit shuffled his feet in the dirt. "Not well. He's not, as they say, one of my constituents. He doesn't live in the village. His farm is part of the township. Keeps to himself pretty much. We know the kids, because they go to school in town. They've always been good kids.''

"Have you seen him around tonight?''

"Actually, I think I saw him right before it happened. I had gone to use the john when I walked by him.''

"Was he alone?''

"I believe he was.''

"When you came out, did you see him?''

"I don't recall that I did.''

His use of the word recall struck Claire. This happened ten minutes ago; there hadn't been time to forget it. Why would he have to recall it? She decided not to push it right at the moment. "If you remember anything, please let me know.''

"Always happy to cooperate with the police.''

After he walked away, Claire asked Billy about the mayor. "How well do you know him, and what's the deal with his name?''

"Well enough, I'd guess. He's been mayor longer than I've been around. I know he looks like a real softy, but if you've ever seen him in action at a town council meeting, you'd understand. Once he latches on to something, he won't let go of it. Like a pit bull with their smooshed-in snouts. He holds on forever.''

THE COUNTRY CAN BE so dark sometimes, Jenny thought as she watched for a light to appear in the landscape. Brad drove, and they were silent in the car.

That wasn't unusual. Their dad didn't talk much, and they had gotten used to the quiet. Mom had talked. Jenny remembered the sound of her voice, like water on rocks, glistening.

Jenny wanted a light to fasten her eyes onto. Something to draw her across the land as they drove to see Dad in the hospital.

Her dad, dying.

She had wished for it for so long, she could hardly believe it might come true. Don't talk about it. Don't think about it. You'll jinx it.

She thought of taking another Darvocet, but she decided she needed her wits about her at the hospital. She had first gotten the pills when she had had a root canal. After using them for the pain, Jenny found she liked them so much she went back to her dentist, complaining of more pain. Men doctors always thought women needed pills to handle pain. She was glad she had the pills—they sure had made her life easier. Then she had found someone at school who could get them for her from time to time. She had stocked up.

Add a beer or two to the mix, and she was flying.

She wondered if there was a hell. She kinda hoped there was. A hell where her father was kept bent over, weeding row after endless row of sunflowers. Let them go on for absolutely forever. That should be his punishment.

And it would barely make up for what he had done.

She had sometimes imagined that she was not his daughter—that she had been stolen or switched at birth—and that her real father was trying to find her. He would be a man she could love and respect. She would sit and think about this fantasy in school when she had finished her work. But she had always known that her mom was her real mom.

Maybe she should talk to Brad. The idea floated in her head, and she could almost feel her mouth opening, ready to move, but then she saw a light. A farmhouse light. She watched it as they drove by. Someone had left it on for the last person to come home. How nice.

"You okay?" Brad asked.

"Usual."

"How much you drink tonight?"

"What's it to you?"

"We have to be together on this thing. If Dad, you know, doesn't make it, they might try to split us up and put us in foster homes or something. We might lose the farm. We can't let that happen."

"We won't let them split us up."

"Well, yeah, but you have to get it together, Jenny," Brad said urgently. "Think of Nora. You have to help me out here."

Jenny sat up straighter. She liked the idea of helping Brad out. He had tried to be a good brother, and he never really asked her for anything. He had always been the big brother, and she the little sister who needed him.

Staring out the window again, Jenny thought about her brother. For her, Brad was like that yard light on in the dark countryside. You always knew where he was, and he'd help you find your way home.

As RICH APPROACHED his car, he saw Leonard Lundgren sitting in his old Chevy pickup truck. The lights weren't on, and the engine wasn't running. Rich walked over to talk to him.

Leonard was nursing a beer and staring through the windshield at nothing. He had his cowboy hat pulled on tight, and his ears stuck out underneath it. A dark jean jacket was pulled on over a Lone Star T-shirt. A stylish man Leonard would never be. Big and bruising, he got into fights whether he wanted to or not. Usually he did.

"Hey, Leonard."

"Well, if it isn't Rich Haggard. Don't see much of you around."

Rich thought to say that he didn't hang out at the bars, but decided it would be better to jump straight to the question. "You know anything about what happened to Jed Spitzler tonight?"

"That son of a bitch. 'Bout time someone stuck him." Leonard looked over at Rich, and his look dared him to say different.

"You didn't care for him?"

Leonard started laughing. "You always were a smart-ass, Rich."

"Were you there when it happened?"

"Close enough, my friend, close enough."

"You see who did it?"

Leonard took another swig of beer and said, "Listen, my man. I know who you're hanging with these days. She can come and ask me questions any old time. But I don't have to tell you a thing."

"That's true. Just wondering."

"You're not about to bring my head on a platter to your true love." Leonard laughed a high, rasping laugh while his shoulders shook.

Reaching down with his keys, Leonard started up his truck. The vehicle sounded like it was only running on half the cylinders. Rich backed away and watched him career down the street. Rich remembered him from school. If there was trouble, Leonard was often in the middle of it.

FIVE

BRAD KNEW HE HAD to keep a sharp eye on Jenny. He didn't know what she had taken tonight, but she had mixed it with alcohol. Needles pricked him all over his skin. High alert. Don't let anyone know what's really going on. He was the oldest. He had to try to watch out for them all.

Brad drove carefully as they approached the hospital. He hadn't been there since he broke his arm two years ago. Don't think about that. Just take care of Jenny and find out what's happening to Dad. Then get them all home.

"Do you want to wait in the car?" he suggested when they pulled into one of the spaces reserved for the emergency room.

"No," she said and pushed her door open.

"You know you don't like hospitals."

"Who does?"

He came around and helped her out of the car. She seemed to be able to stand fine. He got right up to her and said, "Jenny, I'm counting on you."

With as sober a look as he had gotten from her in a while, she stared at him. "You don't have to worry. I won't mess anything up."

They walked into emergency side by side, and he was comforted. The bright lights hit him after the dark night, and the interior of the hospital seemed strangely quiet. Maybe they had beat the Saturday-night after-the-bar rush. He walked up to the counter, which looked like a check-in at a cheap hotel, and gave his name to the dark-skinned nurse. "I think my father was just brought in."

The nurse raised her head and gave him a sad smile. "Are you a Spitzler? They took him right in."

"Right in?"

"To the operating room."

"Can we talk to anyone?"

She nodded. "Go sit down, and I'll send someone out to you."

Brad felt his shoulders tighten up on him. Dad was in the operating room. They must be sewing him up. He tried not to let his mind go there, to the blood. He hated to see blood. But not as bad as Jenny. She'd even fainted when she got her first period. That had been a mess.

But she hadn't fainted tonight.

Brad and Jenny sat down in the waiting room. A white-haired woman sat in a corner, shredding a Kleenex. Jenny picked up a *Good Housekeeping* magazine. That was a laugh. She couldn't even make her own bed in the morning. Once she had tried to bake a cake for Nora's birthday and burned it so badly they had to throw the pan out.

An older woman dressed in white came out and called their names. Brad stood up, and she walked over to them.

"They took him in about ten minutes ago. It will probably be a while. He has a very bad puncture wound. Do you know what happened to him?"

Brad shook his head, but Jenny said, "It looked like someone stuck him."

He shot her a glance, and she lowered her head.

"He's lost a lot of blood. I'll let you know when I know more."

"Are you going to give him some more blood?" Jenny asked.

"Yes, I think they will have to transfuse him."

"Oh, Dad won't like that. Remember, Brad, how he

wouldn't even give blood. Said he didn't want his mixing with anyone else's.''

"Yeah, but this is different."

Then Lola barged into the room. Brad felt like hiding.

"What's going on?" she screamed. "How's my Jed?''

Brad always felt like a small tornado had been let loose in a room when Lola entered. He reacted the same way he did to storm warnings: He looked around for a safe place to take cover. Something to read. He grabbed today's newspaper, opened it up, and ducked behind it.

Jenny yelled back at Lola, "He's dying. That's how he is. Your Jed is dying. What do you think about that?''

THERE WAS NO WAY he was going to fall asleep. Rich felt like his body was lifting off the mattress when he thought about Claire coming over later on in the night. What a dream. Waking to her sliding into his bed. He hoped. He assumed that's what she would do. Maybe she would change her mind and want to go home. Maybe she would not even come over. Maybe she would be hungry, and he would make her eggs and toast. He hated the thought of staying up all night, waiting for her.

He glanced over at his alarm clock. The lighted dial told him it was one o'clock in the morning. He had checked on the pheasants before he came in the house. They were all quietly roosting in the sheds. Some of them were large enough to start selling, but he would probably wait another month or so. Take some to the farmer's market in Red Wing. Sell them to the local restaurants in the area. The Harbor View Café had a standing order for them all through the fall. What they did to pheasant was amazing.

He should cook a pheasant for Claire one of these nights. Cook it the way his grandmother taught him. Sauté it in oil and butter in a big cast iron pan, season it well with salt and pepper, then put the lid on, turn the heat down, and cook it until the meat fell off the bone. An old-fashioned way to cook, he knew. Now everyone did everything so fast. Seared the meat. But he still liked it the slow-cooked way. It seemed succulent to him. So good that you had to lick the bones when you had eaten all the meat.

He wondered if he was hungry, thinking of pheasant. He thought about what he had eaten that night and then realized what he was feeling was all about Claire.

He was hungry for her.

He wanted her so bad, he felt like his body was strung to play a song that only she could coax out of it. Think of something else. This will not help you fall asleep.

Leonard. He must tell Claire about Leonard. He would tell her about what he did a few years ago. It would show her what she needed to know about his character.

Shaking his head on his pillow, he tried to relax. The night was streaked with the rays of the full moon. He could see the lake glint in the silver light out his window. The moon floated on its surface like a coin waiting to be picked up.

SHE WOULDN'T STAY LONG, Claire had decided before she even walked into the emergency room with Billy. She would take a short statement from the children and then tell them she would talk to them in the morning.

This part of her job, which she had taken for granted in Minneapolis, felt more invasive down in the country. You were supposed to bring people hot dishes and words of consolation when a loved one was in trouble, not ask them disquieting questions. But the job must go on.

"Why don't we divide up?" Claire suggested to Billy as they walked in the door. "You talk to the boy, and I'll take the girl. I think they'll respond better that way, and it certainly will go faster. What's the girl's name again?''

''I think it's Jenny.''

The nurse nodded them through when they mentioned Jed's name, and they found Jenny sleeping in a chair, Brad sitting next to her reading the paper, and Lola pacing the floor. Lola was talking, but no one appeared to be listening to her.

Billy tapped the paper that Brad was reading and sat down across from him to ask him some questions.

Claire sat down next to Jenny and looked at her for a few moments before waking her. Passed out is really what the girl looked like. Claire guessed her age to be fifteen and wondered if Jenny would be doing better if her mom were still alive. She felt the urge to push back the girl's tumbled straw-blond hair, to arrange it behind her ears so she could see her clear face. The girl had lovely skin. But she herself was not lovely. If she took care of herself, she would be attractive, but her fair looks could be destroyed all too easily.

Claire put a hand on her shoulder and shook her. The girl's eyes flew open, and her mouth rounded itself. A slight compression of breath came. Claire recognized the signs. Fear. She had been waking with the same sense of panic all summer long. Fear of what you might wake to.

''It's okay. I'm sorry to startle you. My name is Claire Watkins. I'm a deputy sheriff here in Pepin County. I need to talk to you about what happened to your dad.''

Jenny leaned forward, shook her hair over her face, and rubbed her hands, palms open, into her eyes. Then, just as suddenly, the girl whipped her hair back off her face, wiped her face with her hands, and said, ''What do you want to know?''

''I heard you found your father.''

"Brad and I did."

"Did you see anyone with him?"

"It wasn't like that. We weren't paying attention. We were actually watching the band and talking, and all of a sudden we looked down, and there was Dad."

"Was anyone else around?"

"There were a lot of people, but it was dark, and no one was real close or anything. I didn't notice anyone."

"What did you do?"

Jenny thought for a moment, her sight turned inward as she recalled the scene. "I tried to figure out what was going on with Dad, why he was lying on the ground. He was making a weird noise, like a stuck pig."

"I don't know what they sound like."

"Hope you never hear one. It isn't really a squeal, it's more like a moan. A high-pitched moan." Then, for the edification of her audience, Jenny let loose with a sound that was halfway between a moan and a squeal.

Brad looked over from his conversation with Billy and shot her a dirty look.

Jenny clapped a hand over her mouth, then lifted it off and said, "I think he was trying to breathe."

"Did you see anything? A knife of any sort?"

"No."

"Do you know who might have done this to your father?"

Jenny rubbed her fingers, staring at her hands. "I got blood on my hands. Brad helped me wash them off."

Claire repeated her question.

This time Jenny answered it. "Not really. Dad kept to himself. I don't think anyone knew him well enough to dislike him."

"Anything else you can tell me?"

Jenny shook her head. Then she ran her fingers through

her hair and looked up at Claire. "But what if he has to stay here, in the hospital? Will they let me and Brad take care of the farm?"

"Where's your mom?"

"She's dead. Farm accident."

Jenny's answer threw Claire for a moment, then she asked, "How old is Brad?"

"Nearly eighteen."

"You have any family close by?"

"Nope."

"I would think so. Can you manage on your own?"

"Oh, sure. We do it all the time."

"Is your father gone a lot?"

"No, he just thinks that we should be able to do most of the work on the farm. That's all."

Claire stood to leave. She wanted to hear what Billy had learned from Brad, see if their two stories matched. Jenny had slumped back into her chair and would be asleep again in no time at all.

Then a nurse walked in. In her fifties, she was dressed traditionally, all in white. Her shoulders were broad, and her face was solid. She stopped inside the doorway and looked at the two teenagers. Jenny's eyes popped open, and Brad dropped the paper. "I'm sorry," she started, but was interrupted by a wail from Lola, who had finally settled in a corner of the room.

Brad stood up, and Jenny looked up at him.

"Is he—?" Brad asked.

The nurse nodded her head. "Yes, he died. He didn't make it through the surgery. I think he had lost too much blood."

"Maybe Dad knew that would happen. Maybe that's why he guarded his blood so carefully," Jenny said to Brad.

Lola slumped into a chair and cried. She was quieter, and

neither of the children looked at her. Claire was surprised by how they acted as if she didn't exist.

"Would you like to come and see him?" the nurse asked.

Jenny turned a panicked eye to Claire. "Do we have to?"

Claire's heart went out to the poor girl. "No, you don't. But often it helps people to see someone after they have died. To get a chance to say good-bye. To know for sure that they are gone. It might be a good idea."

"Will you go with us?" she asked.

Claire looked over at Billy. He shrugged his shoulders as if to say, It's your call. She decided it wouldn't hurt her any to help out these children. "Sure, I'll walk down with you."

Lola started to follow, but the nurse stepped in her way and said, "Let's let the children go first."

Claire was surprised at this act of sensitivity. If Lola went with them, it would all become a scene, her scene.

"Billy, why don't you ask Lola a few more questions?"

He nodded and sat down next to the crying woman.

Claire and the children followed the nurse down the long, quiet hallway. "He's still in the operating room. We put a sheet over him, except his face. You don't have to be afraid of what you might see."

Jenny was walking with her shoulders up near her neck and her arms wrapped around her body. Brad was stiffly walking right next to her, but they weren't touching. They seemed horribly lost to Claire. Was it any wonder? Both parents dead, and both in violent ways. What must the world seem like to them? Unstable, unpredictable, full of danger.

DAD LOOKED more peaceful than Jenny had ever seen him before. His head was tilted back and his eyes were shut, his lips were cracked open a bit as if he were still breathing through them, but she knew that was not so. The room seemed to shimmer with departure.

As the nurse had promised, he was covered with a white sheet, and there was no blood to be seen.

Jenny stood at the doorway and watched Brad go up close to their father and stand at attention near him. The good son. Doing what was expected of him. Brad's shoulder shook, and Jenny knew he was crying. Unlike other boys, Brad wasn't ashamed of crying. It was one of the things she liked about him.

Jenny could tell the Darvocet had worn off, and so had most of the beer. The world was a sharper place when she wasn't on anything. She could see the edges to everything—doors, the sides of the gurney—even Dad's nose came to a crisp point. Like he was made of wood. It scared her to see the world so clearly, which was one of the reasons she usually took something. To soften it all. To make the world marshmallowy.

But Dad looked crisp and clear. She walked up and stood next to Brad and looked down at her father. She wondered where he was right now. Maybe he didn't have to go to hell. Maybe limbo would be bad enough. She knew what that felt like. Never knowing what was to come. Waiting and waiting for it to end. Trapped in a situation. Yeah, that might be a good lesson for him.

She reached out and touched the end of his nose. Something she would never have dreamed of doing when he was alive. She leaned down toward him and said, "Good-bye, Daddy."

She never called him Daddy. She did it for everyone who was watching. Give them the show of the grieving daughter. Tears squeezed out of her eyes.

He was really dead. Gone from their lives forever. She felt incredible freedom. She could now make her father be the dad she had always wanted him to be.

SIX

"YOU LOOK GOOD TONIGHT, Claire." Billy drove easily in the dark, leaning back in the worn seats of the patrol car. He knew the coulee country so well. "I don't think I've ever seen you out of uniform. Now, don't take no offense."

Claire laughed. "I won't file a sexual harassment claim. Thank you for the compliment."

"That top and a little makeup really transform you."

"Thanks, Billy. I don't think they had Coco Chanel design our uniforms. In fact, I know that a female body was never meant to wear them."

"You might be right about that."

They were driving upriver toward Fort St. Antoine. The moon lit the way, but Claire couldn't help watching out for deer even though she wasn't driving. She had had a close call one night when a herd had jumped up on the road in front of her. Somehow she had slalomed through without hitting one, but it had left her ever watchful.

"I hate it when some of the other guys cut you down just because you're a woman." Billy shifted in the car seat next to her.

Claire took his statement in the gut. She knew that went on, but she hadn't realized it was so prevalent. "Oh, don't pay attention. I don't."

"I think most of them are just jealous. Stewy tries not to show it, but it's clear he's a little partial to you. You know, like when he made you investigator. But I think he should be. You've had more experience than the rest of us put together."

"Hey, you can stop a drunk like nobody's business."

"You know what I mean. I dig it that you know so much. I think it's exciting working with someone that's done all the things you've done." Billy paused for a moment, then continued. "It might be easier for me because you were already in the department when I started. First woman and all. I suppose the other guys just aren't used to it. That's their problem. I like working with you."

"I like working with you too, Billy. I feel like I can be myself with you. But don't think you need to stick up for me with the other guys."

He nodded.

Claire brought up the investigation. "Before we get to Fort St. Antoine, I want to hear what you thought of Brad. What did he tell you?"

"Not much. He said Jenny and he were just wandering around at the dance. She was drinking a beer, even though she's underage. He was keeping an eye on her. He said that Jenny could be a little wild."

"I don't doubt that."

"He said they were watching the band, and then they saw their dad on the ground. He was making noise, so they knew he was still alive. Jenny touched him, and they saw where the wound was. But he said they didn't move him at all. They knew not to do that."

"What did you think of Brad?"

"I think he's a nice kid. A little uptight, but a straight shooter. Hard to read emotionally. But, hey, that's not so unusual with us male types."

Claire laughed. They didn't partner up in the sheriff's office like they had in the police force in town, but if they did, she wished she could have Billy as partner. Being able to laugh with someone got you through the worst of it.

"What about Jenny?" Billy asked.

"She told basically the same story." Claire thought of Jenny again. It would be a while before she would forget the look on that girl's face when she turned and asked Claire to come with them when they went to see her dead father. So in need of rescuing. "Hard to know what goes on in that girl's mind. She's on her way to becoming addicted to one substance or another. She's so uncomfortable with herself, it's kinda painful."

"I know what you mean. She looks like she might break if you said the wrong thing."

"Yeah, maybe. I think she's stronger than she looks. I don't know how those two are going to make it through their father's death. What a legacy that family has had."

They were approaching Fort St. Antoine, and she needed to tell him that she didn't want to be dropped off at home, but rather at Rich's house. She liked to keep her life private from her work, but often it was hard as a deputy. A small lie would have to do the trick.

"Could you drop me at Rich Haggard's house? I left my car there."

"Sure, no prob. You two dating?" He looked over at her as he asked the question, probably to see her reaction. Cops did love to ask the probing questions.

"Yes, I would say we are."

"He seems nice. Don't really know too much about him. He's so much older than me. I think my dad went to high school with him."

Claire sat and waited to hear what more he had to say on the subject.

"Dad always said that Rich could do anything he wanted to do. He figures he works with pheasants because they're nicer than most people."

THE FIRST THING he felt was a hand on his forehead, cool and gentle. Then he was being kissed like a soft rain falling

on his face. He basked in it and sighed. Then a whisper in
his ear told him, "You don't have to wake up. Just move
over," and she was in his arms, under the covers. His mouth
full of hair, his body at the ready, and soft, warm skin all
around him like he was swimming in it. It had been so long
since he had been with a woman.

Her mouth found his, and they kissed. She bit his lip, and
he said, "Claire." She rubbed against him and gave a deep
throaty chuckle.

He never opened his eyes. He didn't have to. He knew
her smell, her feel, her sounds. She sang to him, sighs and
coos from the feel of his hands on her body. When his hand
went between her legs, he felt how ready she was for him,
and then he made her wait a little longer. He stroked her
and sucked her and nipped her until her sighs became higher
in pitch, until he knew she was nearly ready to ask for it.

She was down under him, and he rested up on his arms,
his legs locked around her hips. She guided him in, and
then he held still. So they could both be there together. After
this moment of quiet, he started rocking into her, sure and
steady.

She felt like the earth and the sea beneath him, as necessary for his life as anything else in it. For one instant the
boundaries between them disappeared, and then he exploded. He was sent high, and stars danced in his head.

When he moved off and curled around her, he was ready
to fall back into sleep.

He heard her ask, "Was that good for you?"

What a silly question, he thought. It set him off. Instead
of answering, he started to laugh. She rolled into him and
laughed too. Their laughter took the last of their energy,
and they fell asleep wrapped around each other, only to
separate gently in the night, bodies floating loose on the
bed, touching in spots.

SEVEN

ELLA GUNDERSON, retired schoolteacher, walked down the road with the use of a good sturdy walking stick. She knew she looked older than her sixty-eight years, but she was determined not to let that stop her from getting in her daily walk. She figured the reason she looked older was that she walked like she was ancient. Stooped over, hesitant, watching the ground as much as she could. She walked like she was eighty years old. Doddering.

It shamed her, but she knew if she quit walking, she would start to move slower, and her life would become more limited. She walked two miles a day. Had since she retired. She didn't care what the weather was like. If it was forty below zero, like it was a couple of winters ago, she dressed for it. Down jacket, moon boots, glove liners inside polar fleece mittens inside leather choppers. Even a mask so she could breathe the cold air without damaging her lungs.

The cold days actually weren't so bad. They were usually clear and bright, the sun a bright pebble in the sky. The days that were harder on her were the mid-thirties, overcast, wet. The cold penetrated her bones, and she couldn't see worth a darn. But she still walked her two miles.

She knew her route by heart. She never varied it, so there were no surprises. As she walked, she might have heard a cardinal calling from the trees, a hawk screeching overhead. She wouldn't see them, but they were still in her life.

She took the time of her walk to think of her life and organize her day. She tried to read a bit, but more and more she relied on Books on Tape. She wrote some. Before her eye problem, she had had all these plans of what she would do when she retired: write her family history, volunteer at the county historical society, take trips to various places in the world she had never been. But her life was much more circumscribed than it had ever been. Being alone had never bothered her much until she began to lose her eyesight. Being alone and sightless was scary.

Night was the hardest time. She knocked things over, couldn't go out, certainly couldn't drive. So she stayed in and listened to the TV, but relied on Wisconsin Public Radio more and more for her news and entertainment. Bless them for their talk shows and their short stories and their music. What would she do without them?

This morning she was edgier than usual. She wondered how Jed Spitzler was. It was too early to call anyone. She hoped for Jenny's sake that her father would not die. The poor girl had suffered so many losses.

Ella remembered how sweet Jenny had been as a student in her class. One day she had brought Ella a poem about what she thought her teacher's hair looked like and proudly recited it to her. Ella still remembered a line from it: "White as snow, it seems to glow." Ella had cherished it. She probably still had it in one of her files.

Unfortunately, what was really bothering Ella was what she had seen last night. Although she could not see clearly straight ahead, most of her vision was still fairly good. She had been listening to the music when she saw a flash of light out of the corner of her eye. What she had been seeing, she realized later, was the knife that had killed Jed Spitzler.

She hadn't said anything because she wasn't sure Jed hadn't deserved what he got. Plus, she didn't think anyone would take her account very seriously. She knew her testimony would never stand up in court. What defense lawyer wouldn't have a heyday with her loss of vision?

But maybe she should tell someone what she had seen.

RIGHT BEFORE Claire woke up and opened her eyes, she felt fear shoot through her body like a knife twisting in her side. She bolted upright in bed, not knowing where she was for an agonizing moment. Sun painted a landscape of brightness on the opposite wall. Rich's house. His bed. She was okay. Don't flip into panic. Not here, not where Rich can see what it does to you.

Putting her hand over her heart, she willed it to slow down. Sometimes she feared it would give way under the adrenaline flood. Gradually the beating lessened. She sank down into the bed and relaxed.

She crawled back under the covers for a moment and tried to calm down. She wanted to bolt, throw her clothes on, and leave Rich's house immediately, but she would not let herself do that. Her fear was not to control her life. If she was to overcome it, she must fight it off and not let it rule her.

Forget about the dream. Stare at the sunshine.

She was wearing a large T-shirt of Rich's, and it smelled like him—earthy and sweet. In the pit of her, she ached slightly from the lovemaking last night, or rather, early this morning. Wondering what time it was, she tried to find her watch, which she had placed on the bedside table before she had climbed in with Rich.

Eight. Good. She could take her time. Even though she wanted to leave and go home, she would stay and at least have coffee with Rich. Officially she wasn't working today, but Meg would be coming home, and she did want to check in on Jed Spitzler's case.

She could hear Rich downstairs, moving around. What a

pleasant sound. A man stirring in the morning, probably putting coffee on, reading the paper. How long it had been. Domesticity. She missed it.

After a long moment or two of trying to enjoy this instant in her life, she rose from the warm bed. Pulling on her jeans, she decided to keep his T-shirt on. To show that she was not exactly the woman she had been before. To acknowledge his presence in her life. Besides, it felt comfortable. A trip to the bathroom, where she washed her face, swished water around her mouth, and pulled her hair back, and she was ready to meet the quiet world of Rich's kitchen.

"Hey, how'd you sleep?" Rich asked her as she descended the stairs.

"Great," she told him—and she had, until the end. He didn't need to know about her dream. He wouldn't understand.

He walked up to her, wrapped his arms around her, and kissed her. Then he pulled back and said, "I assume you need coffee."

"Desperately."

"I have some of Stuart's delicious caramel rolls. Would you like one of them with your coffee? Or I could scramble up some eggs?"

"I could eat both."

Two old white plates sat on the pine table with knife and fork next to them. Rich poured her a mug of coffee. "I know you like it black."

She sat down at the table and felt touched by his hospitality. She watched as he pulled out a small cast iron pan and poured some oil in it.

"Do pheasants lay eggs?" she asked.

"Yes, but only in the spring. So you'll have to make do with plain old chicken eggs. But these are very free-range chickens, as you will see by the color of their yolks."

"What's different?"

"They're bright orange. Startlingly so." He broke one in a bowl and brought it over for her to see.

"What a beautiful color. Like the sun."

"Yes, regular storebought eggs look so pale by comparison. The color comes from the iron they get by eating grass and other weeds, I think."

Suddenly it occurred to Claire that Rich didn't know what had happened last night. "He died, Rich. Jed Spitzler died. Lost too much blood."

Rich gently poured the eggs into the hot oil and then stirred them slowly. "I wondered. Were you there?"

"Yeah. The kids took it pretty hard. They're on their own now. I felt so sorry for them. Did you say there was one more?"

"Yeah, they have a little sister. I don't know her name. She must be nearly twelve."

"Close to Meg's age." Claire thought of Meg all alone in the world. It had almost happened. She pushed the thought away. "At least they have each other. The three of them. And the oldest boy is nearly eighteen."

"They can't manage that farm on their own," Rich said.

"I don't know. They seem to think they can."

Rich pulled the eggs off the stove, delivered two to her plate, and brought out the caramel rolls. "Tuck in."

She took a bite, and he watched her. "Have you eaten already?"

"Yeah. I got up a while ago. I don't last an hour without some food in me. But it's time for my midmorning break. I'll have coffee and a roll." He paused, then said, "It's odd to be going out with a deputy. What a strange life you lead."

Claire nodded. "Stranger than I thought it would be. When I graduated from the academy, I was young and enthusiastic. My uncle had been a cop. I idolized him when I was young. Recently, looking back on his life, I see how destructive police work had been to it. He was divorced twice, drank too much, smoked too much. But what are you going to do? At first the adrenaline of a new case is exhilarating. I loved it. I'd work all night long, drink far too much coffee. Then have to drink something stronger even to get to sleep. But now I see how that adrenaline takes its toll on the body.''

"Even working down here?"

"It's better, definitely. But you saw last night. I'm not supposed to be working today, but I'll probably run into the office and check out Lola's ex-boyfriend, Leonard something.''

"I talked to him last night," Rich told her after taking a sip of his coffee.

"You what? Rich, you are full of surprises."

"I knew you would ask about him, and I've been preparing.''

"Really?"

"Yes. When you ask me about people around here, I always feel like I have nothing to tell because I've known these people all my life." Rich paused and sipped his coffee. "You gotta understand, when you live in one spot with the same community around you, you assume everyone knows what you do—because they do."

"You've got a point."

"Last night he didn't have too much to say except he didn't care for Jed Spitzler. But I assume you knew that. While I was waiting for you to come here, I put my mind to what I had to tell you about Leonard. Three things occurred to me that you should know. First, and this is just to give you some background, he and Lola have been on again, off again for going on a decade now. They've never been married, but they've lived together and such. Lola's younger than Leonard. She was a friend of his kid sister's. So I do think he feels like he owns her.''

"Lola was sure pointing the finger at him last night.''

"She'd like to blame everyone but herself for the state of her life.''

"Wouldn't we all? What else?''

"Two, Leonard's been known to drink too much and act rashly. He's not alone in that behavior around here. One night, this is about four or five years ago, he was drinking at Barb's Bar, you know where that is? Down by the river, other side of the tracks, between Pepin and Nelson. Anyway, this guy name of Buddy Purdy pisses Leonard off. They're sitting drinking at the bar next to each other. Pretty soon, Leonard gets up and leaves the bar. Buddy looks out the window and sees that Leonard is driving Buddy's car down to the shoreline and then out onto the ice. I forgot to mention it's winter, the lake is frozen over. He drives it about fifty yards out, and the ice starts to crack. Leonard barely gets out of it in time. The car sinks through the ice.'' Rich swirled his coffee around in his cup. "I don't think they towed it out until spring.''

"How did Leonard get the keys to this guy's car?''

"Buddy did what most everyone down here does. He had dropped the keys under the front seat.''

"And what's the last thing?''

"This happened long ago, but I think it's pertinent. Leonard went out deer hunting with his best buddy when the two of them were just out of high school. So we're talking twenty-some years ago. They went bow hunting. The season's longer. It was early morning when this happened—hunting starts at first light. Leonard shot his friend in the neck with an arrow. The kid died.''

Rich unrolled part of his caramel roll and buttered the

piece, then took a bite. Claire waited for him to finish eating it. She knew he had more to tell her.

Rich continued. "There had been some talk of his buddy cheating with Leonard's girlfriend, but it might just have been talk. Sheriff called it an accident. It might well have been."

Claire took a sip of her coffee and waited. When Rich didn't look like he would add anything, she couldn't stand it. "What did you think?"

"Well, it being so early in the morning, it was a safe bet, unless they had been at it all night long, that they hadn't been drinking. That time of day it is hard to see. But with bow hunting, you tend to be closer to your target before you shoot. I thought about it all when it happened. To tell you the truth, I was just never sure. But I can tell you this. I would never go hunting with Leonard Lundgren."

NORA MADE BREAKFAST for herself. She was pretty good at it. She made everything just the way she liked it. She toasted her bread and then let it sit for a while until it cooled off so the butter wouldn't melt on it. She liked the butter to stay whole. Then she slathered strawberry jam on the toast. More than her dad ever let her put on.

She poured herself some milk, but she poured it into a coffee mug. She stirred a little sugar into it. She liked to pretend she was drinking coffee. Sometimes Brad would make her a very weak cup of coffee. He would heat up milk and then pour enough coffee into it to make it turn color. Then he would let her put a couple spoonsful of sugar in it. The best.

Everyone else was sleeping. It didn't happen very often that she was on her own. Like last night. What she would do was pretend that her mom was there, in the other room.

Otherwise, sometimes she was afraid. But if her mom was there, then she would be all right.

Nora worked hard at remembering her mom. She had her picture right by her bed, and every night she kissed her good night. She said prayers to her mom. She believed in her mom more than she believed in God. Maybe that wasn't right, but since they rarely went to church, she figured she hadn't had much practice at believing in God.

After she finished her breakfast, she cleaned up her dishes.

She went out and fed the chickens and gathered all the new brown eggs they had laid early that morning. She loved to hold the eggs against her cheeks. They felt so smooth and warm.

She walked down to the end of the road and got the paper.

Then she watched TV quietly for a while.

They had all gotten in late last night. Very late. When she heard them come home, she had taken her mom's picture out from under the covers where she had put it for protection and set it next to her bed. Then she went back to sleep.

She was surprised her father wasn't up yet. He never slept in, not like Jenny, who tried to sleep in every morning. Then Dad and she would fight. Nora hated their fights. She often went and hid in her room when they fought.

Nora went upstairs and walked down the hallway to her father's room. The door wasn't shut all the way, so she gently pushed it open. No one. Empty bed. Hadn't even been slept in. Maybe he had gone to stay at that woman's house. He had a couple times before. But usually Lola stayed at their house.

That Lola. Lola had bought Nora a Barbie doll for her birthday. The doll sat on the top of her bookshelf now. Nora had never really played with dolls. Besides, she'd rather read or run around outside. Nora got the feeling that Lola would like to make her her own little girl.

Sitting on the edge of her dad's bed, she waited for something to happen. As if on command Jenny's door opened, and she came stumbling down the hall.

When Jenny glanced into their father's room, she let out a scream. Nora glanced around and wondered what she had seen.

"Jenny, it's me." She ran out to her.

Jenny grabbed her into her arms and said, "Thank God. It's only you."

I do have moments of happiness. You asked me, and I do.
My roses, blooms so heavy they lean toward the earth. Hawk soaring off the bluff. My daughter running up the hill. She can never walk.
It's as if I forget for that moment.
Their deaths leave me. They are not in my sight, in my presence. I no longer carry them.

They are heavy?

Intolerably.

What can you do about that?

I don't like these questions where you know the answer and I'm wandering around in the dark.
I just want to forget.
The deaths to have never happened. It all to go away. A good wind, that's what we need is a good wind to blow it all away.

Where would that leave you?

I would be the rose, heavy with only my own beauty, the hawk soaring over the land, my daughter.
I would be like my daughter again, running up every hill.

Has she forgotten what has happened?

No. I know she hasn't.

Is there another way?

I hope so.

EIGHT

SUNDAY MORNINGS the sheriff's department was as quiet as a morgue. Tonya was answering the phones, a couple of the squad cars were out, but no one else was around the office. There just wasn't a lot of call for the police on Sunday mornings in this small county. Claire could hear the bells from the Lutheran church down the street chiming a hymn. Ten o'clock. Time for service. She almost felt like she knew the words to the hymn, but they stayed a vague memory.

As Claire typed his full name into the computer, *Leonard Lundgren,* she tried to remember him and his manner last night. He was a big man, over six feet tall, broad through the shoulders and chest. He probably had done a lot of heavy work in his time. Much bigger man than Jed Spitzler. But last night he hadn't seemed particularly belligerent. When Lola had pushed him away, he had backed off and left her alone. Maybe he had been aware of all the eyes on him.

Their computer was hooked into all the important databases in the state, and she wanted to see what would come up for Leonard. Information started to appear on her screen, and she read through it, sifting it in her mind.

He was in his late forties, born July 9, 1952.

Graduated from high school.

Never married.

In jail once. Drunk driving. Before they did much about it. He was just given a warning and a night's stay.

Three speeding tickets, but spread out over nearly thirty years of driving. That wasn't bad.

Sued someone over a damage deposit on an apartment. Lost.

No children.

No surprises.

She printed it out for her file, but didn't think it held any information worth keeping. Obviously the man whose car he had driven into the lake hadn't pressed charges. And the shooting incident wasn't on his record. Claire knew it was the way it should be, but it frustrated her that she wouldn't even know of these incidents if it weren't for Rich. She would have had a much less complete picture of Leonard.

But she did know. She was going to keep checking into him. She had a feeling he had been up to no good. From what she had heard from Rich, it was obvious that his relationship with Lola was volatile.

Claire wanted to get a look at his truck, at his house. Whoever stabbed Jed Spitzler must have gotten sprayed with blood. There would be traces, and she wanted to find them before it was too late.

If she wanted to get a search warrant on Leonard Lundgren, she would need a little more ammo. The judge didn't hand them out easily. Claire would need to go in with a good probable cause—at least motive and opportunity, preferably an eyewitness.

She sat back in her chair and looked over what she had printed out, but her mind started to wander back to last night with Rich. He had surprised her as a lover. Maybe because he was awkward and quiet moving through the world, she had thought he would be the same in bed. Not the case. He was a thoughtful, thorough lover with just enough of an edge to be very interesting.

"Hey, Claire." Steve Walker, the other deputy who had shown up at the dance last night, poked his head into her cubicle. "What're you doing in here?"

She felt herself blushing as if Steve could read her mind. To give herself a chance to recover, she showed him the file she had printed out. "Checking on the Spitzler case. What about you? You on duty again?" she asked him.

"Just getting off."

"Long shift. How'd it go last night at the dance?"

"You know about what I know." He perched on the edge of her desk. "We found nada. No knife, no bloody clothes. No one seemed to have seen it. Pretty strange."

"I'm glad you think it is. I'm having a hard time believing it. Even his kids, who found him, didn't see anyone."

"It was dark. There was a band. I suppose that can explain some of it."

"What do you know about Leonard Lundgren?" Claire asked him. "Do you know where he works?"

"I think I heard he's working at that new sand pit that opened up past Maiden Rock. Other than that I don't know much. Big guy. But not so bad as he looks. I caught him speeding once, barreling down Thirty-five. It was about two in the morning. I pulled him over. He had been going seventy. He was actually pretty agreeable about it. Didn't seem to have been drinking. Said he deserved the ticket. I sent him on his way."

"He had been drinking last night. I wonder if he's one of those people who become Mr. Hyde when they drink."

"Who's Mr. Hyde?"

Claire looked up at him to see if he really didn't know. He waited for her answer. "The side of us we want no one to see."

"BRAD, WAKE UP. I think someone's here."

Brad had been having a very bad dream, and he woke feeling like all the muscles in his body were clenched, as if he were fighting hard against something unmovable. When he opened his eyes, Nora was staring down at him.

"Who?" he asked her.

"I don't know. I don't recognize the car. A guy."

Brad scrambled out of bed. He hadn't even taken his clothes off from the night before. He and Jenny hadn't gotten to sleep until around five in the morning. "What time is it?"

"After noon."

"Where's Jenny?"

"She went back to bed." Nora was wearing a white T-shirt and a pair of polka dot shorts. Her hair was a mass of curls. He sat up in bed and reached over and tousled her hair.

"Is it true about Dad?" Nora asked him.

"Did Jenny tell you?"

Nora nodded.

"It's true," he said. He remembered seeing Dad stretched out in the operating room, pale as a ghost. The blood had flowed out of him.

"Who's going to take care of us?" Nora asked.

"We'll take care of each other."

"What about when I go to school? You and Jenny are already gone. I'll be by myself."

"But you're a big girl."

She ran her hands down her T-shirt and said, "Yeah, I guess I am. I'm in the top grade now in my school."

"We'll figure it out."

"I wish Dad didn't die," Nora said, and she started to cry. Brad rubbed her shoulders and said, "Don't cry. Let's go fix some lunch."

"We're orphans now," Nora said as she walked out of the room with him.

What a weird thought. No parents, all alone in the world except for each other. He was glad he had two sisters.

A banging came from the front door. The doorbell hadn't worked for a few years. Dad never had felt like fixing it. Brad went to see who it was, and Nora tagged along.

A thin man in a clerical collar and black jacket stood at the door with a casserole dish in his hands. "Are you the Spitzler children?" he asked.

Brad said yes.

"I'm Pastor Wilkins from the Calvary Covenant Church. I don't know if you remember me. I haven't seen you in church in a while. Probably since your mother died. Anyway, your mother is buried in our church, and I know you have another plot there, so I thought you might want to use it for your father."

Brad felt like he should introduce himself. "I'm Brad, and this is my sister Nora. Our other sister is still sleeping."

Brad let him into the living room. It wasn't in too bad shape.

"May I sit down?" the man asked. "Oh, and my wife made this for you children." He handed Brad the casserole. "It's tuna hot dish. Should still be warm."

Brad thanked him and took the casserole dish, setting it on the coffee table on an old pile of newspapers.

"I'm here to talk to you about the funeral. Do you have any relatives that can come and stay with you?"

"No," Brad told him. "Mom was an only child. Her folks died a while ago. Dad's family I don't know too much about. We've never kept in touch with them."

"Are you the oldest?"

"Yes, I am."

"Then let's go over the arrangements."

Brad pretty much agreed to everything the pastor suggested. A short service on Wednesday. A luncheon served in the church basement made by the Ladies' Club.

"And then I think your father had purchased two plots when your mother died. So we can just bury him next to her."

"No." The word popped out of him before he had time to think. He wished Jenny were there to help him.

The pastor looked at him in surprise. "Do you have another plot?"

"No, but we can buy another. Can't we? Is there another one for sale in your cemetery?"

"Yes, I'm sure there is. But why don't you want him in the plot you already have?"

Brad thought fast. "Because Dad promised Jenny that she could be buried next to our mother. And I know he wouldn't want to break his promise."

CLAIRE KNEW THAT Bridget and Meg would be along any minute. Once she had gotten home to her empty house, she had missed Meg. They were hardly ever apart.

It was such a lovely day, warm wind, in the low eighties, fluffy clouds floating overhead. She needed to be outside. She decided to go and work in her garden for a while. She would do what always needed doing in her garden—weed. The soil in this area of the state was dark and amazingly fertile. In one of her gardening books, Claire had read that nettles are an indicator plant for fertile soil. She had a fine crop of nettles on the back end of her lot.

Actually, some of the weeds that came up in her flower beds, she ate. Purslane and lamb's-quarters were nice in salads, and sometimes she even cooked the lamb's-quarters like spinach. She loved the idea that even the weeds in her garden were tasty and good for you.

She looked over the leaves of her roses. They got these

nasty little green worms on them if she didn't spray them every week or so. She used an organic spray that wasn't toxic. If she used one of the more toxic sprays, she would probably not have to spray as often, but she didn't mind the excuse for puttering around.

Her gardens were small and usually gathered around something. She had three beds next to the house, one around her clothesline, two next to a shed, and then one by the garage. She felt more comfortable working off an already established building. She read the books and knew this wasn't the correct way to make gardens. They should be seen as pools of light in the lawns, beds that have their own shape and form. But she didn't feel brave enough to start digging up the middle of her yard.

One of these years.

Her roses were blooming again. Landers, her neighbor, who had taught her much about gardening but had died early spring, would have been proud of her. She had done everything right this year. Deadheaded them vigilantly after they bloomed in the early summer, fertilized them, watered them although they had had nearly enough rain, and now most of their long waving wands of growth were festooned with clumps of lovely red-pink roses, a soft faded red color that she would love to find in old silk fabric and make into a blouse.

She picked a blown rose and smelled—the soft fragrance of nutmeg. Sleeping with Rich had stirred up dark feelings in her, her sense of vulnerability and danger. To love someone was very dangerous.

Two years ago her husband had been killed by a drug gang in the Twin Cities. It had blown her life up. So she moved down to Fort St. Antoine and started over. But the trouble followed her in the form of her old partner, Bruce Jacobs. She had discovered that he was behind everything.

He had been the infamous "Hawk," the leader of the drug gang, and he had been responsible for her husband's death. Worst of all, she had loved him. In a showdown, she had killed him in self-defense and then, to save his reputation, concealed what he had been. No one knew she had killed him. She felt trapped in his death.

How could she even think of getting involved with another man, considering her track record?

She heard a car drive into her driveway and stood to watch Bridget's car pull in. Meg bounced out of the car as soon as it had stopped. "Mom!" she shouted.

"Here, sweetie." Claire waved at the two of them, glad to be pulled out of her dark thoughts.

Bridget extricated herself from the car with care. Another inch or two on her belly, and she would not be able to drive. She slowly walked behind Meg, rocking side to side.

Meg flung herself on Claire, and Claire grabbed her up and twirled her around. "Is Auntie Bridget tired of you?"

"I doubt it," Meg said. "We had a blast. She let me stay up late and watch a scary movie. *Frankenstein*. Have you ever seen that? Totally cool. Kinda sad at the end, when they burn him to death. The monster, I mean. It's really the doctor's name that is Frankenstein, but everyone always gets that wrong."

Bridget came up to them, smiling at Meg's description of their night together. "I didn't make it through the whole movie. Meg had to wake me at the end."

"Hey, Mom, I tried to call you this morning, but you weren't here. Did you stay over at Rich's?"

Claire wasn't quite ready for this. She didn't believe in lying to her daughter, so in good splitting-hairs fashion she sidestepped the question. "I had to go into work for a while this morning. Sorry I missed your call."

"Oh, I was kinda hoping you stayed at Rich's. You know, that would show that you really liked him."

Claire bent down to be Meg's height and looked her in the face. "I do really like him."

"Yeah, I know. But I'm waiting for you guys to get to the next step. The sleep-over step."

"Where do you learn these things, Meg?"

"At school. TV. Books. Aunt Bridget and I had a good talk about you and Rich last night."

Over Meg's head, Bridget rolled her eyes. Claire would check in with her later.

"I'm glad you are so up on everything."

"What's for lunch? I'm hungry."

Bridget chimed in. "So am I."

"Tomato soup. Grilled cheese sandwiches. Meggy, you run in and start the soup. It's sitting on the stove."

Meg ran ahead of them, and Claire walked with Bridget. "I hope she didn't wear you out."

"Not at all. She is a constant stream of chatter, but she's quite interesting. I need distraction right now. I feel like a whale. Actually, I feel bigger than that. Like the *Titanic*. I'm afraid that if I hit something, I would sink."

"Not long now." Claire reached over and wrapped an arm around her shoulder.

"That's what I'm really afraid of. I can't imagine this child trying to get out of me. Gives me the shakes."

"When the time comes, you'll want it out."

"I'll want it over, is what you mean." Bridget stopped. "Before we go into the house, not to change the subject, but give me the lowdown on last night."

"Wouldn't you know, a guy got stabbed at the dance we went to."

"No. Did you have to work? Did that ruin your evening?"

"Yes, I did have to work. He died a few hours later in the hospital."

Bridget said, "Oh, I'm so sorry, Claire. I know how much you were looking forward to last night."

"But it didn't completely ruin my evening." Claire smiled.

"Well, that's good to hear." Bridget studied her. "Sister of mine, you look like a satisfied woman."

Claire simply nodded.

LOLA WAS DONE with her shift at the Bluff Bar and Grill. All the customers were gone, and her area was all set for the evening shift. She had eaten a cheeseburger with fries and decided to have a beer with it. What the hell. She almost hadn't come into work today. What with Jed killed and all, she would have had a good excuse, but she desperately needed the money.

She sniffed into a napkin when she thought of Jed. Things hadn't been great between them recently, but for a while he had treated her so good. They had met at the bar about six months ago. Not that she didn't know who he was—she had seen him around all her life, but he was quite a bit older than her.

But about six months ago, he sat in her section and she waited on him. He had been in a good mood, and she had flirted with him. Before he left, he asked her out for a drink. That started it all. He had taken her out a few times before he made any kind of moves on her. She had been surprised by how slow he was about it, especially considering it had been a few years since his wife died. Then, when they made love, he always wanted her to start by going down on him. It seemed to be the only way he could get aroused. She didn't mind, but it surprised her. He wasn't that old, but still getting close to fifty.

She wasn't getting any younger either. In two years she'd be forty. She had hoped that they might marry. Brad would be moving out this year, and Jenny wouldn't be far behind. That would leave her and Jed and Nora. A nice little family. Since she couldn't have kids herself, she had really looked forward to raising Nora, dressing her up and taking care of her.

Now it would never happen. She would have to waitress the rest of her life. She lit a cigarette and looked around the bar. Maybe it was time to leave. Get out of this area. Everyone knew her and her business. And Leonard would never leave her alone.

Just as she thought of him, he walked in the door. The last person she wanted to see, Leonard. She would have known it was him just by the sound of his big boots on the floor. Leonard never picked his feet up, he dragged them. Him and his big stupid cowboy hat. Nobody wore a cowboy hat anymore. What did he think he was, some kind of Western hero?

He walked up to her and said, "Lola, I gotta talk to you."

"Get out of here, Leonard!" she yelled at him.

Jim, her boss, came out from the kitchen. "You two take it outside. I don't need your fighting in here."

Leonard grabbed her wrist and started pulling her outside with him. She kicked him in the leg, and he kept pulling. She kicked again, and he yanked her so hard that she almost fell.

"Jim, stop him!" Lola yelled.

"I don't want to hear about it, Lola. You get rid of him."

She gave in and went outside with Leonard.

"I want to talk to you."

"Let go of me. I'll only listen if you let go."

He dropped her wrist, and she thought of running back

inside, but Jim was obviously going to be no help. She might as well get it over with. "What?"

"Lola, you need to get away from that guy. I'm worried about you. You're not thinking straight."

"Listen, Leonard. I told the police all about you last night. You were seen with Jed right after he was stabbed. I'm surprised they haven't picked you up yet for killing him. Did you know he was dead? He died in the hospital. Now are you happy? You killed him."

Leonard stared at her as he let her words sink in. Surprisingly, he did not get riled up. He pushed his hat back on his head and said, "Spitzler got what he deserved. You're the blind woman around here. Jed Spitzler was no good, and I don't mean to speak poorly of the dead, but it's the truth. You'll just have to get over him."

"Get over it. The man I loved is dead."

"You said you loved me once. Doesn't seem to mean much to you."

Lola decided to tell him her big news, even if she was pushing the truth a little. He thought he knew everything. "We were going to get married."

Leonard stopped at this. "Married?"

"Yes. We were talking about it. Probably sometime this year."

Leonard took a step back from her, looking her over. "You would have married that creep?"

"Hey, I would've been able to quit work, stay at home, and raise his little girl. He would have taken care of me."

"Right. Just like he took care of his first wife." Leonard turned to walk away. Lola was surprised. Usually he didn't give up so easily. Then he turned back and said, "I think you are one lucky woman."

NINE

"MY FAVORITE GHOUL." Dr. Lord smiled and nodded as Claire walked in the door to the morgue, which was in the basement of a deconsecrated church. He was sitting at his Mission-style desk, a small laptop open in front of him. The two objects looked so incongruous that Claire chuckled. That typified Dr. Lord. He seemed able to live in many worlds at the same time.

"My favorite necrotomist," she replied.

"What an apt term." He stood up from his desk and walked toward her. "I bet you've come about Mr. Spitzler. Jed. Am I right?"

"As always."

"Looks like someone killed him." He ran his fingers through his hair, but there wasn't much there. Dr. Lord was in his sixties, and his hair was thin and white, but his demeanor was robust.

"You're not beating around the bush today."

"A knife in the guts isn't usually an accident. Although"—he stopped and thought for a moment, his index finger touching his lip—"I do recall a very strange incident where a man fell on his knife as he was gelding a horse. But I don't think he died."

"Thank you for that little tidbit. Well, as you've probably heard, the stabbing happened at a street dance."

"Yes, I had heard." Dr. Lord waved toward the back room, where Claire could see a body lying in state under a sheet. "I'm sorry you missed my big performance, but I got to him sooner than I thought I would. No surprises with him. He was stabbed in the guts, right under the rib cage. The person either knew what they were doing, or they were lucky in their placement of the knife, or they were shorter than him."

"So they would naturally jab him in the right spot?"

"Might be something like that. But the blade of the knife cut right up into his lungs and under his heart. He bled out pretty fast. I'm surprised he even made it to the hospital alive."

"His daughter said he sounded very odd. She was at the scene. She described him as sounding like a stuck pig."

"Yes, that would be about right. Trying to get his breath while the air is leaking out of him on the inside. Must be a horrible feeling." He bowed slightly and said, "Would you like to have a look-see?"

Claire thought about it. "No, thanks. I don't think that will be necessary. I saw quite enough of him last night. I located the wound, although it was gushing blood, as you surmised."

He motioned to his desk. "The blade of the knife was probably about six inches long. Pretty standard for any kind of long-bladed knife. So that's not much help. I was just writing up my notes. I'll get you a copy of them as soon as I'm done. But I think it's time for my midafternoon break. Can I persuade you to join me for a piece of pie?"

"I planned it that way."

They walked across the street to the small café that Dr. Lord frequented. Claire had had dealings with the doctor several times since she had joined the sheriff's office. He treated her with respect and was a delight to be around, but he also had several weaknesses, and one of them was any sort of pie.

They settled into a booth by the window, and the dyed blond waitress automatically brought over two coffee cups and a pot of coffee. "What'll it be today, Doc?"

"What do you recommend, Doris?"

"The apple streusel looks good, and I know you always like the double chocolate fudge pie."

"I think I'll go with the chocolate and a dollop or two of whipped cream."

"I'll have the coconut cream," Claire announced. She hadn't had a piece of coconut cream pie in twenty years. But once she saw it on the menu, it sounded perfect.

Dr. Lord poured them both cups of coffee, and Claire poured some milk into hers. She needed to get her calcium.

"How are the Spitzler children doing?" Dr. Lord asked.

"I'm not sure. They were in deep shock last night. I'm going out there next to check on them. The boy is nearly eighteen, so we've left them on their own, which makes me feel uncomfortable. Maybe a relative will come out and stay with them."

"No one came when their mother died. It was a good thing Jed worked at home, or I don't know what he would have done."

"I'm glad you mentioned that. I keep hearing references to her death, but what exactly happened to Mrs. Spitzler?"

"Her first name was Rainey. She was a pretty woman. Fine, slim figure, golden hair, light complected." Dr. Lord rubbed his nose thoughtfully. "I hate to remember that day they brought her in to the morgue. Unlike her husband, she did die on her way to the hospital. I heard the kids were hysterical. I think they had to sedate the older girl. Jenny? Is that her name?"

Claire nodded. "Yes—I think she's been sedating herself ever since."

"Both of Rainey's hands were smashed. Total trauma. Every bone in her hands and her arms up to her elbows was broken, nearly pulverized. Several fingers were pulled right off her hands. She had been working with the two oldest

kids and her husband and had fallen into the machine that
squeezes juice out of sorghum. Have you ever seen a sorghum press?''

''No, I don't even know what sorghum is,'' Claire said.
''I haven't spent much time on farms.''

''Dangerous places. I could tell you stories.'' He shook
his head. ''Well, sorghum is a tall grass. Its stems are
crushed to extract juice, which is then boiled to make a
syrup. A sorghum press is made up of three metal rollers—
two on top and one on the bottom. You feed the sorghum
through it, and the juice drips out the bottom. Rather simple.
Very effective. And like much farm machinery, if used in-
correctly, quite dangerous.''

''How did that kill her?''

''Well, it wasn't a pretty sight. Everything was mangled
and mashed. It was as if she had slit her wrists from the inside.
Once they released her from the machine, she started to bleed.
From what I've heard, Jed carried her to the car, had the
children manage her while he drove into town. He didn't call
an ambulance. I don't think it would have made any difference. I heard the children blamed him for her death. Said if
he would have acted faster, called for help, they might have
saved her. I tried to talk to them once. I told them I didn't
think she could have been saved. She was in very bad shape.
And there was certainly no saving those hands—they were
smashed beyond repair. What kind of life would she have had?
I have to wonder. But that's beside the point.''

The waitress brought their pie, and Claire was glad to eat
something sweet and not think of farm accidents. Her coconut cream pie was light and tasty, the coconut flakes car-
amelized on top of the meringue. Dr. Lord ate his chocolate
pie with a certain amount of reverence, and Claire let the
silence settle on the table. She found him such a comfortable man to be around.

When he was done, he pushed his plate back, poured them both a little more coffee, and said, "Now I can finish my day. I always seem to need a little boost in the late afternoon. With my impending old age, I indulge myself."

"Anything more you can tell me about the knife used on Jed Spitzler?"

"Sometimes I forget you're a policewoman, and then you rudely remind me." He smiled at her. "The knife? Nothing special about the knife. An ordinary long-bladed knife that everyone has at least one of at home. I'll be more specific in my report."

"Something used around the farm?"

"Possibly. Are you suggesting this might be, in another form, a farm accident?"

THE DAYLIGHT hurt her eyes. Her body ached as if every bone were being pulled on. Jenny sat in the living room with the shades drawn and slowly drank a cup of coffee. Halfway through the second day with no Darvocet, and her mind felt like a balloon about to burst. Withdrawal was no fun.

Nora sat on the floor, drawing a picture of their farm. Brad and Jenny had decided to let Nora stay home from school today with them. Jenny noticed that Nora was drawing all the animals lined up, like in a parade.

"What's that one?" Jenny pointed to a small brown animal that looked like a cross between a beaver and a pig.

"That's the groundhog that lives in the culvert."

"You're even putting the wild animals in."

"I consider him a pet. He's pretty friendly."

"Not to the dogs."

Nora continued to draw, humming a little tuneless tune under her breath. She had cried a few times yesterday, but so far today she didn't seem too upset. Jenny looked down at the small head of tousled blond curls and didn't know if she was up to taking care of her sister.

"Where's Brad?" Jenny asked.

"He's out doing chores."

Brad had been very quiet yesterday. He went to bed early and got up early this morning. Being the good boy, taking care of everything. Jenny often found him very hard to talk to, even though in many ways they were quite close. If they were going to keep the farm together, they would need to learn how to talk to each other.

"Oh, the police are coming over," Nora announced. "This woman called while you were in the shower. She said they'd be over before suppertime."

Suppertime. Jenny wondered what they'd eat tonight. She really should try to take care of that. She wasn't a good cook, but maybe it was time she learned how to do it right. They still had all Mom's old cookbooks.

"What do you want for supper?" she asked Nora.

"Pancakes."

Pancakes sounded good. Mom used to make pancakes and eggs for supper sometimes, for a treat. Eating breakfast for supper was kind of fun. Jenny felt like they hadn't had pancakes since her mother died. That couldn't be true, but she couldn't remember eating them in the last four years. So many things had died with their mother.

Jenny went into the kitchen and got out the Betty Crocker cookbook. She propped it open on the kitchen counter and then cleared off the rest of the counter.

"I'm going to make pancakes. Can you do the dishes?"

They had never gotten a dishwasher. Mom had wanted one so bad, but Dad said they were a waste of energy and water. He never did anything to make Mom's life easier. Nora ran a sink full of hot water, piled all the dirty dishes into it, and washed away.

Jenny lined up all the ingredients like the animals in Nora's picture: salt, flour, oil, egg, milk. She found the measuring cup and the measuring spoons. Then she got out a big blue bowl, the one Mom had always used when she made pancakes.

Slowly and carefully, Jenny put everything she needed in the bowl. Nora pulled up a stool and watched her. Then she stirred it all together. Just as she was done, a knock came at the door.

"I'll get it," Nora sang out, jumping off the stool and running for the door.

Jenny covered the pancake batter with a towel. She remembered her mother doing that. Her mother said that pancake batter was always better if it sat for a while. Jenny looked around the kitchen. It was a pigsty. Her mother would be so ashamed if she could see her kitchen. Maybe, after the police left, Jenny would try to clean it up.

Jenny walked out into the hallway and saw the woman deputy that had been at the hospital when Dad died. She had been nice to them. She was dressed in a uniform with her dark hair pulled back and no lipstick on, but she was easy to recognize because she had a big, full smile.

"Hi," Jenny said.

"Hi, Jenny. I don't know if you remember me. My name is Claire Watkins."

"I remember you. You went with us to see Dad."

"How are you doing?"

For some reason, the woman's question drew tears to Jenny's eyes. It was the concern in her voice that did it. The understanding. It made Jenny think for a second of getting down on the floor, on her hands and knees, and telling everything. But then she saw the gun the woman carried and the badge she wore. There was no way this woman would understand. It was her job not to.

"Okay, I guess."

"I know it's hard. The first few days you feel like you've been run over by a bulldozer, but you're still numb. Then it gets worse."

Jenny nodded. She remembered how it had been when her mom died. She had wanted to shut her brain down. She wanted the world to stop. She hated everybody. Absolutely everybody.

"Jenny, I need to ask you and Brad some more questions. I'm afraid, as you've probably figured out, that someone killed your dad. We're going to try as hard as we can to find out who did it. We need your help."

"Nora, go get Brad." Jenny watched Nora scamper away. Then she turned to the woman deputy. "Can I get you something? Coffee? I just reheated a pot. It doesn't taste very good, though. Never does when you reheat it."

"You know, I just had a couple cups with a big piece of pie. I think I'm fine for the time being."

Jenny turned on the tap and filled a glass full of water for herself. She seemed to be craving water today, as if she needed to flush her system clean. Then she led the way to the living room and offered Claire a seat.

"Is that your mother?" Claire asked, pointing to a family picture sitting on the fireplace mantel.

Jenny said yes. The photograph had been taken right before Labor Day, the last picture anyone had taken of Mom. Her mother looked thin and a little worn, but still beautiful. Jenny hated the way her own hair looked in that picture, thin and flat to her head. Her eyes looked enormous, and her teeth were huge. A normal ugly twelve-year-old. Nora was a lot cuter than Jenny had ever been.

"She's very pretty," Claire continued.

Jenny knew her mom was pretty, but it seemed like such a lame thing to say. The picture didn't show how gentle her mother could be, or how scared. Just a one-dimensional, smiling woman with her hand on Jenny's shoulder.

Brad walked in and took his boots off right by the door. Their mother had taught them to do that. He walked up and said hi and shook Claire's hand.

"Thanks for helping us last night," he said. He always knew how to act. Especially around adults.

"You're welcome. As I've already told Jenny, I'd like to ask you two more questions. Anything you can think of that might shed some light on what happened to your dad—who might have stabbed him—please tell me."

Claire took them through the night, step by step. How Dad had seemed, when they had gone to the dance, when they had last seen him. Then she asked them about Lola. "Were your father and Lola getting along?"

Brad shrugged. Jenny decided to say something. "I think they weren't getting along as well as they had at first."

"What makes you think that?"

"I can just tell with Dad. He was always snapping at her. He didn't even want to go to the dance last night. Somehow she persuaded him."

"What about Leonard Lundgren? Do you know who he is?"

They both nodded.

"Has he made any threats to your father?"

Brad answered. "Not that I know of."

Claire turned to Jenny.

Jenny answered. "I should tell you something. You said to tell you anything that might shed some light. This happened about three weeks ago. That guy, that Leonard, he was here on the farm. Remember, Brad?"

Brad nodded.

"It was dark out. Lola was over. We had finished supper and were watching TV. I went out to put the chickens in, and I heard something over in the barn. I just thought it was an animal, so I walked over to see what it was. I saw him. He was digging around in Dad's tools. I yelled at him, and he slipped out the back way."

"Did you tell your father?"

"No. But I told Brad."

"Why didn't you tell your father?"

Jenny stopped for a moment and thought how to phrase what she was about to say. "Dad gets mad kinda easy. And Leonard was gone. When Dad gets mad he takes it out on anybody. I didn't feel like dealing with him. Anyway, I just think Leonard was here sniffing after Lola. I figured with any luck Dad and Lola would break up pretty soon, and he could have her back."

CLAIRE FELT LIKE she had Lundgren now. All she had to do was fill out the affidavit requesting the search of Leonard Lundgren's house, outbuildings, and vehicles. She needed to list it all. In the country, many people kept more stuff in their outbuildings than they did in their houses, and she could search only the places she had listed.

If she could get all the documents to the courthouse before Judge Shifsky left, they might be able to get over there tonight. Catch him at home just as he got off work. That would be good, although he would have had all of Sunday to clean up any mess.

Tonya walked up to Claire's desk and deposited a pink slip on it. "While you were gone...," the slip read, and Tonya had filled in: "Lover boy called." Claire felt a smile pull at her lips.

"Lover boy? Mine or yours?" she teased Tonya.

"You know who I mean. That Rich guy. He sure has a nice voice. Smooth and deep, full of promise."

"My goodness, Tonya, you could become a romance writer with that kind of language."

Tonya flipped her long hair away from her face and said, "You think?"

"Hey, is Billy still around?"

"I think he's out back, dinking around with the squad car that's on the fritz."

"Could you run out and ask him if he has time to run out to Lundgren's house with me? I'd go ask him myself, but I'd really like to get this search warrant in pronto."

"Sure."

Claire looked at the slip with the message from Rich, folded it, and put it in her purse. Later. She'd call him later.

She went back to the affidavit: List what will be searched for. A knife or any long-bladed instrument, any bloody clothes, any blood in the vehicle, and blood in the house. That should give them the amount of leeway they would need. Once in a case early in her career she had been too specific; they had found incriminating evidence, but it had not been listed on the warrant, and so they couldn't take it. She would never forget that.

Tonya ran up to her desk. "I got Billy. He says he's ready to go whenever you are."

"Great, Tonya. Now, can you call the crime lab and ask them to be ready to meet us there? I think we'll want them to go over his truck."

Claire looked over the two affidavits and the three search warrants. All t's were crossed, all i's dotted. A glance to her watch told her she had fifteen minutes to spare. The courthouse was two minutes away. Just hope that Shifsky hadn't had a light load today and left early.

She walked briskly over to the courthouse. In her mind, she was already searching the premises. She wanted to get to Leonard first. Then the vehicle. Rich had said he was driving a truck—a Toyota, early nineties. Tan. It was important to know which vehicle he had driven the night of the dance, because most people around these parts had more than one.

Judge Shifsky was in her office, poring over a big law book. Her hair was pulled back into a braid, dark with threads of white sewn through it. She was a small woman with an impressive face, a sharp nose, and deep-set eyes. She looked up when Claire knocked on the edge of her door frame, since the door was open.

"Come in, Deputy Watkins. What do you have for me this late afternoon?"

"A search warrant, Your Honor."

The judge held out her hand, and Claire delivered all the papers to her.

"Mr. Lundgren," Judge Shifksy murmured. "Don't think I know him. Has he been in trouble before?"

"Not really, Your Honor."

"You feel good about your probable cause?"

"Yes, Your Honor. He has motive—his ex-girlfriend was dating the victim. He had opportunity—he was seen at the crime scene."

"As was half the county," Judge Shifsky added.

"He was seen next to the body."

Shifksy nodded.

"And, as I write on the affidavit, he was seen by the victim's daughter trespassing on their property." Claire wondered about that statement. She wasn't sure she believed Jenny, but it served her purpose at the moment. It wasn't up to her to determine if a witness was lying.

"That doesn't sound good."

"No, Your Honor."

"He probably should be checked out."

"That's how I feel."

Judge Shifsky signed the warrants and kept her copy of the affidavit. "Let me know how it turns out."

TEN

LEONARD LUNDGREN was leaning over an old truck in his backyard, tinkering with it, when they arrived; his broad back covered in red-and-black-checked flannel looked as big as a blackboard. He stood up and faced them as he heard the patrol car pull up behind him, no hand raised in greeting as they got out of the car. But neither did he appear overly hostile.

Claire was glad he was outside. She didn't like barging into people's houses.

"We need to look around your place, Mr. Lundgren, and I'm afraid we're going to have to impound your Toyota." Claire handed him the search warrant.

He took the piece of paper and looked at it as if he could not read. For a moment Claire supposed it was a possibility, then she saw him glance down the page, and he read out loud, "You're looking for knives. Fuck, what guy who lives around here doesn't have a shitload of knives?"

"That was the weapon used on Jed Spitzler, who died yesterday of a knife wound to the abdomen."

Leonard Lundgren wiped off his hands on the tail of his flannel shirt. "That little worm. I wouldn't have bothered to step on him if he were in my path."

Since he was talking, Billy proceeded to push him a little further. "We'd like to ask you some questions."

"You guys really think I had something to do with this. Who've you been talking to? Lola. So I can have a lawyer if I want to."

Billy nodded.

Leonard laughed. "I'm not paying nobody nothing when I haven't done a thing. They just want your money. I have nothing to hide. Ask your questions."

Claire decided to go for it. The man seemed forthcoming. "You didn't like Jed Spitzler, did you?"

"No, but neither did anyone else around here. The man kept to himself, never helped out a neighbor, never joined in when something needs to be done, got his kids half scared to death. Sure, I know it's hard, your wife dies on you and leaves you with three kids to raise, but he doesn't even know enough to ask for help."

"But you particularly didn't like him because he was seeing your ex-girlfriend, Lola."

Leonard lowered his head and shook it with a sense of weariness. "I guess that would be true."

"You were at the dance Saturday night?"

"I was."

"You were seen next to Jed after he was stabbed."

"I was there. But not right after. Not soon enough to see what happened to him. You know what I mean—who did it and all."

"Did you stab Jed Spitzler Saturday night?" Claire decided to ask the direct question.

Leonard shuffled in his heavy work boots and kicked at something on the ground. "I don't understand all the rules here. What I can say, what I can't say. I'm afraid I'll say the wrong thing the wrong way, and then you'll think you've got me. So let me be as clear as I can be. I didn't stab Jed Spitzler. I'd thought about it in the past, but, to tell you the truth, I didn't think he and Lola were going to be together that much longer. Jed ain't really Lola's type. She thinks she wants to settle down and play house, but that's really not what she wants. She'd be bored of ironing and cooking before too long, and she'd be finding her way down to the bar without Jed.''

''Thanks, Mr. Lundgren. Can I ask you to go sit in the back of the patrol car while we search your house and out-buildings?''

''Awfully polite and all. Sure, I'll go sit in the patrol car. Help yourself. Everything is open. I got nothing to hide. Try not to make too big a mess.''

Billy walked Lundgren to the patrol car and put him in the back.

Claire proceeded to the house, a small, tidy clapboard dwelling that sat on the edge of a hill. When she walked inside, she was struck by how neat it was. But on closer examination, she noticed that it wasn't spotless.

Two bedrooms, one upstairs, one down. A small bath with a shower and a galley kitchen. Nothing special about it, but every room was so well organized. Every thing had a place and was in it: the newspapers all stacked in a wooden box next to the couch and close to the fireplace, fireplace tools all hung up next to the mantel, slippers placed right at the doorway, boots lined up in the closet. It reminded her of the word *shipshape*.

She wondered if he had been in the military. She didn't remember that being in his record.

He had been right about the knives. She found a number of long-bladed knives in his kitchen drawers and then more in the utility closet by the back door. As she found them, she placed them in evidence bags. By the time she was done with the kitchen, there were over a dozen bags sitting on the counter.

The crime lab truck showed up about a half an hour after she and Billy had started searching the place. Clark Den-forth, whom she had worked with before, was in charge. She asked them to do Lundgren's truck. If they were going to find any trace evidence, it was going to be in that vehicle. She wanted the experts to go over it.

A few minutes later, Denforth walked into the kitchen, holding an evidence bag with a knife in it. "Look what I found."

Claire pointed at all the bags with knives in them on the counter.

"All very nice," Denforth said, "but this one has blood on it. You can see it in the hilt. Might be something."

"Where'd you find it?"

"Tucked right under the front seat."

"Why wouldn't he get rid of it?"

"I just find evidence. I don't claim to understand the criminal mind. That's up to you detectives."

She had Billy finish up the house while she looked through the outbuildings—a woodshed with wood stacked tidy as Lincoln Logs, another shed that housed a riding lawn mower, a snowmobile, and an old motorcycle. Men and their toys.

Then she opened the door to the last outbuilding and found herself in Lundgren's woodworking shop. The room was entirely paneled with warm old pine. A dark Jodul woodstove sat on a hearth of red bricks. Above the long workbench hung row after row of tools. She didn't know the names of half the instruments that hung from the wall. She would have to bag some of them—the ones that resembled knives.

She was starting to feel like they were headed down the wrong road. Lundgren hadn't acted like a murderer, facing them evenly when they drove up in the patrol car, not fussing when he was put in the backseat. And she knew it was not smart to make decisions based on intuition, but she just had a hard time believing that someone who took as much care as he did with his tools would bloody one of them by stabbing it into Jed Spitzler's guts.

She looked through every drawer in the workshop and bagged every knifelike tool she found. She bet they were leaving this man's property with over thirty knives. What a haul. But, from the looks of it, most of them, except the one found under the seat of the car, were spotless. The lab would find out.

Before going to the car, she checked in with Denforth. His crew had the truck ready to be towed back to Eau Claire. He felt that the place had been gone over thoroughly. "Might get lucky on this one," he said. "That knife looks very promising." He told her he hoped he would have something for her in the next day or two.

Claire got into the patrol car, and Leonard turned to look at her from the backseat. "So you're going out with Rich Haggard?" he asked.

"I'll ask the questions."

"He's a nice guy. Not too many of them around."

She agreed with him silently. "What about that knife under the seat of your truck?"

"I figured you'd find that. I just remembered that I left it there. I forgot about it after it happened."

"Well?"

"I killed a deer with it."

"You killed a deer with a knife? Whatever for?"

Lundgren made a sound halfway between a snort and a laugh. "This stupid woman hit a deer. This is a couple days ago. I'm coming home from work. It's dusk. Like right about now. And she's driving in front of me. A deer jumps up on the road in front of her, and she clips him in the rear. The deer flies into the ditch, the woman pulls over, and so do I. Just to check it out. Anyhow, this woman is hysterical. Bawling. She can't even get out of the car. The deer is flopping around in the ditch. There's nothing to do about it but put it out of its misery. I take my knife and slit its throat. End of story.''

"Did you know the woman?"

"Never saw her before in my life. She had a Minnesota license plate, probably just a dumb tourist.''

It was a good story. Claire didn't know if she believed it or not, but she had enjoyed it. "Nice place you've got here. You sure are a good housekeeper.''

"That's the way I like it.''

Claire mentioned something else she had noticed about his place. "You don't have a single animal here. Not even a dog.''

"I don't like animals. I know that everybody else does. But I think they're a waste of food and time. And they make a mess. I hate a mess.''

Claire wondered how he could tolerate Lola. She also wondered why he was taking this all so calmly.

GLOAMING. She had always liked that word, the way it filled the mouth. Liked it in the poems of Robert Burns. But now her world seemed to be in perpetual twilight. Little light. Half-light. Encroaching dark.

Ella Gunderson sat in her rocking chair and didn't bother to turn the lights on yet. It was nearly dark, but she was using this time to think about what she should do about Jed Spitzler's death. She believed in acting, and yet she did not like to think about what her actions might lead to. She felt like there were many layers to what had happened to him, and she was only aware of a few of them. Was that enough?

The phone rang, and Ella Gunderson stood up to get it. She didn't need to see where it was; it always sat right on the edge of her kitchen counter. She could find it in the dark, or in the gloaming.

"Good evening," she said into the phone.

"Mrs. Gunderson, Pit Snyder here."

"Well, hello, Mr. Mayor. To what do I owe the pleasure of this call?" She had wondered if he might not call. He had been in her fifth-grade class thirty years ago. Nice boy. Stubborn, but fair. She had always liked him. It tickled her no end to call him Mr. Mayor. Like Mr. President.

"Another beautiful day."

"Yes, it was indeed. I have heard that we are to have a mild fall. That's what the weatherman has been promising."

"I'll take it," he said.

She knew he hadn't called to discuss the weather with her, but it was good manners to start a conversation with such a discussion. It allowed people to gather their thoughts. "What can I do for you?"

"I'm worried about those Spitzler kids," Pit Snyder said.

"Yes, I am too."

"I thought you might be. You know they've got no one. No family, no nothing. I hate to think of them all alone up at the farm without anyone to talk to or watch over them. It doesn't seem right."

Ella Gunderson wondered where he was going with this all. "They are resourceful young people."

"Yes, they are. But they are still kids. They're too old for us to force them into foster care, plus I don't think that's how this should be handled. But it occurred to me that you might be able to go up and stay with them for a week or two. Just to get them over this hump. Make sure they don't fall apart. Talk to them about what has happened. You know. You're good at that."

Ella stretched her head back as she thought. She hated to leave the comfort of her own home. She knew every step of this place by heart and didn't need to worry about what she could see or not see. But in a big old farmhouse, it would be more difficult for her.

"I could try it for a day or two."

"That would be just great, Mrs. Gunderson. Maybe that's all they would need. It sure would make me feel more comfortable about their situation. Do you want me to call them and see if it would be all right?"

"No, I'll do it. I'll talk to them at the funeral. It's tomorrow. Are you going to it?"

There was a long pause at the other end of the line. "I suppose I should. I didn't like the guy, myself."

Ella bent her head at his words. "I understand. But he's gone now. I don't think we go to funerals to say anything more to the dead; we go to give our love and comfort to the living."

RICH KNEW IT WAS important that they find someone to plow the streets this winter. But they had been discussing this issue for the last hour and seemed no closer to resolving it. Board meetings were supposed to end at nine, which was only five minutes away.

What irked him was that the board just didn't want to pay anyone enough money to do a good job of it. But they would be the first to complain when the idiot they did hire did a lousy job. He would do it himself if they would pay him ten bucks an hour. But it was an insult to offer someone six dollars an hour to work out in the cold in the early morning to plow everyone out. He had already had his say on it, they hadn't listened to him, and now he'd let them try to find someone for that insanely low amount.

This was his second year on the board, and he wasn't sure how much longer he wanted to sit on it. It wasn't like he was so busy that he didn't have the time, and he did believe it was his civic duty, but he never felt he was much good at it. He tended to disagree with everyone else on the board, except Stuart. Then, when he didn't get his way, he would just clam up and let the other members hash the problem out.

What he had come to see about himself was that he didn't like working with other people. He found them slow and thoughtless. Usually irritating. He just wasn't a company man. A loner was what he was.

Lou Johnson, the youngest board member, spoke up. "Hey, guys. I'd plow the roads myself for eight bucks an hour."

Rich decided it was time to step in. "Let's hire him. Enough said. Eight bucks an hour is a bargain, and we know Lou will do a good job."

Lou turned, not sure that he had actually heard a compliment coming from Rich Haggard. A goofy smile spread across his broad face. "I will do a good job."

"And we'll know where to find him, if he oversleeps," Stuart added.

Everyone laughed at that remark. Stuart was good at saying the right thing at the right time and making everyone come together on an issue.

"But it's more than we have in the budget," Lester Krenz, the mayor, pointed out.

"I think there's some flexibility there, Lester," Stuart said. "We might not even get much snow this winter. If we do, I think we can dip into the campground funds to help out. After all, we've been talking about raising the camping fees."

"But we need a motion."

Rich was pleased to see it carry. Lou wore a grin the rest of the meeting. They adjourned just after nine o'clock. Stuart walked out the door with Rich and asked him if he wanted to go get a beer at the Fort.

"Not tonight."

"You seeing Claire tonight?"

"Don't think so. She's working a case."

"Spitzler?"

"Yeah, you read about that in the paper?"

"Hell, who needs to read about anything when the postmaster knows everything before it happens."

"Did you know Spitzler at all?"

"Couldn't even tell you what he looked like. I don't think he frequented my establishment." Stuart ran the bakery in town.

"Probably not. His farm is about ten miles away from here. He'd go into Durand for baked goods."

"So it's keeping Claire busy."

"I guess."

As Rich walked away, he wondered if there'd be a message from her on his machine. They had only been seeing each other a couple times a week, but after Saturday night he found himself wanting to talk to her more often. He wondered how sleeping together would change their relationship. Usually it was the woman who wanted to move in and get close and comfortable. But he thought with Claire it might well be different.

He walked the half mile back to his farm along Highway 35. There wasn't much traffic at night, and the late-summer air was still warm, but the first smells of autumn were in the air. A slight tang of leaves falling. A bit of a snap in the air. The softness of summer was leaving.

When he was down the driveway from his house, he noticed that there was a dark pile of something sitting on his front steps. He couldn't make it out. He tried to make it a pile of leaves, which didn't make any sense. Maybe a bird had flown into the window of his back door and landed in a pile of feathers on the stoop. But as he walked closer, he saw a hint of color. Red. Something red.

He came to the bottom of the steps and saw what had been placed in front of his door.

A bouquet of roses. Red roses. In a glass vase. There was only one person who would have done that.

No woman had ever given him flowers.

He lifted the roses up into his arms and smelled their dusty sweetness. His heart lifted up in his chest from happiness. He was in love with a generous woman.

Then he saw the note: ''Rich, can't see you for a while. Real busy with case. Claire.''

If only I hadn't become a police officer.

If only I had never met Bruce.

If only I had gotten the mail, my husband wouldn't have walked out to get it, the truck wouldn't have hit him, he'd still be alive.

I know this all sounds utterly absurd.

But what scares me the most is when I say, It should have been me who got hit by the truck. It should have been me that took a bullet in the chest.

It makes this whole thing we're doing, this life we're living, seem a game. I feel like if I had moved two steps in a different direction at a certain time, everything would have turned out differently. Do you know what I mean?

Yes, of course I do.

Do you feel that?

It's close to despair. I do feel it sometimes.

I don't know if I told you, but I'm seeing someone. We've been friends for a while, and now we're getting closer.
And I realize I don't know if I can do it.
The other night I thought, for a second, that maybe if I gave Rich up, if I promised not to see him anymore, then I could get my husband back.
Isn't that ridiculous?

The feeling isn't.

Can't you tell me what to do?

I talk to you, I tell you all this, but what I want from you, what I need, is some task to do that will change how I feel.

If you would tell me to climb a mountain, or go work for the homeless, or give away all my money.

It sounds like you think you should do some kind of penance. What is it that you need forgiveness for?

You don't get it. You just don't get it.
I didn't die. I'm still alive.
I can love someone else. I can be happy again.
That isn't available to either Bruce or my husband. I took it away from them.
It isn't fair. It isn't fair.

No, it's not fair. Fairness is just something we humans dreamed up. It has little to do with the reality of the world.

I know I need to accept what has happened, but sometimes I feel like I'm fighting so hard that my stomach knots up, waiting for a punch.

What do you want, Claire?

I want to go on with my own, good life.

ELEVEN

DOWN A LONG HALLWAY, Claire was leading Leonard Lundgren toward the cells. The corridor in the jail was dimly lit. One of the bulbs must be out, she thought. She wasn't talking to Leonard. He was walking in front of her. She stayed close behind him. When they got to the door of the cell, he stepped to the side to let her unlock it. She kept an eye on him. He had been quiet, but she wasn't sure she trusted him.

As the door swung open, she touched his shoulder with her hand to usher him into the cell. Then it happened. A dance. He spun away from her, got behind her somehow so fast she couldn't believe it was possible.

And he had a gun.

Why hadn't Billy frisked him.

What the hell was he doing with a gun?

The gun grew larger in his hand. He shoved it into her belly. She stepped back. He was pushing her toward the cell. She didn't want to go into the cell. She was afraid she would never leave it. He would lock her in and leave her.

She tried to scream, but no sound came out. She was choking. The scream had gotten stuck in her throat. She couldn't breathe. Black air rose up from the floor and filled the room. She couldn't see anything.

Suddenly, she broke through into night—the quiet night of her bedroom. Her heart galloping in her chest like a runaway horse. Her body covered with sweat. Her hands tingling with the hyperventilation. She clasped her hands over her chest to slow herself down, to reassure herself.

It was only a dream. There was no gun. No cell. Lundgren was safely locked up. She would see him in the morning.

Breathe slowly. That was the first thing to do. Stop breathing so fast and breathe in deeply. She focused on the air moving in and out of her body, pulled it in deep, held it in for a count or two, let it out slowly. Her therapist had taught her this method of breathing; it was supposed to be calming. Especially good for panic.

Claire hoped she hadn't screamed. She listened intently for any noise coming from Meg's room, but heard nothing.

She knew there would be no getting back to sleep for a while. She might as well get up and have something hot to drink. Her therapist had said to get up and shake the dream off. She couldn't stop them coming, but she could remain calmer after they had gone. Not give them so much power over herself.

Glancing over at the alarm clock, she saw the time was three in the morning. Hours before it was time to get up. She wished the dreams would come about six and she could just segue into the day, but she really did need another two or three hours of sleep to be able to cope with all the work she had ahead of her. Jed Spitzler's funeral was today, and she felt she should attend.

Claire got out of bed and went to her window. Gentle darkness. The moon overhead had a slice taken out of its side but was still giving off plenty of light. On the bluff behind her house, she could make out the white lines of the birch, thin fingers of trees reaching for the sky.

She wrapped her terry-cloth bathrobe around her, cinched it at the waist, and quietly walked past Meg's doorway. Peeking in, she saw her daughter's sweet profile tipped up, nose pointed at the ceiling, seeming to strain into the air of the night. Meg had been sleeping better of late. Her worries

had died down—and she knew none of her mother's. Claire
was so glad of that.

The world had become a safer place for Meg, and with
help, Claire hoped that it would become a less fearful place
for herself.

THE PASTOR HAD ASKED Brad to say something about his
father at the service. Brad should have turned him down,
but somehow he hadn't been able to. Brad knew he suffered
from trying to please other people. Oldest child syndrome,
according to this psych book they had read in school.

So now he stood in the back of the church, watching the
few people who had come to the service file in and take a
pew, and he held a crumpled piece of paper in his hand on
which he had written a few sentences. Searching around for
something profound to say, he had pulled a few lines from
the Bible, figuring that would be a safe bet. The best he
could come up with on such short notice.

Jenny and Nora sat up front in the pew reserved for family. Some of the people in the church he didn't know, and
he figured they were members of the congregation who had
come to help with the luncheon afterward. He recognized
some friends from school. Their parents probably told them
they could skip school if they went to the service, and they
decided that was a good deal.

Mary Beth Klinger was sitting a few rows from the back.
Brad had always liked her. She was funny and serious at
the same time. The few times he had tried to make a joke
in her presence, she had understood it. She was a grade
behind him in school, but their school was so small that
everyone knew everyone.

As he looked at her, she turned and smiled at him. Maybe
he should ask her out. What a thing to think about at a
funeral. It sure was nice of her to come to his dad's funeral.

She had met his father only once, but as Brad recalled, his father had been decent to her.

Brad had been working on remembering the good times with his father, stockpiling them up against all the other memories. His favorite time was once when he was seven or eight, they had gone together to cut down a Christmas tree. Dad had let him take the first few swings at the trunk and then had praised him for the job he had done, cutting a deep notch into the tree. They had dragged the tree back over the snow-covered land to the truck and hoisted it up into the back. On the ride home, his father had whistled a Christmas carol. Snow had sifted down out of the sky. Brad had looked out the window and felt warm inside.

More people were filling the church. Brad was glad. He would have felt embarrassed if no one had come to mourn his father's passing. He knew many of these people were coming to offer their support to him and his sisters. Pit Snyder, the mayor of Little Rock, was there. He was sitting in the very back row. Mrs. Gunderson had come, and she had marched right up front and sat behind Jenny and Nora. She was patting Jenny on the shoulder right now.

Then that woman deputy was here, in uniform, sitting with another deputy, the one who had asked him questions. What the hell were they doing here? It seemed like an insult to have the police at his dad's funeral, but maybe that was part of their job.

Then Brad saw Lola walk down the aisle. She aimed herself at the front row and pushed Jenny and Nora over. Dressed all in black, she had pulled her hair back so it didn't look so messy. Actually, black suited her. It made her look more elegant than she usually did. But her face was a mess. Mascara-streaked cheeks. One more production by Lola. Maybe now they'd be through with her.

She had come out to the farm yesterday and asked Brad

if he needed help going through his dad's stuff. He had told her no. He wasn't ready to even go into his father's room. But she had seemed to need something, a memento. So finally he told her she could go in and take something to remember his father by. He had stood in the doorway and watched her. He didn't trust her much. She had gone through the closet and, after digging around, finally pulled out an old flannel shirt and clutched it to her chest.

After hugging Nora and crying for a while in the middle of the kitchen, she had finally left. He hoped she never came back.

The church was more than half full. The organ started playing, and the pastor came forward and started the service with a hymn, "Asleep in Jesus."

Brad walked to the front and slid in next to Mrs. Gunderson. Lola was taking up enough room in the front row. Mrs. Gunderson reached over and squeezed his hand, then let go. He had never had her as a teacher, but she had always been nice to him. She seemed to know how to give a person room to breathe.

Brad couldn't focus on what the pastor was saying. It had always been like that for him when he went to church. As soon as the pastor started talking, his thoughts flew out the window. It was something about the singsong sound of the pastor's voice. They never talked like regular people; they always had an odd cadence.

After the next hymn, the pastor motioned Brad to come forward.

Brad stood up in the pew and walked toward the pulpit. He unfolded the paper he had kept in his hand and smoothed it out. He looked at the words he had written and read them out loud in a clear, strong voice. He didn't have much to say, but he could let everybody hear it.

"My father raised us kids the best he could. We always

had food on the table and clothes on our back. He loved farming and he wasn't bad at it. Once he won a blue ribbon at the county fair for his feed corn. As the Bible says, 'Honor your father and your mother, as the Lord, your God, has commanded you, that you might have a long life and prosperity in the land which the Lord, your God, is giving you.'" For a moment, standing there, Brad remembered the next commandment: "Thou shalt not kill."

He took a deep breath and looked out at the faces of all the people in the church, watching him as if he were about to announce something really important. "That is all I have to say."

AFTER THE FUNERAL, the pastor invited everyone to join them for a light luncheon in the basement. Billy and Claire had agreed that it was worth sticking around to see if anyone had anything to tell them, so they had walked down the linoleum-covered stairs into the basement with the crowd.

Claire looked over the food spread out on two long folding tables. Every form of hot dish known to mankind, and it all looked good to her: tuna casserole, macaroni and cheese, bean dishes, spaghetti, green beans with potato chips crumbled over the top, meatballs and scalloped potatoes. She had only had coffee for breakfast.

Billy nudged her. "I could go for some grub. How about you?"

Claire turned to him and nodded. "Someone's got to eat it. The church ladies have outdone themselves."

They both walked over to the end of the line. Within minutes they were up to the table, had picked up plates and loaded them up. Billy found them a place to sit at another long table, and after setting her plate down, Claire went and got them both cups of coffee.

After they'd been eating for a moment, Pit Snyder walked

up to the table and asked if he could join them. He pulled out a folding chair and sat down in it carefully, as if he were afraid it might break under him. Claire was surprised by how little food he had on his plate: carrot and celery sticks, an unbuttered roll, and some green beans.

"Not enough hot dish on your plate," she told him.

"Hey, I'm on a diet. I don't like it, but my wife has threatened awful things if I don't lose a few pounds. If I even look at anything with fat in it, I gain weight."

He bit into a carrot stick while watching them eat their hot dishes. After gnawing it down to nothing, he said, "I heard you took Lundgren into custody."

"Yes, we brought him in last night."

"Isn't that a little premature?"

Claire was surprised by his comment. "Actually not at all. Most murder cases that are solved are closed within the first few days. So we're right on schedule if we're going to get this one figured out."

"You think he did it?"

"Wouldn't have gone in with a search warrant if I didn't think it was a possibility. Forensics will let us know in the next day or two."

"What does he say?"

"Not much. Says he didn't do it." Claire looked over at Snyder, nibbling on a roll with no butter on it. "What do you think?"

Snyder threw the roll down on his plate and shoved it away. "I wouldn't pick Leonard Lundgren for a stabber. He might sock someone and give them a concussion by accident, but he doesn't strike me as someone who would knife someone to death. This has a premeditated feel to it, don't you think?"

"You've been giving this a lot of thought, haven't you?" Claire asked.

"It's my town. I've been mayor here for over ten years. What I'd like more than anything else is to find out that someone who came into town from out of the county took a dislike to Jed and stabbed him. I'd like this thing to be pinned on someone I've never heard of."

Billy shook his head. "Not likely, Pit. I didn't see too many strange faces at the dance. Mainly the local yokels."

"Yeah, you got that right." Snyder sighed, then out of the blue said, "It'll be four years this next week since the Spitzler kids' mother died. She died on the thirty-first of the month."

Rainey Spitzler. She kept coming up in this case. Claire wasn't surprised to learn the deaths had happened so close to the same date, years apart. Somehow the two deaths seemed tied together. This woman's death was certainly haunting her.

"How do you happen to remember that?" Claire asked, pushing her plate back. She hadn't quite finished, but she no longer believed in the clean plate club, figuring it was partly responsible for all the overweight midwestern folks.

"I was on the ambulance crew."

Claire thought back to what Dr. Lord had told her. "But I heard that they hadn't called for an ambulance. I was told that Jed just piled her in his truck and drove her in to the hospital himself."

"Yeah, the stupid bastard did. Sorry to speak poorly of the dead, but I don't know what he was thinking. Sometimes I've wondered if he didn't call the ambulance because he knew I was part of the team. Be just like him. But I went out to the farm later that day."

"Why?"

Snyder didn't answer at first. His eyes were turned inward, as if he were seeing the accident scene all over again.

"Dr. Lord called me. He wanted me to go out and retrieve what was left of her hands from the sorghum press."

LONG TABLES in dark basements with deep bowls of food were not easy for Mrs. Gunderson to make out. She stood at the end of the table, held her plate in one hand, and decided there was only one way to get what she wanted, as hard as it was for her to do sometimes, and that was ask for it.

"Excuse me, Nora." Mrs. Gunderson looked down at the young girl next to her elbow. "Have you eaten already?"

"Yes, ma'am, I have."

"My, what nice manners you have."

"Thank you. My mom taught me."

"She was a real nice lady, your mom."

"You knew her?"

"Oh, yes. I knew her well, and I was very fond of her." Mrs. Gunderson touched Nora on the shoulder. "I have a favor to ask of you."

"What?"

"Could you tell me what is in each plate on this table? I can't see very well anymore."

Nora looked up into her face. "Your eyes look fine."

"Yes, I know they do, but they don't work so good anymore."

"Sure, I can do that. I'll tell you what I liked and what wasn't so good, too." Nora reached up and took her hand.

"That would be nice. Why don't you just tell me what you like?"

So Mrs. Gunderson came to find herself holding a plate full of Jell-O salads and brownies and date bars, but she had managed to get a ham sandwich. Nora had declared the sandwiches okay.

"Should we go sit with Jenny?" Mrs. Gunderson asked her when they were done filling her plate.

"Sure, she's right over there." Nora took Mrs. Gunderson's arm and led her to the far end of a table where Jenny sat picking at her food.

"How are you, my dear?" Mrs. Gunderson asked as she set her plate down.

Jenny shrugged.

"Please speak up. I have trouble reading body language."

"I'm peachy," Jenny said with a nasty tone in her voice.

"I rather doubt that."

"I'll just be glad when this day is over."

"It nearly is." Mrs. Gunderson bit into her ham sandwich and wished that it had a little mayonnaise on it. Awfully dry. She managed to swallow the first bite, then asked, "How are you doing at home?"

"Awful."

Mrs. Gunderson could hear the slurring in Jenny's voice. She wondered if it was caused by pills or alcohol. Whatever it was, it would need to stop. Jenny was simply too good a child to throw her life down that pit of despair.

"Well, I was wondering if I might come and stay for a week or two. Just to be there for all of you. To help get you settled."

Jenny didn't say anything, and Mrs. Gunderson took a bite of some kind of Jell-O. It had an orange color to it, and she could taste those little mandarin oranges that come in a can. It was not bad, quite sweet and fluffy, but tasty to eat.

"We're not easy to live with," Jenny finally said.

"Nor am I, I imagine. I've been on my own for over twenty years now."

Jenny finally said grudgingly, "We could use some help."

"I'll come up in the next day or two, and we'll see how it works out."

TWELVE

LIMA BEANS.

If she squinted her eyes just right, her toenails looked like a row of pale green lima beans.

Jenny sat on the top of the stairs, staring at her bare feet. She had always liked her feet. They were the one part of her body that didn't make her puke. It was midafternoon, and she was waiting for Nora to get home from school. Jenny hadn't felt up to going to school. Brad had tried to make her, but she had stayed in bed despite all his begging and screaming.

One more day, she thought, give me one more day. Then maybe I'll be ready. Brad was worried that if they didn't behave, the county would step in and take them all away. But now Mrs. Gunderson was coming, so he didn't need to worry about that. Jenny picked at her toes.

Maybe she would do some cleaning today, she had thought, get the house a little more presentable for Mrs. Gunderson. But somehow the hours had floated by without her doing much of anything. She had eaten a piece of toast about eleven. The pill she had taken had smoothed out all the rough edges of the day.

After she had gotten up this morning, she had gone and stood in the doorway of her father's room. The bedclothes were tossed back. He never made his bed, though Lola would make it sometimes when she stayed over. She had certainly disappeared from their lives. Not that Jenny cared, but still, it had surprised her that Lola didn't come around at all except that one time. Her father's work jeans were on the floor at the foot of the bed. Jenny knew that if she opened his closet, not much would be hanging up in it. Most of his clothes would be in piles on the floor.

Mrs. Gunderson would have to stay in her father's room. Jenny thought she would try to clean it up, but she found she did not want to go into the room. It smelled like him: dirt, oil, and beer. Not a horrible smell, but it reminded her too much of her father.

Hearing the school bus pull up down the road, Jenny lifted her head up from her contemplation of her toes and watched Nora get off the orange vehicle. Nora made it all worthwhile. That's the way Jenny felt about her. Maybe that was the way Brad felt about both of his sisters.

Nora waved, and Jenny waved back.

RICH FINISHED CUTTING a pile of firewood and stacked it into the woodshed. He put the new wood at the back of the pile. He still had enough wood left over to get through most of the winter, but he liked his wood aged at least a year. The wood he was cutting up was over half a year old. It should be dry enough to burn by the time he needed it.

The weather was balmy, but he could tell the days were getting shorter, and he knew that winter could descend upon them anytime after September. He even remembered snow in September. It didn't stick, but it could make the roads a mess.

Rich stood in the middle of his yard and saw that a few leaves were coming down off the black walnut tree, always the first to lose its leaves in the fall and the last to get them in the spring. There was a scent of fall in the air, a smell of sweet decay. He was done with his morning chores, and he had a phone call he wanted to make, so he headed into the house.

He still hadn't talked to Claire since the dance and the

morning after. And he was feeling uncertain if he should, after the note she had left him. He felt slightly awkward calling her at work, but she had assured him it was okay. "If you don't call me there, you might never catch me."

He poured himself a last cup of coffee, sat down at the table, and dialed her number. It rang only once before she picked it up. Her voice, clear on the line, announced, "Deputy Watkins, Pepin County."

"This here is Mr. Haggard. I'm calling to report an assault by a rose bouquet." His attempt at humor.

Her laughter broke over the phone, and he relaxed. "Did you like them? They were all from that bush in front of my house."

"Of course. They smelled almost as good as you."

"Rich, I'm at work."

Then he asked what he had called to ask, what he had been thinking about for days. "I know you said you were busy, and I appreciate that. My busy season is about to start too. But…when can I see you again?"

Claire didn't say anything for a few moments. "How about dinner tonight?"

Her answer took him by surprise. "Tonight?"

"Is that too soon?"

"Hardly soon enough."

"What would you like?"

"Whatever you're having. The only two things I don't like are tripe and eggnog."

"It won't be exotic. Meg likes her food plain and simple," Claire said, then asked, "Why don't you like eggnog?"

"You don't want to know. Let's just put it this way: A bit of blood floating in a glass of sweetened yellow milk wasn't my idea of holiday cheer when I was a kid. Put me off it forever."

"Yuck. No eggnog."

"Can I bring anything?"

"Just yourself and your wide store of Pepin County history and lore."

"How's the case going?"

"I'll know more by dinner."

He wanted to ask her if he could spend the night, but was afraid she'd say no. It would be easier for him to know beforehand, but he could think of no subtle way of asking. "I've missed you."

Again, there was a pause, then Claire's voice: "Yeah, me too."

CLAIRE LOOKED UP to see Sheriff Talbert standing next to a post near her cubicle in the big room, cleaning his fingernails with the edge of a matchbook. They weren't dirty; it was a habit he had. Seemed to help him think.

"What can I do for you?" Claire asked, smiling up at him.

"Have you heard anything on Leonard Lundgren?"

"Nothing yet, sir."

He pulled a chair toward Claire's desk and turned it around so the back was facing her. He sat in it with his arms wrapped around the top of the chair. His short gray hair looked as if it was mowed every day or two, creating a half-inch of white stubble that gleamed on his pate. He had snapping blue eyes set into deep wrinkles and could bore a hole through a person with his stare.

At the moment, he was smiling back at Claire and looked slightly wicked. "Did I ever tell you about the last time Leonard was pulled in for a murder?"

"Don't believe so." Claire figured he was going to tell her about the hunting accident, but rather than tell him she already knew the story, she decided to hear his version.

He tottered back in the chair and then came forward with a snap and started his story. "This is going on thirty years ago. I was a deputy. Lundgren was maybe twenty years old. I was five years older. It was morning. We got a call that there had been a hunting accident. I drove out with the chief deputy sheriff, and when we got to the so-called scene of the crime, there was Lundgren. His truck was pulled into a dirt track near a farmer's house. That was where he had called us from. He met us at the truck and led us to the body. He had shot the guy right in the neck. Don't think the friend lasted a minute. But what was weird was that after that, he had shot a deer. After he killed his friend, a deer came by, and he shot it. Strangest thing I ever heard."

Claire asked a question that had been bothering her. "So he wasn't too upset about killing his friend?"

"Well, I wouldn't say that. I do think he was upset. They had been very close. Gone hunting every year since they were kids. But I think he just figured you don't waste an opportunity. Not shooting the deer wasn't going to bring his friend back."

"Do you think he shot his friend on purpose?"

Sheriff Talbert rubbed the top of his head. "Oh, you know, there were rumors flying about. Something about a girlfriend. Nothing much I can do about that. It isn't my business. I just get paid to see that someone's prosecuted if they deserve it. Leonard's blood alcohol was not over the limit, but he had some in him. He's a big guy. I bet he can drink three or four beers without going over the limit. His buddy's was higher. They had been up all night long, partying, what have you. Come morning, I don't think they were in very good shape." The sheriff paused, then pronounced, "It was a stupid accident, but, far as I could see, it was an accident."

"What do you think about this case? You think Leonard Lundgren would stab someone?"

"I wouldn't put it past him. I think you had good reason to get a warrant for him, search his place and all. But I'm not betting on him. You never know, though. Keep me posted."

"I'll do that, sir." Claire returned to her paperwork. She had been sitting tight at her desk, waiting for the phone to ring from Eau Claire. Leonard Lundgren was starting to think a lawyer might be a good idea. She wanted the forensic results before they listened to him too seriously.

Five minutes after the sheriff had stopped by, the phone rang again. Claire finished the sentence she was writing, then picked up the phone.

"There was blood on the handle of the knife, as we suspected," Clark Denforth told her after they had exchanged minimal pleasantries.

"That's good."

"Except guess what kind of blood it was?"

Claire didn't need to guess. "Deer?"

"Good guess. Deer blood. How'd you know?"

"Lundgren told us what he had done with the knife on the ride back to the station. I thought of calling you, but knew you'd have to check it out no matter what. What about all the other knives?"

"From what the technicians could tell, a couple of the knives might have had faint remnants of beef blood, but it was likely they were used for cutting up meat. For dinner. Nothing else showed up. Sorry."

Claire hung up the phone and stared into her empty cup of coffee. No more for her—she could feel how it jangled her. Her therapist recommended she get off the stuff completely. Told her it wasn't helping her anxiety at all. But Claire still felt that she needed at least a cup or two in the morning to get her going. She had cut back to decaf after lunch.

Sitting at her desk, she thought of putting her head down on her desk and having a brief cry, not a good sign. This stupid case. She felt like she didn't know enough, didn't understand what had gone on before. She knew she had done what she should do—Lundgren was a logical suspect, and she had checked him out. She had needed to do that. But now what?

She needed to talk to more people. She had always felt that the children—Brad and Jenny—were not telling all they knew. Were they protecting someone? Would she have to look more closely at the two of them? She hated the thought of that, after all they had gone through.

And then there was Rich. He was coming for dinner tonight, probably happy at the thought of seeing her again. If it could only be that easy. She hated to do what she had to do tonight, but she could see no other way at this moment.

She kept imagining her life as a clean-swept prairie, where everything was easily seen and nothing could sneak up on you. But she was not there. Rather, she was in some kind of deep hole, dark and claustrophobic. How to get out, she did not know.

THIRTEEN

CLAIRE HAD KEPT it simple for dinner. Meat loaf, roast potatoes, a salad, and chocolate pudding for dessert. Meg liked all these foods, and that would make dinner easier. At the moment, Meg was in the bathroom getting ready for Rich to come. She had told her mother that she had to look in the mirror and see if she looked pretty.

"You always look pretty."

"Oh, Mom, you just say that because you're my mom. Sometimes I know I don't. When my hair's all ratty and I have dirt on my face."

"Even then you are adorable."

Meg looked at Claire carefully and cocked her head. "You could use a little lipstick, I think. I'll go get it."

Now she could hear Meg singing to herself in the bathroom. She was so good at entertaining herself. She always had been. She could play by herself in her room for hours.

The meat loaf looked almost done. It should sit for a few minutes, then it would cut better. She had poured the chocolate puddings into parfait glasses and set them in the refrigerator. The potatoes could use another few minutes. She knew this wasn't elegant dining. You weren't supposed to shove dinner at company the minute they walked in the door. Where were hors d'oeuvres and drinks? But she liked to get Meg fed near six o'clock so she had a little time to digest before she went to bed.

She heard a knock at the door and went to answer it. She could see Rich looking down the road, then he turned and smiled. His hair was still wet from a shower, and he was wearing a light wool Pendleton shirt in a soft brown plaid that suited him. As she opened the door, she heard footsteps running up behind her.

"Hi, Rich," Claire said. He said, "Hi," but his eyes weren't on her. They were on her daughter, behind her.

Claire turned to see what he was looking at. The bright, makeup-covered face of her daughter Meg resembled a trampy clown. Obviously, she had decided to use Claire's makeup. For a first try, it wasn't too bad.

"Are you practicing for Halloween?" Rich asked innocently.

"Rich, I dressed up for you."

SHE HAD GONE OVER her questions in her mind so she wouldn't forget them when they went on their walk. Rich had promised her a walk after dinner, and her mom had been happy to get rid of the two of them so she could clean up the kitchen.

As they walked up to the shore of Lake Pepin, Meg picked the top question on the list. "So how is King Tut?" King Tut was her pet pheasant that Rich had given her in early spring. He had lived in a castle with a high wall around it all summer long, dining on fresh greens and seeds that she would hand-feed him. About two weeks ago, Rich told her that he thought it was time for King Tut to go back to the flock. He had assured her that King Tut would reign until he died a natural death.

"He seems to be adjusting well. Happy to be with other pheasants. It's not good for anyone to live alone."

"You live alone." Meg felt like she had to point this out. It led into her next question.

"You're right. I do. But who knows what the future will bring?"

"So are you and my mom boyfriend and girlfriend?"

Rich picked up a rock and threw it as far out as he could into the lake. The rock dropped into the calm lake, and wavelets rippled out until they faded away. He was taking his time answering Meg's questions, just to tease her. "Did you ask me to go for a walk with you just so you could quiz me about my relationship with your mother?"

"No. I have other questions."

"Oh, that's reassuring."

"So?"

"So your mother and I are becoming good friends."

"That sounds good."

"Let me ask you a question. Do you have a boyfriend?"

Meg reached down and picked up a rock. She heaved it into the water about five yards away. "I'm not a very good thrower."

"I could show you how to do it better."

Meg turned and faced him and said, "There's one boy I like and one boy who likes me, but they're not the same boy."

"These things happen."

She decided to ask him her big question and get it over with. "Have you ever been married?"

"Yes."

"What happened to your wife? Did she die?"

"No, we got divorced. It was quite a few years ago."

Meg had suspected that he might have been divorced. But she knew she should not stop asking her questions at this point. She needed to go on and see how he would respond to one more. After all, if she didn't watch out for her mother, who would? "Whose fault was it?"

Rich walked over and sat down on the huge cottonwood stump that was near the water's edge. Lightning had hit the tree, and it had fallen last winter. "Some hers, some mine. We wanted different things. I was a lot younger then."

"So you feel like you've changed?"

"That I can say for sure. I have changed."

SHE WOULDN'T SETTLE.

That was the first thing that he noticed about Claire's behavior when she came downstairs from putting Meg to bed. She kept walking around the house, picking up pieces of clothing, hanging them up, straightening a rug, looking out the window. Through all this, she was talking to him, but not about anything important. What Meg had done at school, what the weather was supposed to be like tomorrow, how the meat loaf had turned out. She was avoiding any serious subject.

It came to him that she reminded him of a bird, scouting around, nervously pecking. And that is how he knew how to handle her. He had worked with birds all his life. If you walked toward them, they backed up. If you were aggressive, they flew away. He knew to stay calm, keep his voice low and soothing, and do nothing to startle her. He could wait her out.

Finally she sat down. But not next to him—in the armchair by the window, not on the couch where he was sitting. She perched. She stopped talking and gave out a sigh.

"How's the case going?" he asked. She always seemed willing to talk about her work. She had mentioned that she missed having a partner, someone she could discuss the case with at length. He knew she often used him as a sounding board.

"One step forward, two steps back. Doesn't look like it was Leonard Lundgren who knifed Spitzler. I keep going back to the wife for some reason. She keeps coming up, and it makes me wonder if the two deaths are linked. Maybe it's just me who thinks that. I can't stop thinking about that horrible accident. What was she like? Did you know her? Rainey, her name was.''

"Not really. I knew who she was, but she went to a different school. She was pretty, I remember.'' Rich thought back to high school, so many years ago. ''You know who knew her real well was Pit Snyder. He played football in high school. We have so few guys in our schools that they take anyone who goes out for football, and actually he wasn't bad. A block of a guy. Fairly fast on his feet. She was a cheerleader. Classic romance. Anyway, he went out with Rainey through high school. Then he joined the service, served in Vietnam, and when he got back, Rainey had married Jed.''

"Jed isn't from around here, is he?''

Rich thought back over what he knew about Spitzler. "No, not sure what brought him to this area. That farm was Rainey's family's farm. Jed hasn't done so bad with it. Some of the farmers laugh at him for the things he tries to grow, like sorghum and now sunflowers, but he tries different things. Got to give him credit for that.''

"So Pit Snyder went out with Rainey. I wonder if he held a grudge against Jed for taking his girl away.''

"After all these years, I doubt it. As far as I know, Pit's pretty happily married himself. He got married about ten years ago. Nice woman. Works in Durand, I think.''

"Does seem awful after-the-fact.''

"Maybe the knifing was just a fluke,'' Rich suggested. "Remember how Jed bumped into me when we were getting beers? Maybe he had too much to drink and was a little out of control. Said something to someone he shouldn't have. So the guy pulls out a knife and stabs him.''

"It could be, but you would have thought there'd be more of a fight for someone to be provoked that badly. That

someone would see something. That's partly why I think
the knifing was premeditated.''

"What else makes you think that?''

"Just who Jed Spitzler was. I feel that at least one person
wanted to kill him.''

"Not very scientific of you, my dear Sherlock.''

She wrinkled up her face at him. "I wish I were Sherlock
Holmes. I often feel I have more in common with Watson.
I bumble around until something hits me over the head.''

"I've never seen you bumble.''

She shrugged, and they were both quiet for a few moments.

Seeming uncomfortable with the silence, Claire asked if
she could get him something, anything.

Rich thought about what he wanted: her in his arms, here
on the couch, up in bed, wherever. He said he was fine. Let
her come to him. Let her make the move. Be patient, he
kept telling himself.

"I have something to tell you,'' she started.

It scared him, the way she said it. An announcement.
Something she had thought about. Often thinking didn't
help a relationship. They were still so new to each other.
Maybe she had thought him out of her life. He nodded for
her to continue.

"I haven't told anyone. I guess I feel a little ashamed.
But I wanted to tell you.'' She took a deep breath. "I'm
seeing a therapist. A woman in Red Wing. She was recommended by my former police department.''

"Oh,'' Rich said, relieved at what she had to tell him.
"I think that's good.''

"Yeah, I guess it is. I mean, I know people do this. I just
never thought I'd do it, you know, go to a therapist. But
things have been kind of hard lately.''

"Like what?''

"Well, this is more stuff I haven't told you, but I've been having panic attacks."

He wasn't sure what those were, but they didn't sound good. "Panic attacks? How do you mean?"

"I've been told that panic attacks can take different forms. Mine mainly come at night, when I'm sleeping. I wake up totally scared, heart racing, mind spinning, body jumping around. Petrified. The first time it happened, I thought I was having a heart attack. I nearly called nine-one-one. But sometimes they happen during the day. When I'm on the job, driving around. I have to pull over and let them pass. I feel like I can't breathe, like I'm going to die."

"Die?"

She leaned toward him, anxious for him to understand. "Yes. That's how I feel sometimes."

It took great strength not to go to her and swoop her up in his arms. But he stayed seated on the couch and said, "That sounds awful."

"It is."

She ducked her head, and he let another silence happen. Then he asked, "Is there anything I can do?"

She raised her head, and she had tears in her eyes. "I know you don't want to hear this. I don't want to say it, but I think I just need a little time here, Rich. I like you so much. I want to see you and all, but it's scaring me."

Rich felt his heart sinking in his chest. His lips tightened. He nodded.

Claire went on. "You see, the therapist and I have been talking, and one of the triggers for me might be feeling strongly for someone."

"So you feel strongly for me?" he asked.

She nodded and continued, "The last two men I've loved have died. I feel like they've died because of me. I need to figure this out, work it through, somehow get over it."

So she had loved Bruce, her old partner. Rich had met him once, and he was sorry to hear that she had loved him. He had never trusted the guy. Something snaky about him. "Do you think that will take long?"

Claire pulled back her hair. "God only knows. Some days I feel like I'm making progress, but then other days I feel worse than ever. I know this Spitzler case is getting to me. A murder that feels like it might have been premeditated. The wife's death four years prior. The kids' involvement. Layers of history in this community. And I'm trying to figure it all out."

Rich had to ask. "So what are you telling me? Are you saying you don't want to see me for a while?"

"I think so."

Rich had to ask again. He had feared something like this when he had gotten the note, but he still couldn't believe it. "Not see me at all?"

Claire squeezed her eyes shut and then opened them and looked right at him. "I don't want to have to do this, but I see no other way. Whenever I feel myself opening up to you, I panic."

Rich stood to leave.

Claire rose from her chair and watched him walk to the door. "Rich, I'm afraid if I love you, you will die."

FOURTEEN

ELLA GUNDERSON looked in the mirror, squinted her eyes, and patted her hair. She couldn't risk putting on lipstick because she really could not make out the outline of her lips anymore. There was nothing that made a woman of her age look like a senile old lady quite as much as smeared, crookedly applied lipstick.

Her bags were packed and waiting by the door. She had taken enough clothes to stay for several weeks, optimist that she was. Pit Snyder said he would come by for her around noon.

This morning she had watered her flower garden, the blossoms just blotches of color for her, but she still enjoyed them. Her neighbor, Tina Ludvig, promised that she would water them if they needed it.

She had no cat to leave food for, no dog to fret about. The mice would probably come in and take over her kitchen while she was gone, but that was nothing that couldn't be fixed when she got back. And yet she was worried about her house. Sometimes she felt like the small house was a being, had some sort of soul, it was so much a part of her. She had lived in it for nearly forty years.

She loved the smell of it when she walked in from the outside, a hint of sweet spice, the warmth of oil and wood fires. She had painted every room all by herself at least once. She was leaving it clean and tidy: new sheets on her bed, the bathrub rinsed out, all the dishes washed and put away, her violets watered, her floors swept. Once a month she had a cleaning lady come in and really do all the floors because she just couldn't see the dirt, and she knew it would congregate in corners if she didn't get help. But the day-to-day cleaning she managed well.

She heard a horn toot out front and checked her purse one more time. She had her pills with her, her checkbook, her magnifying glass. She had asked the postmaster to forward her mail to the Spitzlers' farm for the next few weeks. Brad could drive, so he could bring her into town and even back to her house if she needed. She would try not to be a burden on him, though; he was already shouldering so much.

A rap came at the door, and she pulled it open. She could recognize Pit by his shape, a stocky short body and a bullet head.

"All set?" he asked.

"I hope so."

"Let me get those." Pit picked up her two bags and waited for her while she shut and locked her front door. "This is awful good of you, Mrs. Gunderson."

"Think nothing of it, Pit. I'm glad to be able to be a help. Not so very much I'm good for anymore."

"You have served as a role model for countless scores of children. It's your turn to relax and enjoy your retirement." He opened the passenger-side door for her and waited while she got in. Always the gentleman.

After he came around to his side and got in the car, she responded, "You know, retirement is all well and good, but I have to tell you truthfully, Pit, I'm mighty bored sometimes. I used to hate it when any of my students said they were bored, and now I find the word popping into my mind. I miss conversation."

"Well, I think you'll be kept busy up at the Spitzlers'. And those kids could use some loving, too. The last few years with their father have been awful rough."

Ella decided to take the bull by the horns. "Do you still miss Rainey?"

Pit started the car and pulled out of her driveway. "I do at that. You know we grew up together. I always thought we'd be together the rest of our lives. Didn't happen. What can I say?"

"Do you think Jed had something to do with that accident that killed her?"

Pit didn't answer at first, turning onto County Road N, which took them to the top of the bluff. "It's hard for me to talk about that sensibly. I have no proof. Nothing concrete. I know Dr. Lord said it was an accident, as far as he could tell. The kids both said she fell into the press. But I've got this gut feeling that it was somehow Jed's fault. Now, I'm not saying he pushed her. But why was he having her feed the stalks of sorghum into that press? That's not a woman's job, and besides Rainey wasn't that big a woman. Jed should have been doing that. Maybe he criticized her, made her go too fast, something. Somehow I have always felt like he was behind her death. I think he's regretted she's gone when he has to raise the kids on his own. But I never sensed he was really mourning."

"Well, you'd probably be the last to know that, wouldn't you?"

"I guess."

Mrs. Gunderson had had Jed in for conferences the year that Rainey died, when she had been quite worried about the change in Jenny's behavior. He had yelled at her. Told her she was a silly old woman and to mind her own business. Said he'd pull Jenny from her class if she didn't watch it. She would never forget his abuse. She never told anyone about it, but she tried to help Jenny as much as she could that year.

"I didn't like him either," Mrs. Gunderson confessed.

"He was an A number one shit," Pit said.

Mrs. Gunderson didn't like it that he swore. But more than that, she heard the loathing in Pit's voice when he talked about Jed Spitzler. "Still and all, he shouldn't have been killed."

BRAD WAS SO MAD when he got on the school bus that he didn't sit with anyone, even though Peter Crenshaw had saved a seat for him. He walked to the back, slumped down in one of the last seats, and stared out the window. He felt like slamming his hand against the glass, but he would never do such a thing.

Brad had felt so happy this morning when he got up. He could smell something cooking downstairs, and he knew that Mrs. Gunderson was up already and stirring around in the kitchen. After their mother died, they had had to fend for themselves in the morning. Dad only ever had coffee and maybe a piece of toast. He didn't care what the kids ate.

When he went downstairs, he found she had made oatmeal for breakfast. Nora was standing right by her side, and she explained proudly that she did all the measuring. "My eyes can't see to measure anymore. Between the two of us, we're quite a team," Mrs. Gunderson had said and patted Nora on the shoulders. Nora had beamed.

This new sense of happiness had all started when Mrs. Gunderson had come yesterday afternoon. When he got home from school, she was there. She had moved into their father's bedroom, which was fine by him. She had stripped the bed of its sheets and opened the blinds for the first time in four years. "I need some light in here so I can see as best as I can."

Having her around felt like a blast of fresh air. Last night they had had bacon, lettuce, and tomato sandwiches using the fresh tomatoes from the garden. Mrs. Gunderson said they were the best tomatoes she had ever eaten. She had brought out some ice cream and root beer, and after dinner they had all made floats.

Then she told them the rules: They needed to clean up the house and keep it clean, they needed to get their homework done every day, and they needed to respect each other. "That means no swearwords, no tantrums. We're all in this together, and that's the only way it's going to work. It doesn't mean you can't get mad or feel bad, but then we'll talk about it."

Mrs. Gunderson was totally up front that her eyes were fading out on her, but she didn't mind if you helped her out, and she seemed comfortable asking for help. She actually couldn't do that much cooking or cleaning herself, but she encouraged them and talked to them, and they all had cleaned up the whole kitchen last night after dinner. It had been fun. Except for Jenny.

And that's why he was steaming mad, sitting on the bus in a seat by himself.

Jenny had been sober but strung out yesterday. He could always tell when she was trying to go straight—she'd fidget and pick and jerk around. She didn't seem to know what to do with her hands.

She had promised him that she would go to school when Mrs. Gunderson came to stay. And, in fact, this morning she had dressed and come down for breakfast. But she had looked like shit. Her hair was stringy, dark circles ringed her eyes, her eyes were bloodshot, her hands shook as she tried to spoon sugar on her oatmeal.

Mrs. Gunderson had asked her how she had slept, and she said lousy.

But Jenny had walked down to the bus stop with him. He had been proud of her. He knew how hard things could

be for her. She wasn't especially well liked at school, and
she was very sensitive to what the other students said about
her. But he also knew that everyone would be nice to her,
because of their father's death.

They were standing at the end of their road, waiting for
the school bus. They could see the orange bus circling the
fields on County Road R. It would pick them up in about
five minutes. There was one stop before theirs.

Jenny had looked up at the sky and then at Brad. "I can't
do it, Brad. I can't go to school yet. I feel like everyone
will be staring at me."

"No, Jenny, no one will stare. Everyone's been really
nice to me."

"Well, they're always nice to you. That's nothing new.
I'm the freak in the family. You and Nora are the perfect
kids."

"Listen, Jen, it will only get harder. The longer you put
it off, the more people will notice. Just go to school today.
I'll walk in the building with you, even to your first class,
if you like."

"I don't need your help. I need to do some thinking
today. I won't go back to the house until you come home
from school. I'll just hang out. Mrs. Gunderson won't have
to know I didn't go."

She never even gave him a chance to argue with her. She
had just turned and walked away, cutting across one of the
fields of sunflowers.

He knew where she was going. It was where she always
went when she was feeling bad. She would go down into
the coulee that ran along the back of their land. He suspected she had a hiding place down near the edge of the
wash. Once she had told him she had seen a black bear in
there, walking through the underbrush.

He thought everything would be better after his dad had

died, but Jenny didn't seem like she was doing any better at all. He was worried that something bad would happen to her, and then there would be only Nora and him left in the family.

MRS. GUNDERSON could see the sunflowers. Their bright yellow heads bobbed in the sunlight. If she had tried to hold a head in her hands and pick the seeds out, she wouldn't be able to do that, but scanning the field, she had a good visual sense of it. Colors seemed to flood her eyes more than they used to. She took special joy in the bright yellow of the sunflowers and felt like she understood van Gogh's work better than ever.

There were so many ways to see. She had been sad to lose her eyesight, sad to be unable to read much anymore, but sometimes it wasn't a bad thing to be reminded of how precious our senses are. In full sunlight, looking out over a colorful field, she didn't even notice that there were holes in her eyesight.

She stood in the farmyard and took some deep breaths of the late-summer air. It had started cooling down a bit. They were moving into September. The nights were lengthening and getting chilly. She didn't look forward to winter.

And she didn't look forward to what she had decided to do next.

She had made up her mind last night that she would call the police and tell them what she saw.

They could do with it what they would, but her civic duty would be done.

The truth, she believed, was worth some sorrow and pain. After watching Jenny last night and this morning, she didn't think that young girl could stand much more pain. The sooner they found out who had killed her father, the better it would be for the children—and for the community. They could all get on with their lives.

She walked slowly back into the kitchen. Going up stairs wasn't so hard for her, but she really had to watch it coming down. She had fallen once or twice when she thought she was at the bottom and then realized, too late, that there was one more step.

The kids had all worked hard last night, and the kitchen looked a lot cleaner than when she had come. Nora had helped her with breakfast, but she would need to insist that Jenny help out too.

She had brought some groceries from town, and when she got out to the farm, she found they had a fair supply of food in the pantry. Brad had told her that they also had a freezer downstairs. She'd have to go look and see what was in there, but not today.

It felt a little odd to be sleeping in Jed Spitzler's bed, but there really wasn't anyplace else for her to sleep and no good reason not to sleep there. She didn't believe in ghosts, and it was just a bedroom. She had opened the two windows in the room and was airing it out. She had put her suitcase on a chair at the foot of the bed and would live out of it for a while. She wasn't quite ready to have the children help her empty out their father's drawers and closet. But maybe this weekend. Brad could keep anything that might fit him, but then they might as well drive the rest of it in to Durand and give it to the Goodwill. Someone could get some use out of his old clothes.

She went to the phone, which was attached to the wall, and picked up the receiver. She would need to get the number of the police from directory assistance, since she was unable to look it up herself in the phone book. The woman was very nice and even said she could connect her directly to the police.

When a young woman answered, Ella gave her name and then said, "I'd like to talk to the woman deputy sheriff. I think her name was Watson."

"It's Watkins."

"Oh, dear, that's a bad mistake," Mrs. Gunderson felt herself start to laugh nervously and pulled herself together. "Yes, Watkins sounds right."

When Deputy Watkins came on the line, Mrs. Gunderson explained who she was and why she was staying out at the Spitzlers'.

"Oh, I'm so happy to hear someone is out there with the children. I've felt so badly about them being on their own."

"Do you have children of your own?"

"Why, yes, I do."

"I thought as much. You talked like a mother and not a deputy sheriff there for a moment."

"I don't know. Us deputy sheriffs can be pretty caring when we set our minds to it."

"I don't doubt that. Are you still investigating Jed Spitzler's death?"

"Yes, we are."

"Well, I have something to tell you. Could you possibly drive out to the farm this afternoon and have a talk with me?"

"About one?"

"That sounds just fine. I'll put some water on for tea."

FIFTEEN

JENNY WOKE with a start. Sunshine streaming through trees. Her body was cold and sore from lying on the ground. She got up on one elbow and waited until her head stopped spinning. She had fallen asleep in the shade of an oak tree. That must have been hours ago. As soon as she had gotten to the coulee, she had taken a couple pills. After not sleeping all night long, she had been exhausted, and she knew that school was out of the question.

She stood and walked out to the edge of the overhang— a rock outcropping that overlooked the coulee. In many areas the wash was not very deep, but here it dropped away and cut deep through the limestone. If there was significant rain, a small waterfall would form under the rock overhang. She loved to come and watch the water pour over the edge of the rocks. Liquid silver. Gentle force.

She shook and moved back from the edge, knowing she wasn't too steady on her feet. She didn't want to be like the Indian maiden.

On Lake Pepin, there was a spot on the bluffline called Maiden Rock. The legend went that an Indian maiden was told that she had to marry an old Indian chief when she was in love with a young warrior. The night before she was to be wed, she climbed up to this rock, which was more than twenty stories high by Jenny's calculations, and jumped, falling to her death.

Who could blame her? Being forced to marry some old geezer would be horrible. Jenny never had understood young women who married old men. No matter how much

MARY LOGUE   135

money the old man had stored away, she never thought it
would be worth it. But then Jenny had yet to find a young
man who did much for her either. Sometimes she wondered
if she was a lesbian, but she thought she would know for
sure by now if that was the case.

Jenny had always thought the story of Maiden Rock was
pretty cool. Very dramatic. And when you think about it,
how else could an Indian commit suicide—fall on an arrow?
Not very effective. They probably knew of poisonous plants
and berries that would kill them, but a lot of them could
produce pretty painful deaths.

Jenny looked down into the coulee. It must be three or
four stories high here. Enough to do some pretty serious
damage. With the tree branches and all, it might not be a
guaranteed death, though.

She dumped out her bottle of pills into her hand. She had
about ten left. She'd take a couple more, just to get her
through the day and help her sleep tonight, and then she'd
come off them. She'd go to school tomorrow, and then the
weekend would allow her to get through the withdrawal.

She swallowed two more pills. She didn't even need water to swallow them anymore. Looking up at the sky, she
thought it must be getting close to three o'clock, and Brad
would be coming home on the bus. She'd walk home in a
little while and join up with him near the house.

"THE BEST WAY to explain macular degeneration is, a small
blood vessel in the back of my eye bled out, and as a result
I have a hole in my vision." Ella Gunderson poked her
finger at her eye. "It makes it difficult to read, hard to do
any close work. I have trouble cooking, and I couldn't knit
anymore to save my life. But I can see things far away fairly
good. With my glasses on. Your mind kind of fills in where
the hole is. So I don't notice it. For example, I'm staring

up at the blue sky. There isn't a hole where the sky should be, it's all blue. But if a bird happens to be flying in my blind spot, I don't see it. My mind just fills in more blue.''

"So basically, you see what's there, but not everything. So if you see something, it was there." Claire wanted to understand Mrs. Gunderson's vision problem and determine if it would make her an ineffective witness. But from what she had heard so far, it didn't appear it would.

"Yes. That's right." Mrs. Gunderson poured her some more tea. "Would you like another Fig Newton?"

"One more would be fine. Then are you ready to tell me what you called about?"

"I am ready. I'm sorry I didn't tell you before, but I had to think about it. It's difficult in a small town to turn in someone you have a lot of respect for. And I certainly have a great deal of respect for Pit Snyder.''

"The mayor of Little Rock?"

"Yes. Let me explain." Mrs. Gunderson shifted on the couch and then straightened up her back, ready to start speaking. "I was sitting in my folding chair, watching the band. I was getting tired and wasn't going to stay much longer. But it had been so much fun to be out amongst them, as my mother used to say. Anyway, I didn't lie to you when I told you that I hadn't seen what had happened. I heard Jenny scream, and that's when I knew that something terrible had happened. A moment later, Pit Snyder walked by me at a good clip. And this is what I wanted to tell you. I'm sure that I saw a knife in his hand.''

"A knife?"

"Yes, it flashed in his hand. I looked at it twice. At first I thought it was a flashlight or something. But when I got another look at it, I saw that it was a long-bladed knife and that the lights for the dance were shining off of it. I thought that maybe he had needed to cut something open. Then I heard what had happened to Jed Spitzler.''

''I see.''

''I don't know if you know this, but Pit was in love with Rainey Spitzler.''

''I had heard that, but I thought it was long ago, when they were in high school.''

''Yes, that's when it started, but I think they took up again, after Rainey was married. There was a bad stretch in there, after Brad was born, and I think Pit and Rainey were seeing each other again.''

''How do you know this?''

Mrs. Gunderson looked toward the sunshine coming in through the kitchen window. ''There isn't much that goes on in a small town that is secret. You haven't lived in this area long enough to find out, but it's the truth. It doesn't take much for people to put two and two together. Rainey and Pit were seen together once or twice; it got all over town. Then it ended. I don't know how or why. But Pit met and married his wife not long after that. I think he's been happy with her. But I know he has always felt like Rainey was something special.''

Claire finished her tea and looked at the bottom of her cup. Only a couple little leaves lying there, not much to read by. ''Thank you for telling me this. Please don't let anyone else know that we've had this conversation. I will check this out with Mr. Snyder within the day.''

''Might you let me know what happens? I feel so responsible. He's a good man, Pit Snyder.''

''Yes, I will keep you informed.'' Claire was standing up when she heard a crashing noise by the kitchen door.

''Whatever can that be?'' Mrs. Gunderson stood up.

''Let me check it out, ma'am.'' Claire walked to the door and pulled it open. Sprawled out in front of the door was

Jenny Spitzler. Her eyes were closed, and her head was twisted at an odd angle. Claire knelt down next to her and ascertained that she was still breathing.

As she was bending over the girl, Jenny's eyes opened and she screamed, "Too much blood! Too much blood!"

—➤ ◄—

I was crying the other night—

Meg had gone to bed, Rich had gone home—and all of a sudden I wished that every tear, every stupid tear that had ever coursed down my cheeks, was a thin sliver of glass.

Why?

So that they could accumulate, count for something. I could pull out my bowl of tears and have something to show for all my sorrow.

I'm sick to death of crying.

Okay.

Do you just say okay to keep me going? So that I know you've heard me?

Or does it mean something—is it truly okay to be sick of crying?

What do you think?

I think I think too much.

At the moment I'm disgusted with my life.

Two men have died because of me and the other I've sent away.

I've gone from having a good job with a big-city police department to being a deputy in a podunk county. And I can't even solve the case I'm working on.

Sounds like you're frustrated.

Frustrated? No, that's when a kid can't open a box. I'm

furious. I want to stand in the middle of my field under the bluff and scream my lungs out.

About what?

We kill each other.
We humans take guns and knives and rocks—whatever is handy—and we kill each other.
What is wrong with us?
What is wrong?

SIXTEEN

"I DON'T LIKE THIS one bit," said Judge Shifsky, sighing, as she signed the search warrant.

Claire had found the judge in her chambers. Her judicial robe was off, revealing a short red dress, which made Claire wonder where she was going after work. Odd to think that Judge Shifsky had another life.

"I know." Claire nodded in agreement. She knew that most people liked Pit Snyder, and this was not going to go down well in the community.

The judge handed back the copy of it and kept her own copy. "Treat him with kid gloves."

"I'll do my best."

Judge Shifsky shook her head. "I hope you don't find anything. He's a hell of a good guy."

"That seems to be the consensus." Claire was ready to head out the door, but she saw that the judge was not done with her.

"One time, this was five or six years ago, Pit was nominated to be the grand marshal of the River Parade. Quite an honor. I was on the committee that had made the selection, and I was asked to deliver the news. When I told him he had been nominated, he suggested that we pick Bud Schilling—you probably don't know him. Bud was getting up in years, and Pit was afraid that if we didn't have him as grand marshal that year, we wouldn't have another chance. Bud was grand marshal. He died three months later. I've never forgotten that. We asked Pit to be grand marshal the next year, and he accepted. There isn't anyone around these parts that doesn't like the guy.''

''I have to act on the information I've received.''

''Of course you do.''

Claire left the judge's office. On the way out the door, she glanced back and saw Judge Shifsky staring out the window at the blue sky above her shutters. She seemed to be gazing at something out of reach.

''Hi.'' A SMALL WOMAN opened the door and smiled at Claire. Gentle looking, she wore her dark brown curly hair piled on top of her head in a messy bun. An old forties-style dress hung loose on her thin frame, and beaded moccasins adorned her feet. She looked about early thirties, which Claire figured would be about fifteen years younger than Pit.

She wrinkled her nose and brushed back her hair, then said, ''I'm in the midst of something. Can I help you?''

''Are you Mrs. Snyder?''

''Yes, I'm Ruth.'' She turned and smiled at Billy. ''Hi, Billy, haven't seen you in a while. What's this all about?''

Claire handed her the search warrant and explained who she was and why she was there, ending with, ''I'm sorry to be interrupting you.''

''What does this piece of paper mean?'' Ruth shook the paper at Claire. ''This is a real search warrant? Does this mean you can come in and look anyplace you want to in my house?''

''Yes, it does, ma'am.''

The woman narrowed her eyes. ''I don't understand all this language. Why are you here?''

''You know that Jed Spitzler was killed. We need to check your house for the murder weapon.''

"Ha," Ruth burst out with a genuine laugh. "That is the most ridiculous thing I have ever heard."

"May we come in?"

"Well, I need to check that this is legitimate."

"Do you want to see our badges?" Claire asked. She turned back to look at Billy, and he just widened his eyes.

"No, I know Billy. We went to school together. I want to call someone. Is that okay? Pit would be pretty upset with me if I just let anyone into our house. So may I call someone first?"

"Who are you going to call?"

This stopped Mrs. Snyder for a moment, then she said, "Well, Pit's out on a job, I think. I might give my dad a call. He's a lawyer in Durand. He'll know what I should do in this situation."

"Fine. I'll have to come in with you while you make that call."

"Why?"

"Because once I serve the search warrant, I cannot allow the area to be tampered with."

"You think I might get rid of something? This is so ridiculous. Oh, come on in. Billy, you come in too. Either of you want some coffee?"

Claire had never had a search begin on this amused, neighborly note. The woman wasn't going to be pushed around, but she didn't seem worried that they would find anything. She and Billy followed Ruth into the kitchen. It was a large room with a round oak table that was covered with an unfinished quilt.

"Let me clear this off. I was just putting together this quilt when you came. What do you think?" Ruth held up the quilt top.

Claire was astounded by the quilt. "What a lovely thing."

Black and white and gray blocks of fabric seemed to tumble down the quilt as Ruth held it up. What a wonderful way to spend your time. Claire hadn't sewn since she was a kid, making clothes for her dolls and once an A-line skirt for home ec. Maybe she needed a hobby. For a moment she imagined herself sitting in a sunny spot in her house with such a quilt spread out over her knees and her hands sewing quietly while she contemplated her life.

Ruth smiled at the compliment. "It's called Tumbling Blocks. An old Amish design, but I think surprisingly contemporary. I want to get it finished for Christmas. It's for Pit—he does know about it, but he hasn't seen it yet. I only work on it when he's gone. I have another project I sew on at night when he's here."

Claire reached for the other end of the quilt, and they folded it together. Then Ruth swept the rest of her sewing equipment off the table and handed them two cups of coffee, pointing to the sugar jar on the counter.

Then she took the phone and dialed a number. "Mr. Torseth, please." Pause. "Hi, Dad. Sorry to bother you at the office, but two deputies are here. They want to search the place. They think Pit might have had something to do with Jed Spitzler's murder. I know. Yes. Okay."

She hung up and turned to them. "He said he'd be right here."

Claire stopped drinking her coffee. "This isn't up for discussion. We need to begin our search. We are not waiting for your father to get here."

Ruth Snyder waved her hand. "No, I didn't intend for you to wait. But he is coming over. I just wanted you to know."

Claire heard a little more of the steel in the woman's voice. She wasn't laughing anymore. Maybe she had started to realize this was serious.

On the way over to the Snyders', Claire and Billy had discussed where they would like to start. Now Claire asked, "Could you show me to your husband's workroom?"

"Oh, sure. That's in the back of the garage."

Claire turned to Billy. "You're taking the basement?"

"Right," he said, and nodded.

Claire followed Ruth out to the garage. Another neat, orderly workroom. Pit appeared to have a project going, a long piece of narrow wood stretched out on his workbench with newspapers under it. It looked as if he had varnished it.

Ruth saw where Claire was looking and explained, "That's a stretcher for one of my quilts. We're going to hang it in the living room."

There was an awkward moment when Claire started opening drawers and Ruth stood behind her watching. Then Ruth turned and left. Claire was glad to have her gone. She knew this was her job, but with someone as nice as Ruth, it did feel like she was violating their house, digging through their business.

It didn't take Claire long to go through the workspace. Everything seemed in its place. She heard the doorbell ring and assumed that Ruth's father had come. She might as well go in and talk with him. Get it over with.

She perused the workshop one more time, but it all looked in order. Maybe she would find nothing. Everyone would be happy. She could sit down with Ruth and ask her about quilting.

Claire turned to go. When she reached the door from the garage leading into the house, on impulse she looked back at the work area. That was when she noticed the plastic mat on the floor that stretched the length of the workbench. It was black and looked industrial, like flooring you would see in an airport. But there was a very slight bulge at one end. She walked back over and lifted up the edge. There, tucked into a joint in the cement floor, was a knife. Long-bladed. She put on her gloves and lifted it up.

A rusty brown darkened the place where the blade met the hilt.

JENNY WAS ASLEEP, breathing deeply.

Mrs. Gunderson stood in the doorway, listening to the girl pull air into her lungs and then out again. She had had such a scare today. She had been afraid that Jenny had come close to overdosing on her pills, which she found out were called Darvocet.

Thank goodness that quick-thinking policewoman had been with her when Jenny collapsed on the doorstep. Between the two of them, they had managed to get Jenny to stand, and they had brought her into the house. Then Jenny had told them what she had taken, and Deputy Watkins had called poison control.

Poison control asked for the dosage, asked if she took this medication frequently, and then told them that the narcotic wasn't a problem. She hadn't taken enough to make herself anything but very sleepy. Get her to throw up if they could. Let her sleep it off.

So Mrs. Gunderson and the deputy had hauled Jenny to the bathroom and made her stick her own finger down her throat. After Jenny had thrown up, they had helped her up to bed. She had slept off and on all the rest of the afternoon. Once she had come down for a glass of water, and Mrs. Gunderson asked her how she was feeling. It hadn't been much of a conversation. Jenny's end was decidedly mono-syllabic.

When Brad had come home, he had been quite tight-lipped on seeing his sister's condition. He slammed around the house and then went out to do all the chores. Nora had come home sunny as anything, and when told to entertain herself, she had gone outside and built a fort with bales of hay in the barn.

Nora reminded Mrs. Gunderson so much of how Jenny had been when she had been that age: sweet, innocent, and full of life. Whatever had happened to Jenny had happened to her the year her mother died, the year she had been in Mrs. Gunderson's class. Mrs. Gunderson suspected that it had not been her mother's death that had changed her, but rather her father's unrelenting supervision, and maybe, she feared, inappropriate behavior.

She could almost remember the day she had noticed the change. It had been right before Christmas. The children were all running around, getting ready to put on the Christmas pageant. Jenny had stayed at her desk, drawing. When Mrs. Gunderson had gone over to encourage her to join the others, she had seen what she was drawing. It was square after square after square. They filled the lined sheet of paper. Some of them were squares within squares, but most were lined up right next to each other. When asked what she was doing, Jenny replied, "I'm just drawing rooms with no doors."

That's how shut off Jenny had become from that day on. It had been horrible to see. Mrs. Gunderson had tried to talk to Jenny about it, but there was no way in to the little girl.

Mrs. Gunderson left the door of Jenny's bedroom open a crack and went downstairs to see how the other two children were getting on with their homework. They had established a routine of her helping them with it every night.

She was very careful about going downstairs. She counted the steps—there were twenty-two—and put her foot down carefully so as not to miss one. So far, so good. She hadn't fallen in the house yet.

When she was halfway down the stairs, the phone rang.

"I'll get it," Nora sang out.

"Fine, if it's for me, tell them I'm coming."

A moment later, Nora's voice: "It is for you. Deputy Watkins. I asked them who they were."

Mrs. Gunderson felt the last step and carefully stepped down onto the main floor. She walked over to where Nora held out the phone, took it, and said, "Hello."

"Hi, Mrs. Gunderson, I'm sorry to bother you, but I did say I would call." Deputy Watkins's voice sounded somber.

"That's fine. We've just gathered in the kitchen for homework. Jenny is sleeping upstairs. She seems fine. I'm sure we won't see any more of her tonight. What news do you have for me?"

"I found a knife at Snyder's."

"Oh, dear. I so wished you hadn't. Does it look suspicious?"

There was a pause at the other end. "I would say it does. I need to ask you again, Mrs. Gunderson, not to say anything to anyone about this. We will know more in a day or two."

"I understand." Mrs. Gunderson hung up the phone and decided that she didn't understand. She didn't understand the nicest man in the county being suspected of murder, she didn't understand the sweetest little fifth-grade girl turning into a drug addict, she didn't understand women losing their hands in farm machinery.

Ella Gunderson went to the sink and washed her hands. She looked out the window into the yard, but the darkness had swallowed everything up. She hoped she had done the right thing.

She turned to Brad and Nora, who were sitting next to each other at the kitchen table doing their homework, and said, "What can I help you children with?"

CLAIRE SAT IN A CHAIR in her porch and listened to Meg working away in the kitchen. Her daughter was singing "Michael Row the Boat Ashore." Meg was proud to be doing the dishes all by herself. Claire had recently started letting her do them from time to time. It took her forever, she made a total mess of the kitchen—water everyplace— but she seemed to completely enjoy it. Meg viewed doing the dishes as a treat, and that was fine with Claire. Meg was more than old enough to start doing some chores around the house.

Claire turned when she heard a noise close behind her and saw her daughter holding out a big yellow bowl.

"Where does this go?"

"With the pots and pans in the bottom cupboard."

Meg stood looking at her. "I'm not very happy that you broke up with Rich. I think it stinks."

"Oh, you do, do you? Well, I didn't really break up with him. I told you, we're just taking a break."

"Breaking up, taking a break. Sounds the same to me."

"I hope it's not."

"Me too." Meg went back into the kitchen.

It was nice that Meg liked Rich as much as she did. Claire remembered how badly the Spitzler kids had treated their father's girlfriend, Lola—not that she didn't deserve the treatment.

Claire thought about Jenny Spitzler. Her mind went to the girl like a tongue goes to a sore tooth. Her worst nightmare would be that Meg would start taking drugs at that age, lose herself somehow, and that Claire wouldn't be able to pull her back. When Jenny was straight, Claire could tell that she was a decent girl, but damaged. It scared her to think that losing a mother could do that to someone. She needed to keep going to therapy so that Meg would never lose her mother.

From Jenny Spitzler to Rainey Spitzler was an easy jump to make. Claire found herself thinking about Rainey Spitzler often and wondering what had happened to her that she had fallen into the sorghum press. Next time she was out at the Spitzlers', she would ask Jenny and Brad a few questions about it. Get them to show her the press itself so she had a better idea of how it might have happened.

While Meg was slopping away, standing on a footstool pulled up to the sink, Claire looked down at her hands and wished she had a quilt in them. Was she going to turn into a Martha Stewartite even though she was a deputy? At a certain age did all women want to make something valuable with their own hands? Claire had never liked sitting and simply watching TV or listening to the radio. It felt like a waste of time. She would often clean house or paint walls or scrub floors while listening to the radio. She would iron and watch TV. But if she was quilting, then it would make it totally fine that she was watching TV because she would be doing something productive.

Also, the idea of working on a project that you could do a few hours a day and slowly, over a week or two, see progress, seemed like a wonderful idea to her. Police work was endless, and even after a case was solved, it still went on forever with appeals and all. And sometimes the culprit got away with it.

But with a quilt, at some miraculous point, it would be finished. You could hold it in your hands, put it on a bed. You could walk past a room and look at it every day. It would enrich your life.

Her therapist said she needed to get more solace in her life. Claire hadn't even been sure what the word meant. She knew generally, but not specifically. So she had looked it up when she got home. The dictionary said, "An easing of grief, loneliness. A comfort."

She liked the second definition: a comfort. Quilting would be a comfort. She could quilt a blanket for her daughter's bed. A magic blanket that would only let her have good dreams.

Then she would quilt one for herself. One with red roses tumbling all over a white background. A lovely quilt to sleep under with someone you loved.

One day she might even quilt one for Jenny.

SEVENTEEN

PIT COULD TELL this was not going to be a good day. The
boulder looked as big as the mountainside.

Right at the beginning of the project, thank God, he had
warned the couple that they might find such a monstrosity.
The Vernons were adding on to their house, which sat
tucked into a hillside about halfway up the bluff with a
spectacular view of the Mississippi River far below. To add
on to the house, they had decided to go into the hill. And
he had been hired as the contractor.

Pit remembered clearly the conversation in which he told
them that his bid was based on no such boulder being found.
He had even been smart enough to write it into the contract.
It was the Vernons' bad luck that where their foundation
was to be a huge boulder now sat. He had called the blaster.
He had set up the backhoe. It would set them back a week
or two and add probably fifteen thousand to the price of the
addition. But what could you do? These things happen.

When he saw the county patrol car pull up into the driveway, he nearly ran into the woods. This was way worse
than the boulder. Yet more inevitable. He had been dumber
than dumb. Dumber than that stupid gray boulder whose
massive shoulders were just showing above the ground.

He should have gotten rid of the knife. He wasn't sure
why he hadn't. And now it was way too late.

He put a smile on his face and walked toward the woman
deputy. What was her name? Watkins. That's what Ruth
had told him last night.

Ruth and he had made love after dinner. Gone right to

bed and made fast and furious love. She was joking around, saying she'd never done it with a killer before. He had been dead serious about it, trying to get as much of her as he could.

He loved Ruth. If it was possible, more than he had ever loved Rainey. Why would he think of doing anything that would jeopardize his marriage with her?

Why had he thrown it all away?

CLAIRE LEFT PIT SNYDER sitting by himself in the interrogation room, otherwise known as the coffee room, the fax machine room, the document room, the supply room, depending on what you needed. She poured him a cup of coffee, allowed him his one phone call, and let him stew for a while.

Stewing was as good for suspects, she had found, as it was for an old piece of beef. It softened them up for the questions that were to come, it tenderized them, as tough as they might be. While she didn't think Snyder was particularly tough, he was at core a strong man, and she wanted to give him time to think about what he had done and what he had to say about it.

What she wanted was for him to confess and explain so she could come to understand why he had killed Jed Spitzler. She wanted to get it over with cleanly so there wouldn't be a trial, the children could get on with their lives, and the community wouldn't get all riled up about charges being brought against a prominent citizen.

Sheriff Talbert called her into his office. "Hear you've got Pit Snyder in the waiting room."

"Is that what that room is called?"

"Oh, you know, whatever. Has he said anything yet?"

"No, I haven't asked him anything. This is going down by the book. I don't want any mistakes to happen."

"You're sure about this one?"

Claire hated that question. She asked herself the same thing far too often. "I'm never sure. Not even when I've seen the crime happen myself. But he's got motive, he's got opportunity, and now he's got the murder weapon. What do you think, Sheriff?"

"Don't look good for Pit."

"Would you like to be present at his questioning?"

"No, but thanks for asking. I'd like to stay fairly far back from this one. I'm not sure the voters are going to like it." Sheriff Talbert pinched the bridge of his nose. "You've done good work here, Claire. I'm glad you don't have to worry about your job like I do."

"Me too. I'll let you know what happens."

She went back to her desk and gathered her notes. She often scribbled down points she wanted to clarify with suspects when she sat down to interrogate them. She didn't want to forget anything and have it come back to haunt her.

Billy had gone to get the tape recorder and make sure it was all ready to take Snyder's statement. It probably hadn't been used in a while; they didn't have an opportunity to interrogate someone very often. She told him to be sure and check the batteries. When he presented himself at her desk, she stood up, gathered together her notes, and said, "Let's do it."

When they walked in, Pit was sitting very still, both hands wrapped around the ceramic coffee mug Claire had filled for him, although it looked like he had not taken a sip of coffee, and he was staring at the wall.

Claire and Billy sat down opposite him. Claire nodded at Billy to turn the tape recorder on. "We're going to be recording this, Mr. Snyder. We've read you your rights. Do you acknowledge this?"

He looked at her for a moment and then nodded. His eyes lacked shine; if possible, they seemed turned inward.

"Please say yes for the tape recorder."

He spoke up calmly. "Yes, I know my rights."

"Do you want a lawyer?"

"I don't believe so."

Claire took a deep breath and started at the beginning. Don't skip the easy questions, she had learned, they are the rock foundation of an investigation. "Where were you the night of August twenty-fifth?"

"I was at the street dance in Little Rock. I was there with my wife, Ruth." Pit spoke slowly and clearly, as if he were aware of being recorded. There was little hesitation in his voice as he answered the questions.

"When did you see Jed Spitzler?"

"I saw him once at the beer stand, but we didn't speak. Then I saw him later on in the evening by the Porta Potties."

"What happened that second time?"

Pit took a sip of the coffee. It must have been cold, Claire thought; it had been sitting in his hands for over fifteen minutes and had probably started out lukewarm. Pit was giving himself a moment to think how to answer the question best.

"He had been stabbed. I could see the blood. The knife was there. On the ground. So I picked it up. I'm not sure why. But I picked it up and took it with me."

"He had been stabbed, you said. Had you stabbed him?"

"No, ma'am, I did not."

"Who had stabbed him?"

For the first time, Pit ducked his head and did not answer immediately. Then he raised his head and said, "I can't say."

"What does that mean—you don't know, or you won't tell?"

Pit ducked his head again. Claire had played poker with a bunch of her buddies when she worked on the police department in Minneapolis, and she knew a lie when she saw one. He was going to lie.

"I didn't see. When I saw Jed, no one was around him."

"I have trouble believing that."

"No one was very close. I didn't notice anyone."

"Do you understand what is happening to you here? You have been arrested for murder. If you can shed any kind of light on who else might have done it, I'd advise you to do it. Otherwise, it looks very bad for you, Mr. Snyder."

"I realize that."

"So, you are telling us that you did not stab Jed Spitzler, but for some reason you picked up the knife?"

"Yes, that's what happened."

"You expect us to believe this?"

"No, not particularly. I don't quite understand it myself, so it might be a lot to expect you to see any sanity in my actions. But that's what I did."

"Was it like a memento for you?"

"Not really."

"Did you wipe it off?"

"Not particularly. It wasn't covered with blood. I think maybe someone else had wiped it off."

"And then you saved it."

"Well, I guess you could say that. I just didn't know what to do with it, so I put it someplace out of the way."

"Why didn't you throw it away?"

"I'm not sure. I was thinking about it, I just hadn't gotten around to it. I never thought anyone would think I had it."

Claire moved on to questions of his past history with the Spitzler family. "Mr. Snyder, it's my understanding that you went out with Rainey Spitzler, Jed's wife, when you were younger. Is that correct?"

"Yes, I went out with her all of high school. Then for a year or so after. And we wrote while I was away in Vietnam. But that was that. By the time I got home, she was already married to Jed.''

"I also have heard that Rainey wasn't happy in her marriage, and that there was a rumor that you and she had an affair. Is there any truth to that?''

"Yes, there is truth to that.''

"Do you care to elaborate?''

"What would you like to know? How I felt about her? How many times we slept together? What we thought might happen?''

"How did you feel when it ended between you two again?''

"Awful for a while. But I knew that Rainey was right. Or I thought she was. I tried to understand. She loved her son—that was Brad. She was afraid that Jed might get to keep him if she left Jed for me. She couldn't have left Brad with Jed. She told me that. So she chose to stay with Jed. Then I met Ruth the next year. We married shortly after. I've been happy ever since then.''

"But you've held a grudge against Jed Spitzler?''

Pit didn't rise to the question at all. He answered it in the same calm but perplexed voice with which he had answered all the others. "I never liked the man, but he wasn't very likable. I didn't like the way he treated Rainey, but there wasn't much I could do about that. But to tell you the truth, after I married Ruth, I tried not to give it much thought. I couldn't do anything more for Rainey. She had made her own choice, and she had made it twice. What more can a man do?''

Claire wasn't sure what more to ask him. He claimed he hadn't killed Jed Spitzler. "Did you do anything else when you saw that Mr. Spitzler had been stabbed? Did you call for help? Try to help him yourself?''

"No, I didn't, and I feel bad for that. But as I've already

said, I never liked him much. I think there was a good
reason he was stabbed. I decided not to interfere. I knew
someone would find him soon enough.''

''A good reason? What do you mean? What more do you
know?''

''Nothing specific. I just figured anyone who put a knife
into Jed Spitzler more than likely had a damned good reason
to do it.''

''I have to tell you, Mr. Snyder, that I'm having a hard
time believing that it wasn't you who stabbed him. It seems
to me that you had some very strong, albeit old, grudges
against this man. You never liked the guy. How can you
expect me to believe that you didn't do it?''

For the first time in the interview, Snyder raised his voice
slightly. ''I've never killed anyone or anything in my life.
Even in Vietnam. Why would I let a lowlife like Jed Spitzler
ruin a perfect record?''

A knock on the door sounded in the room, and then the
door swung open. A tall man with sharp features wearing
a suit that looked too small for him came in with his briefcase and held up his hands. ''Let's stop right here.''

He reminded Claire of someone, but she couldn't remember who. She stood up and asked, ''What do you think
you're doing, barging in here?''

''I'm his lawyer, Kent Byron.'' The man sat down in a
chair that was next to Pit and asked him, ''What are you
doing calling your wife? When you get your one call, you
call your lawyer. I can call your wife.''

''I don't need you here.''

''You need me here worse than you even know.''

''I haven't done anything.''

''That's what I mean. Ruth called and told me to come.''

Pit thought about it for a moment. ''Okay.''

As Claire watched the lawyer speak to Snyder, she real-

ized who he looked like—Ichabod Crane. Even though there
was no such person, if there had been, Kent Byron would
be his double.

Byron turned his long thin face up to Claire's and said
clearly, "This interview is over."

THE SUNSETS WERE as gorgeous as they had been a week
ago. Rich knew they were. The sun was dropping down
behind the western bluffs of the lake a little earlier, and a
little farther to the south, but the last red light still poured
across the lake and turned it opalescent, as he liked to think,
like a good oil spill.

His life was solid and good around him. The pheasants
were getting plumper, the air had snap in it, the season of
fall would be upon them soon, and he would be busier than
he cared to think getting his pheasants to market. As he sat
on his front stoop and watched the night fall from the sky
and snuff out the last colors, he knew he was a lucky man.

But he missed Claire terribly. And what he missed even
more was the possibility of her. He hadn't known her long
enough or well enough, she hadn't been woven intimately
enough into his life, that he should mourn her leaving it so
much. However, he realized that he had hoped that she
would be the woman that was going to step into his life and
give it richness and completeness. And then there was Meg.
A terrific kid to fill out the picture. He had wanted it all.
He still did.

He tried to think what he could do. He was embarrassed
to remember what he had done two nights ago. He had
driven by her house, feeling like he was in high school
again. It hadn't been out of his way at all. In fact, it would
have been out of his way to avoid it. But still, it seemed
like such a sophomoric thing to do. It had been after ten
o'clock at night, and he had gone over to Stuart's to play

cards and drink a brew. The lights had been off in all the house except her bedroom. He had actually thought about pulling over and getting out of the car and standing in her yard to look up at her window. What then, Romeo, were you going to warble her a tune?

But the urge to do something, to communicate with her, was strong in him. He had thought about writing her a letter and had even started it, but every word he wrote sounded utterly sappy. *I miss you. I want to see you. I hope you're doing all right. I think about you all the time.* It was all true and stupid. He wasn't a very good writer, so he couldn't expect to think of anything original.

Then he thought of calling her. Just say a quick hello, ask how she was, how Meg was, tell her he was fine. Hang up. Short and snappy. But it seemed like a breach of promise. He had said he would stay away.

He could send her flowers. After all, she had left him flowers. He could give her a pheasant. Bake something. Make her a chair.

But none of that would quite work.

He knew he had to do what she had asked him to do—leave her alone for a while.

The first star shone not far from where the sun had dropped below the horizon. He suspected it was actually a planet. Such a small light, but it did make a difference in the dark sky.

He would leave her be for a while longer. That's all he could promise himself this night. He would make dinner, watch some TV, call his nephew Eric and see if he would come and give him a hand with his first load of pheasants. It would be nice to have someone else around working with him, someone to talk to. He got lonesome now.

Missing Claire made him lonesome in a way that he had never been before.

EIGHTEEN

WHEN CLAIRE DROVE UP to the Snyder home, she sat in the car and took a better look at it than she had last time. Built over a hundred years ago, the house's style was classic midwestern farmhouse, a two-story white clapboard house with a red brick chimney poking out the side of the roof, two gabled windows upstairs, and multipaned glass in all the windows. The house was in good repair—no peeling paint, no broken windows. A tight, compact old house.

Two huge hydrangea bushes flanked the doorway. Their bushy heads were turning brownish red. Claire found this burnished fall color prettier than when they were bright white in midsummer.

Claire raised her hand and knocked at the paneled front door.

When Ruth Snyder came to the door, she had flour smudged on her face and a big floral apron tied over her clothes. Her face registered resignation when she saw Claire. "Yes," she said. "What more can I do for you?"

"I'm wondering if I could come in and talk to you about your husband's predicament."

Ruth wiped her hands on her apron. "Yes, come on in. You must think I'm Miss Susy Homemaker. Every time you come over, I'm in my domestic mode."

Claire laughed and said, "I find it rather inspiring."

"I just didn't know what to do with myself this morning. I feel so helpless, so I decided to bake. It usually makes me feel better."

When they entered the kitchen, Ruth held out a large

plate of twisted rolls. Their smell was in the air, sweet and spicy. ''Cardamom rolls.''

Claire's mouth watered at the sight of them. She hadn't had time to stop by Stuart's bakery on her way to work this morning and so had to skip her morning treat. A bowl of yogurt was simply not enough sustenance to get her through a whole morning of running around.

''Is there any chance I could bring some rolls in to Pit?'' Ruth asked. ''They're his favorite treat.''

''I think that would be fine. They look delicious.''

''Would you like one?''

Claire hesitated. Could this be seen as a form of bribery? Was it ethical of her to take a cardamom roll from the wife of a suspect? Her stomach won out in the argument. ''I'd love one.''

''Please sit down.'' Ruth pulled out a chair and then unwrapped the rolls.

Without even asking, Ruth poured two cups of coffee and got out plates for the rolls.

Claire took a bite of the roll and was delighted with the taste. A lovely spicy, peppery flavor filled her mouth. ''These are delicious.''

''Thanks.''

''Listen, Mrs. Snyder,'' Claire started.

''Ruth.''

''Okay, Ruth. I have come here to talk to you about your husband. I questioned him for quite a while yesterday, and something isn't sitting right with me. Actually, a lot isn't. And I thought maybe you could shed some light on what your husband might be thinking or doing. He claims he didn't kill Spitzler.''

Ruth wiped at her face and then brightly smiled. ''Thank God for that.''

Claire continued, ''Yet he also says he didn't see who

did and that he's not sure why he picked up the knife. But you need to understand that the knife did have Spitzler's blood on it and your husband's fingerprints.''

"I'm really glad you came by. I've been wanting to tell you that you've got the wrong person.''

Claire waited to hear what Ruth had to say. She was happy sipping her coffee and eating her roll. So she simply nodded to acknowledge having heard the statement.

"I've lived with Pit for over ten years. In that time, I've come to know him quite well. He did tell me about Rainey. I know he was in love with her. From time to time, he expresses concern about her children. But he's a good man. He would never, ever kill anyone.''

Claire knew how hard it was for family and friends to accept that someone they loved was capable of murder. She would not waste her time arguing with Ruth. "I can understand you feeling that way,'' she said.

"You see, Pit can't kill anything. And I do mean anything. We live in an old farmhouse in the country. Look around. Like with any other house this age, we often get wildlife in our house. You know what I mean—mice, spiders, bugs, bats, sometimes even squirrels, and once a skunk. Pit insists on setting live traps for the mice. Have you ever heard of anyone doing that? It's ridiculous. But he won't use snap traps. He hates them. We tried once. I set it up, and he went wild at night when it went off and the mouse dragged the trap around the kitchen for a minute or two. He swore never again. So he sets up the live trap and empties it every day. I'd like to put tags on those mice so we could track them. I know they just come in for more food every night and probably enjoy the little ride outside in the morning. He walks wasps out the door on pieces of paper towel rather than swatting them. If I want to kill flies, I have to do it out of his presence.''

"Why is he like that?"

"I have a feeling he was always a kindhearted soul, but Vietnam made him even more pacifist. He was a medic. After he came back, he abhorred any form of violence. Even football—and he used to love to play football."

"Many people wouldn't kill a dog, but they'd kill a human. And do."

Ruth stopped and thought about that. "Yes, I'm sure that's true. And Pit does have a bit of a temper. He's not perfect, and he does get mad and all. But I just can't believe he could take a knife and stab someone."

"So how do you explain his behavior?"

Ruth's eyes teared up. "I didn't sleep much last night. I got up and thought long and hard about what's happened. Pit is mayor of Little Rock, he's been mayor for many years. I think he takes his job very seriously. Maybe too seriously. He sees himself as a protector of the innocent. I think it's one of the reasons he was attracted to me—he saw me as one of the innocents. But I'm not as innocent, nor as in need of protecting, as he thinks I am. So the only thing I can figure is that he's protecting someone. That's the only thing that makes sense to me. I'm sure he would never kill anyone."

Claire thought about what might make a person kill. "What about if it were in self-defense?"

Ruth said firmly, "Not even then."

"What if it was to save someone else?"

Ruth said nothing.

WHEN THE PATROL CAR drove up in the farmyard again, Jenny thought of running and hiding in the barn. But then she knew they would just come and find her. Get it over with, she decided.

Walking into the house, she pulled out her litany of rules

on how not to interact with people. Don't look them in the eye. Think of them sitting there with a squirrel on their shoulder. Have a faint smile on your face. Don't listen to them. And above all, don't let them get to you. Never let them get to you. If you do, it will be all over. It will come flooding in, and there will be no escape.

"Jenny?" Deputy Claire Watkins said her name. They were all sitting around the kitchen table. Mrs. Gunderson had left the room. "Did you see Mr. Snyder by your father's body?"

Jenny snapped her head up and stared past the deputy. "Maybe. It's hard to remember."

"Brad?"

Jenny turned to watch Brad. He was one of the safe ones. Like an island in a river, like a cloud in the sky, a place to put your eyes. She always could trust him. He had tried his best to take care of her. She was curious how he would answer. He had been very upset on the bus when he had told her the news about Pit Snyder.

Brad screwed up his face and thought. Then he nodded. "I think he was there. Off to the side. It's hard to remember. All I could think about was Dad."

"This is very important, you two. We are going to seat the grand jury on this and we will need both of you to testify. I need to know if you can place Mr. Snyder by your father after he was stabbed."

Jenny didn't say anything. She would not be part of this. She would deny she knew anything. It would be up to Brad.

Brad spoke again, and this time there was more certainty in his voice. "Yes, I'm sure he was there. He was standing off to the side when Jenny and I found Dad."

"You would be willing to testify to this?"

"Yes," Brad said, looking the deputy right in the face.

He had such an honest face. Everyone always believed what he said. They never believed her.

Deputy Watkins turned to Jenny. "Jenny?"

"I think I was too out of it. I don't really remember much about that night. It's all kind of a fog."

She hadn't taken any pills since her little incident. Mrs. Gunderson had flushed some of them down the toilet, but she didn't know that Jenny had more stashed away. She might need to take one to sleep tonight. They helped when you didn't want to think about something, when you wanted the troubles of the world to flow away.

"CLIMB UP," Rich yelled at Eric. Eric had come over after school, and they had done the first pheasant drive.

The birds in the first flyway were over twenty weeks old, mature birds, and ready to ship out. Eric had helped him flush the birds out of the covered cornfield and into a narrow fenced-in strip down the middle. From there, they were funneled into the crates. They had loaded the crates onto the trailer, and they were ready to roll.

They were such pretty birds. Since the crates were open to the outside, people always wanted to see the birds if he stopped anywhere on his delivery route. Once a cop had pulled him over to give him a ticket, but once he saw the birds, the cop could talk of nothing else. He let him go with just a warning.

They had loaded up about five hundred pheasants. This first delivery was going to a hunting club that was only a few hours away. More and more the hunting clubs were where he was selling his birds. It was a lot easier than driving them up to the processing plant in northern Minnesota, then staying overnight to bring them back to the Twin Cities for various stores. For the hunting clubs, he just dropped off the live birds, and they let them go in the fields.

Eric was driving with him to make the delivery. Rich could have done it alone, but it went a lot quicker with someone along to help, and it was nice to have the company. Eric was really catching on how to handle the pheasants. He learned when to let them move on their own and when to rush them. He was only a sophomore, so Rich was glad he would have a few more years of his help. He was turning into a real nice kid.

Once they were on the road, Rich asked him, "So how's school going?"

"Boring."

"Not for a smart kid like you. You think at all about what you want to do after you're done?"

"I want to live like you. Big farm, raise livestock, fish and hunt and hang out. Looks like the good life to me."

"But don't you want to go on to college?"

"Naw, I'm not interested in that stuff."

"I'm surprised. You strike me as someone who would want to get out of town for a while. See a bit of the world."

"Did you?"

"Yeah, actually I did. I took a couple years of college, then my uncle died and I inherited this place. But before I started working it, I did manage to get over to Europe for a couple months. Hitchhiked, slept in hostels. I'm glad I did it. I'd like to go over there again. I remember sitting on the Pont Neuf in Paris, eating a loaf of bread and some cheese I had just bought in the market and thinking I'd sell the farm and learn French and move to Paris and paint. But when I got back here, it was just too easy to stay."

"I wouldn't want to go to Europe and not be able to talk to anyone."

"Oh, you'd be surprised how well you'd manage. Most of the girls know at least a little English, and they're dying to know more."

"Oh." They were both quiet for a while.

"Are the Spitzler kids back in school these days?"

"Oh, yeah. In fact, Brad Spitzler went spastic today."

"He did what?"

"You know Brad's usually real quiet. Does what he's told, never gets in trouble. Kind of a brownnoser. Anyways, some kids said something about Pit Snyder getting arrested, and he threw a fit. Slammed his locker, threw his books around. It didn't last very long, and he didn't hurt anyone, but it was real weird. He seems like the kind of kid who just might shoot up the whole school someday."

"What about his sister?"

"She's too out of it to do anything to anyone."

"I CAN'T BELIEVE you drove over here. How did you manage to squeeze behind the wheel?" Claire escorted Bridget to the most comfortable chair on the porch, where she would catch the night breezes.

Bridget lowered herself gently into the chair, gripping the sidearms. When she was in, she raised her long blond hair off the back of her neck, rolled it into a twist, and knotted it. "I just needed to see you. Get a perspective on my life. I get so lonesome. Chuck said he wanted a baby—it was his idea—and now he doesn't even want to hang around with me while we get ready to have it. He went out to a bar tonight with some friends. I'm a drag to him because I can't drink and I don't smoke and I don't like to watch him repair cars or watch football."

"Have you asked him to do some things with you?"

"You know what he's like, Claire. He is the nicest guy in the world, would do anything for me, but never thinks of it on his own. I know that it doesn't prove his love if he can read my mind, but I get tired of being so directive all the time. He thinks we're all ready to have the baby, because the room is all done. And it does look great. You haven't been over since I painted the border, but it is a darling room. But I still have over a month to go, and it's hard. I feel like a log.'' Bridget's mouth quivered, and her eyes filled with tears. She pressed her hands against her eyes as if this would stop her from crying.

Claire walked up to her and rubbed the back of her neck. ''And you're weepy because your hormones are all over the place. Things will settle down when the baby comes.''

''Do you think so? I'm afraid Chuck will find more reasons than ever to get out of the house. What have I done? I should never have married, never have gotten pregnant. If I wanted a kid, I should have just special-ordered one like Meg.''

''Your kid is going to be at least as cool as Meg.'' Claire sat down opposite her in a white wicker chair.

Bridget brushed the last tears away and grumbled, ''I envy those big fat placid pregnant women. They're everywhere. You see them lurking in the grocery stores, malls, content to be this beast of burden hauling around the little unborn in their bellies. As if they've proved their right to exist now that they're procreating. I don't want to be like them.''

''You couldn't be like them if you tried.''

Bridget reached back and untied her hair and fanned herself with the length of it. ''Let's talk about something else. I think I've vented enough. How's your love life? Tell me about it so I can live vicariously.''

''Nonexistent.''

''What happened?''

''Well, I don't think I mentioned it, but I'm seeing a therapist.''

Bridget leaned forward and clapped her hands together.

"Wow. That's big for you, Sis. I think it's a good idea. Are you going because of what happened with Bruce?"

Claire nodded. "Remember I told you that I was scared sometimes?"

"Yeah."

"It escalated into full-out panic attacks. The whole works—heart pounding, ready to burst, breath out of control, arms tingling, hands twisting in on themselves. I knew I had to do something about it. So I decided to get some help. To talk about Bruce and Steve."

"Is it helping?"

"I think so. The woman I'm seeing is pretty straight ahead. She lets me do most of the work, but she steers me so I don't get off track. The hard thing is that I decided that I can't deal with seeing Rich while I sort through all my own mess. He's such a nice guy, he doesn't need to see this side of me. I'd scare him away."

"I doubt it."

"Anyway, it was scaring me to get close to him, so I told him we needed to take a break."

"That's hard. Do you miss him?"

"Yes. More than I thought I would. He is like the earth: solid and reliable. I don't mean to make him sound dull, because he's never that. But when I'm around him, I actually believe that good things might happen."

Bridget rubbed her belly and said, "That sounds better than therapy."

NINETEEN

THE WOMAN WAS walking toward her with long hair streaming down her back. The woman was walking steady. The sky was dark behind her. The sky was dark red, as if the sun was setting. There was no sun. The woman kept walking forward, as inevitably as life, as death. Then she lifted her eyes, and they were red. Then she lifted her arms up, and her hands were gone.

She had no hands.

Claire felt like she had been shot. Electricity coursed down her body. She bolted out of bed. Before she even woke up, she found herself standing upright next to her bed, shivering. She grabbed a blanket off her bed and wrapped it around her shoulders, slumping down onto the floor.

The darkness in the room told her it was the middle of the night. She tried to stop shivering and calm herself. Put her bathrobe on, have something warm to drink, turn on a light. A light would help. She crawled over to her bedside table and turned on her lamp. The burst of brightness it threw out into the room eased her panic. The darkness receded behind the windows.

The woman—Rainey Spitzler—had come to visit. Beseeching. What was she trying to say?

Claire hated the thought of a woman with no hands. This image haunted her. As she sat there on the floor with her feet folded under her, she realized that a woman did everything with her hands. She soothed babies, made beds, cooked dinner, folded clothes, drove a car. A woman without hands was totally powerless. That's what made Claire hate the image so. Looking down at her own hands, she began to cry. What had she done with her hands?

A soft footfall in the hallway made her look up. Meg stood in her doorway, watching her.

"Mom?" Meg's small sleepy voice was filled with concern. "What's the matter, Mom?"

Claire snuffled in her tears and cursed herself for letting Meg see her like this. "I had a bad dream. It's nothing. It scared me, but it was only a dream. You go back to bed, noodlehead."

"Noodlehead," Meg said, laughing. "You haven't called me that in a long time."

"Well, that's what you look like right now." Claire stood up and put the blanket back on the bed. She took her robe down from a hook near the door and put it on. "Back to bed."

"What are you going to do?"

"Go downstairs and make myself some chamomile tea."

"I want some too. I need it to go back to sleep."

Claire thought of arguing but decided it might be easiest if she gave in. Meg would see that her mother was fine, it would be a little nighttime adventure they would share, and it would be over.

"All right, noodlehead. You run down and fill the tea kettle."

Meg ran to the stairs and slid down them on her butt. She loved to be helpful. Claire worried that she was creating a little caretaker. Meg was such a barometer already of how her mother was doing. She hated that she wasn't better able to protect her daughter from her own problems. That's why two people should raise a child. When one was in a slump, the other could pick up the slack.

When she got downstairs, Meg had the teakettle already going on the stove and two mugs out of the cupboard. Claire took out her stash of chamomile tea, bought from the local herbalist. She filled two teaballs, and when the water boiled, she poured it into the two mugs.

"Would you like some honey?"

"Mom, you know I always need honey."

Claire took down the honey jar from the shelf over the stove and handed it to her daughter. "But you're so naturally sweet."

Meg dipped her spoon in and pulled it out full of honey. Then she slowly drizzled it into her tea. "Mom, I just like it."

"I do too, sweetie."

"What was your dream about?"

Claire thought for a moment. She could not tell Meg the truth about her nightmare; she did not want her to have that awful image in her mind. "It was a falling dream. Do you ever have those?"

In her enthusiasm to talk about these dreams, Meg set her tea mug down with a thud. "Yes. Those kind of dreams are horrible. I try not to have them. You know my favorite kind of dream?"

"What?"

"Flying dreams. I'm just walking along, normal as ever, and then all of a sudden I remember I can fly. I run and hold my arms out and up I go. Do you have those, Mom?" Meg turned her face up and smiled.

"I used to have those dreams. It's been a long time since I flew."

"You should work on having one of those."

CLAIRE'S COMMUTE TO the Pepin County sheriff's office from Fort St. Antoine was about twenty-five minutes, which wasn't much longer than she had commuted to work in the Twin Cities, but much more pleasant than driving through rush-hour traffic. She drove along the river and then inland through rolling Wisconsin countryside. There was no traffic. The occasional delivery truck, a school bus, and many pickup trucks. People often waved as they passed you, even if it was only the two-finger wave, hand still gripping the steering wheel.

This late morning, she saw evidence of fall coming. The sumac had turned—it always went burnt red early—the aspen were slowly moving from green to yellow, their autumn color. The once solid green hillsides were dappled with these other glorious colors. For the next month the colors would only get more spectacular, usually peaking in early to mid-October.

As Claire drove, she thought about what she had to do today. She had decided she needed to have another try at Pit Snyder. He was not telling her all that he knew, and she wanted to get to the bottom of this killing. If he did it, she'd like to get him to confess to it; and if he didn't, head them in the right direction.

After a cup of coffee, a bit of jawing with Billy and Dan, she sat for a few minutes at her desk, figuring out her strategy for approaching Pit. His vulnerability was his concern and compassion for other people. He was your basic caretaker. She felt strongly that the way to get to him would be through his wife, and through Rainey. If he was covering for someone, he would not give them up for himself.

Walking down the hallway toward the jail cells, she decided to do it all off the record. Just to see if she could get him talking. It was worth a try. She didn't think she had anything to lose. If he confessed once, he would do it again, and he was more apt to talk openly without the microphone.

Claire stood outside Snyder's cell and asked, "May I come in?"

He looked up from the bunk on which he was lying. "I believe you can come and go as you please."

"I didn't want to be disturbing you."

"Are you serious?" Snyder sat up, and his voice was bordering on sarcastic, but he was too nice a man to be able to pull it off. "I'm locked up, and you're worrying about disturbing me?"

"Okay, it was a figure of speech."

"You can't help yourself. You're just too polite to be a cop."

"Huh, and I was just thinking you're too decent to be a politician." Claire opened the iron door and let herself in. "Let me assure you that I am not too nice to be a cop. Quite the contrary."

She walked over and handed him a cup of coffee. "They don't usually come around with seconds. Thought you might need this."

He took it from her gratefully.

She sat down on the one chair in the room. The cell block was quiet. Friday morning right before the weekend rush began. She was glad there was no one else locked up with him so they could have some privacy.

"I went over and talked to your wife yesterday."

Snyder's head came up, and he said with emotion, "Leave her out of this."

Claire knew she was on the right track. "She's very worried about you. She doesn't seem to think that you are responsible for what happened to Jed Spitzler."

"There's a lot she doesn't know."

When Snyder said nothing more, Claire prodded, "I asked Ruth about your relationship with Rainey."

"It's no secret. I have talked to her about it. It all happened before Ruth, so it doesn't bother her."

"That's what she said. But she seems to feel you're protecting someone. I think she's very scared about what's going to happen to you. Have you thought about what Ruth's life will be like if you continue on this path?''

Snyder dropped his eyes.

''Let me clue you in. The going sentence for this type of crime, for manslaughter, is twenty to life. Ruth's a young woman. How long do you think she'll wait for you?''

Snyder shook his head as if trying to knock these thoughts out of it. ''Can't be helped.'' He sipped his coffee and stared at the floor.

''I like Ruth,'' Claire said. ''Did you get the rolls she sent you?''

''Yes,'' Snyder said. ''Thanks for letting me have them.''

''No problem.''

Claire let the silence stretch on for a while. There was no need to rush this. Let him get used to her, wonder what she was up to, have time to think through what she was saying.

Finally, Claire started, ''I had a horrible dream last night. I dreamed that a woman with no hands came walking toward me. She seemed to want something from me. I feel like you might know what that is.''

Claire saw that she had finally reached him. He bowed his head, and his shoulders shook slightly. ''Rainey,'' he said.

''Ever since I've heard about what happened to her, I've been haunted by it. I know there's a lot of farm accidents. I'm a city girl, so at first it surprised me. But now I'm getting used to seeing farmers with fingers missing, hearing the stories of kids losing limbs. But you know what gets me about this accident? She lost both her hands. I have trouble seeing how that could happen.''

Slowly, Snyder nodded his head in agreement, his eyes lifted up to watch Claire as she talked.

Claire continued. "I questioned Dr. Lord about it. He said that she fell into the press, that she was the one who was putting the sorghum stalks into the press. I wonder why Jed Spitzler wasn't doing that? It sounds like the hardest job."

Pit finally spoke up. "Not necessarily. According to the kids, Jed was lifting the stalks down off the trailer. They had just harvested it, and he was carrying the sorghum stalks over to Rainey. They can be mighty heavy. But I agree with you. I don't know why he had Rainey doing that. It's a god-awful job for a woman, and she wasn't very big. Not as big as you, but a couple inches taller than Ruth."

"What do you think happened? How could she have fallen into the press with both hands? Wouldn't she have tried to catch herself with one?"

"I have thought about it until I've had to puke. I don't understand it either. And I have my suspicions. Always have had. I think Jed Spitzler killed his wife."

"Why didn't you do anything about it?"

"I did, goddamn it." Snyder's temper was rising. "I talked it over with the sheriff at the time. But he had already talked to the children, and they had said it was an accident. Jed insisted it was an accident. Nothing in the autopsy said it wasn't. There wasn't anything we could do."

"What an awful way to die."

"The worst was, I think Rainey knew it was going to happen." Snyder's voice broke as he talked. He cleared his throat.

"What do you mean?"

"She called me the night before the accident. I hadn't talked to her in a couple years. I mean more than saying hi on the street. She asked me to help her. She said she was going to leave Jed. Take the kids. She wanted to know if there was someplace safe she could go. I asked her what was going on, and all she would say was, she had had enough. I told her I'd look into it. That was the last time I talked to her.''

"Did you tell the sheriff that?"

"Yes. He didn't think it made any difference. People have marriage problems. Didn't change his mind. Not with the kids saying it was an accident.'' Snyder calmed. "You gotta understand. I was married to Ruth. I was happy. I didn't want people to start talking again.''

"I'm sorry.''

"Yeah, I've always regretted that I didn't do more. That I didn't push harder. At least get the children away from Jed. But I didn't have anything. No evidence of abuse or anything. I went out and checked on them from time to time. But they seemed okay. Shy. Quiet. Brad's always been a real good kid. But Jenny has turned into a lost soul. I always wished I could have done more for her.''

"How do you think this ties in with Jed Spitzler's death?'' Claire asked him.

"An eye for an eye.''

WHEN CLAIRE HAD FINISHED getting dinner ready—nothing fancy, just BLTs—she went to call Meg and couldn't find her anyplace. Then she remembered that Meg said she was going to visit a friend. Claire had assumed she meant Trevor, so she called over there. They hadn't seen her.

Claire stood in the middle of the kitchen and felt panic start to build. Where was Meg? She tried to calm herself. Meg was in no danger. That was all over with. Meg was old enough to walk around the neighborhood by herself. They had agreed that she could. She would be coming in the door any minute now. But Claire could feel the charges building up in her body, the fear soaring.

Then the phone rang.

Claire picked it up before the second ring. "Hello?''

"Hi, this is Rich. Listen, I have a visitor here, your daughter, and I just wanted you to know she had walked over. I didn't want you to worry."

"Thanks, Rich. I was beginning to wonder."

"If you'd like, I'll bring her home in a few minutes. She said she came to see King Tut, and we've had a nice visit."

"Great."

"You don't mind?"

"Not at all. I'm so glad you called."

She hung up and went to the sink and filled a glass with water from the tap. She loved the water down here, especially after growing up on city water. She had her own well in the backyard that went down a hundred feet to the aquifer. The water had high levels of calcium from the limestone bluffs and was as sweet as anything. She sat down with her water and waited for her daughter to come home with the man that she wasn't seeing at the moment. She could hardly wait to see him.

Fifteen minutes later, Rich's pickup truck pulled into her driveway. Meg hopped out the passenger side, and Claire got nervous that Rich was going to drive away, so she ran out to say hi. But he stayed sitting, with the engine idling, waiting for her.

"Hi there," she said.

"Howdy yourself." He smiled.

What could be more natural than to walk up to him and put her hand on his cheek? But she resisted. Meg walked up to her and leaned into her side. "Sorry, Mom."

Claire wrapped an arm around her daughter. "I'm not really mad at you. I know I told you you could walk anywhere you wanted to in town, but you need to let me know where you're going to be."

"Mom, I told you. I said I was going to visit a friend."

"Right."

"Well, I wasn't sure you would let me go see Rich and King Tut, so I just went."

Claire squatted down and looked Meg straight in the eyes. "You can go and see Rich whenever you want to. I know he's your friend too. And I know you need to visit King Tut. But from now on, tell me. Deal?"

"Deal."

"Go in the house and get ready for supper."

Meg ran up to the house, stopped and waved at Rich, then went in.

"How's King Tut?" Claire asked.

"Adjusting. Meg thought he looked silly with his blinders on, but I explained why I put them on all the birds."

"So they can't see what's all around them. Maybe I need a pair."

"How're you?"

Claire thought for a moment and said, "Not too bad. How're you?"

"Lonely as hell, but aside from that, busy. My season is just starting. Eric's been over to help. Sorry you missed our first pheasant drive."

"Me too."

"Hey, he mentioned the Spitzler kid, Brad."

"Eric did? What did he say?" Claire was more than interested.

"He said that Brad blew up in school when someone said something about Pit Snyder being arrested."

"Brad blew up, huh?"

"Eric said it was quite out of character."

"I would expect so. He's a pretty good kid. I think I need to go talk to him again. Thanks."

"I've got my ear to the ground. I'll keep you posted."

As much as she hated to mislead him, she couldn't help saying, "Maybe I'll be able to make one of those pheasant drives soon."

TWENTY

"I'M STAYING HOME from school today. The sunflowers need to be harvested," Brad said somewhat defiantly.

"Can't it wait until the weekend?" Ella Gunderson heaped some scrambled eggs on his plate. She did a pretty good job with scrambled eggs because the whole point of the dish was that they were scrambled. Her eyesight didn't hold her back from doing that.

"I need to get the combine ready to roll. It probably needs some repairs, and I might need help with them. We've never had sunflowers before. I think I know what to do, but I need to check in with another farmer who has harvested them."

"So you would like to stay home from school and take care of that?"

"Yes, I would. If it's all right with you."

She put some eggs on Jenny's plate. The girl's blond hair was oily and pulled back in a ponytail. Her eyes had a heavy, bruised look to them. She was wearing the same T-shirt she wore to school the day before. It had what appeared to be black notes and the words PEARL JAM written underneath the notes. Whatever could that combination of words mean. Ella had decided not to ask about it. She'd rather not know. But she didn't like Jenny wearing her clothes twice in a row. Ella had washed all the dirty clothes in the house. Jenny had no excuse for that behavior.

"I wish you would change your shirt before you go to school today, Jenny. Please. I put some clean shirts in your drawers."

"I'm not going to school. I don't feel good."

Ella didn't doubt that. Jenny obviously had another stash of pills and was dipping into them. Plus, Ella had found a couple empty beer cans under her bed. It occurred to her that Jenny hadn't put the shirt on for the second day in a row, she simply had never taken it off.

Nora was eating her scrambled eggs quietly, swinging her legs back and forth, a nervous habit she had.

Ella decided it was time to do something.

She let the frying pan she was holding drop to the floor. It hit the linoleum with a loud bang, startling even her. She never behaved like that, but she needed to get through to these children.

Brad jumped out of his seat, Jenny put her fork down, and Nora put her hands over her ears. Poor child, her father probably did such things. They all three were staring at her.

She picked up the frying pan. "I'm sorry about that, but I needed to get your attention. I think we all need to talk."

She put the pan in the sink and turned to find them all sitting at attention, their eyes drilling into her. "Jenny and Brad, neither of you have to go to school today if you choose not to. But as of next week this changes. If you do not go to school every day that I am here, I will have to leave, and I will report you to the truancy officers. I have come to your house to try to restore order and to help you. But I cannot help you if Jenny continues to down pills and leave the world behind and if Brad keeps pretending that everything is all right when it's not. Nora, you've been a good kid. But I think you need to hear this too."

Ella took a deep breath and continued. "I've given you a lot of room to move because your father is dead. I am sorry he's gone, but I think you all can have a good life without him. If you shape up. I miss my own house. I do not want to stay with the three of you unless I get something out of it. When you are all helping me cook and clean, when we do homework together, when you ask me how I am doing, when I feel like we're making progress, then I feel worthwhile.''

She stopped for a moment to let what she was saying absorb into their brains. "I need to feel worthwhile. Everyone does."

She turned to Jenny. "So if you have any pills left, bring them to me, and then go to bed until you feel good enough to get up. At that point, I would like you to take a shower and come and help me around the house. I'm almost ready to start digging out your dad's closets.

"Brad, make your calls and find out what we need to do about these sunflowers. I'll help out however I can. If you can harvest them all this weekend, that would be great."

Ella sat down next to Nora. "And how about you? What would you like to do today?"

Nora's big dark eyes stared back at her with a serious, worried look. "I want to go to school. We read the most books of any class, and so we get to have pizza for lunch as our prize. I don't want to miss that."

Mrs. Gunderson wrapped an arm around her and squeezed her tight. The smile on Nora's face told her that she would be fine. "Good girl."

Jenny stood up. "Don't leave us yet, Mrs. Gunderson. Give us a little more time. We'll try to do better."

"Go back to bed, Jenny. I'll see you in a while."

Brad stood up. "Mrs. Gunderson, we'll all try to help out more. I'm going out to the field and check how ready the sunflowers are to be picked. I talked to a farmer a couple days ago, and he gave me a few pointers."

"While you're out there, would you bring in a few for me to make a bouquet?"

"Sure." Brad turned to go, then stopped and asked, "Mrs. Gunderson, what's going to happen to Pit Snyder?"

"I don't know. I'm afraid he might have to go to jail if he murdered your dad."

Brad's shoulders slumped, and he walked outside, letting the front screen door bang behind him.

PIT SNYDER'S BAIL had been set at a quarter million; the judge had not seen him as a flight risk. He had posted his bail and was to be released later today. Claire didn't think he would stray.

Claire had done paperwork all morning and then ridden around on duty most of the afternoon. She had called Mrs. Gunderson before she went out on her rounds and asked if she could stop by later to see the children. She would tell them all what had happened and watch their reactions.

Pulling in to the farm this time, she noticed how run-down it was. Many of the farms in this area were very well kept up, but at the Spitzlers' all the outbuildings needed paint, and the fences were sagging and broken in places; the windmill had lost some of its blades and screeched when it turned in the wind. The wail of the windmill reminded Claire of Rainey Spitzler. But since the dream of the no-handed woman, many things reminded her of that poor woman.

Chickens scooted across the driveway as she pulled up to the house. She would love to keep chickens and walk out in the morning to gather fresh eggs. Maybe she and Meg should talk about doing that this next summer. Rich might help them get set up. Rich. Not the time to think about him.

Ella Gunderson stepped out the kitchen door and waved at Claire. She was wearing a red sweatshirt and a pair of jeans. Claire had never seen her dressed so casually. On her head she had tied a red bandanna.

"Excuse the way I look," Mrs. Gunderson said as she came forward to shake Claire's hand. "We are cleaning. Jenny and I."

"How is she doing?"

"It's hard to say. She's been in a slump the last few days, but I gave all the kids a pep talk today, and they seem to be coming around. I'm not a counselor. I don't know what to say to them about their dad."

"How do you think he treated them?"

Mrs. Gunderson took off the red bandanna and snapped it in the fresh air. "I'm afraid he was more than strict with them. If I raise my voice, they all quiver and shiver. That's a learned reaction. You know what I mean. They've been taught to be afraid."

"Yes. Do you think he hit them?"

"I doubt it. I don't think that was Mr. Spitzler's style. I would say intimidation was more up his alley. He did it to me when he came in for a school conference. He could be very mean when he set his mind to it. I guess they call it mental abuse."

When they walked into the kitchen, Claire couldn't believe the change that had been wrought in the house. The windows were clean, and the sun shone in. The countertops were swept clear. Dishes were all in their places in the cupboards. A big bouquet of sunflowers sat in the middle of the old round oak table, their heads heavy with dark seeds.

"It looks so nice in here."

"We've all been working hard. I think some of these floors and counters hadn't been cleaned in years. Probably four years. Since their mom died."

Jenny walked into the kitchen and, when she saw Claire, pulled back into the doorway. The teenager looked beaten, her shoulders slumped over, her mouth petulant. Claire felt like giving her a good scrubbing and taking her for a long walk. Get some energy back into her. She was too young to act so weary.

Mrs. Gunderson continued talking. "Nora's my eyes. She points out the dirt and cleans it up. We're quite a team. But Jenny's helping me today."

She walked over to the girl and put an arm on her shoulder. "Jenny's been a big help."

Jenny looked at the floor. "I've hardly done anything."

"Just you making the effort means something to me," Mrs. Gunderson said warmly, even in the face of Jenny's sullenness.

Jenny melted a bit. "Thanks, Mrs. Gunderson. I'm sorry I slept so long."

"We've got the weekend coming up. Don't worry."

Claire spoke up. "Is Brad around, Jenny? I'd like to speak to the two of you."

"Again?" Jenny snapped.

"Yes, this is important. Pit Snyder has been accused of murdering your father. If either of you know anything more about it, I need that information now. Before it's too late."

Brad walked in the door behind Claire. "What's going on?"

"Let's all sit down," Mrs. Gunderson said. "I made some lemonade. I knew we would all need a drink after all the work we've done."

They sat down around the table, and she brought out a pitcher and handed it to Jenny. "Jenny, dear, would you please pour the drinks so we don't need to wipe up the floor after me?"

"Sure." Jenny poured out four glasses.

Claire took a sip and turned to Brad. "Pit Snyder was arrested last night for the murder of your father. I wanted you to know. He has not confessed to this murder, however, which surprises me. Have you had a chance to think about what happened that night?''

Brad was silent for a moment, pulling himself in, and then he spoke. ''I told you what I knew.''

''You told me that Pit was there. Who else was around your father? Did you see anyone else?''

''No, no, no.'' Brad shook his head like he was drowning. ''I don't think Pit killed my father. I know he wouldn't.''

''Brad, you didn't answer my question. Did you see anyone else?''

''No,'' said Jenny. ''We didn't.''

''I thought you were having trouble remembering what happened, Jenny. Is it coming back to you?''

''I don't remember seeing anyone else. And Brad would know for sure. He didn't even drink a beer that night.''

Claire felt like she was getting no place. They weren't going to give her any more information about what happened, so she decided to take a different tack.

''I've been hearing a lot about your mother's death.''

Jenny's head lifted up like that of a deer on the alert.

Claire went on. ''That must have been a horrible thing to watch happen to your mother. Do you still have the sorghum press on the farm?''

Brad nodded. ''Yeah, it's out back in the woodshed. It weighs about a million pounds, and Dad was always too lazy to get rid of it.''

''Can I go take a look at it?''

Brad shrugged his shoulders and gave her an odd look. ''I guess so. I don't know why you'd want to see it. Mr. Snyder came out a few days after Mom died and hosed all the blood off of it and helped move it back in the shed. There's really nothing to see.''

''I've never seen a sorghum press.''

''I'll show you the way.'' Brad stood up.

"Jenny, why don't you come with us?"

"I need to help Mrs. Gunderson."

Mrs. Gunderson waved her hand. "You can go along, Jenny. I'll sit here and take a break until you get back."

Brad led the way. They walked through tall grass until they came to an old shed that had lost all its paint and had weathered dark brown. A rusted metal roof seemed to be holding it together. A stack of wood filled the wall floor to ceiling, but behind it Claire could see a large machine.

"That's it," Brad said and pointed to the press.

Jenny stood near him with her arms crossed over her chest. She looked up in the rafters. "Barn swallows." She pointed a nest out for Claire.

"Could you show me how it worked?" Claire asked Brad.

"I'm sure it's too rusted to work."

"Just explain it to me." Claire walked back toward the hulking machine, stepping over piles of wood. Three metal cylinders sat in a large wooden frame with a huge metal cog on the side. It was nearly as tall as she was.

Brad and Jenny reluctantly followed her. "Where would you put the sorghum stalks in?"

Brad pointed to between the rollers. "They would go in here. The juice would flow out the bottom, and the remains of the stalks would get spit out the other end."

"What were you doing that day?"

Brad answered, "I was helping Dad bring the stalks."

"What were you doing, Jenny?"

"I was watching the juice come out the bottom and telling Mom when we needed to change buckets for the juice."

"Where was Nora?"

"She was in taking a nap. She had a headache," Jenny explained.

Claire leaned against the sorghum press. "What happened?"

Jenny looked at Brad. He looked at the ground.

"How did your mother happen to fall into the press?"

"It happened so fast—" Brad started.

Jenny interrupted. "Brad, we can tell now. Not that it matters. Dad's dead. He can't do anything to us."

Brad swallowed and looked at Claire. "If you want to know what really happened—he pushed her."

"Your dad did?"

"Yeah, Dad hit our mom on the back as she was feeding in the sorghum. I don't know if he meant her to fall forward, but she did. He hit her hard, and she reached out with her hands to stop her fall, and they went into the rollers. They went into the press. Her hands were squished. I ran to stop the machine. She didn't even scream. Her face went blank, then white, and she fainted. The pain must have been so intense." Brad was crying by now. "See, you can't get the press to back up. There isn't a way it does that. So we couldn't get her hands out. We had to pull her away from the machine. We wrapped her arms in a blanket we had out here. Dad took off his belt and my belt and cinched them around her arms. We loaded her in the car. She sat in the back with Jenny and me. Dad drove. But before we left the farm—"

Brad let out a gasp and then went on, "Dad said to us, Jenny and me, that if we told anyone what happened, an accident might happen to us. Maybe to Nora."

Jenny nodded her head in agreement with Brad. "Mom had her eyes open some of the time on the ride to town. But she never talked. Once she closed her eyes, she never opened them again."

In the silence that followed, Claire heard the whir of wings above their heads as a swallow flitted into the barn.

She looked up and envied the bird its easy flight through the soft late-afternoon air. The sky was turning rose red to the west, and in that faded color she saw old blood.

"Your poor mother. I'm so sorry. That should never have happened to you. Your father should never have done that and threatened you like that." Claire felt sick and angry at what these children had gone through. How could a father have treated his children and wife like that? What had he been made of? "Is there any way it could have been an accident?"

"No," Brad said firmly. "They had been fighting, Mom threatening to leave. Dad swore he would hurt her if she tried. She had promised me we would all go away. She said she would never leave us kids with Dad. But she did."

"You must have hated your father," Claire said. Neither of them said anything in response.

Claire pushed them with more questions. "Do you think Pit Snyder knew what had happened? I think he suspected that your father had killed your mother. Is that why he killed your father?"

Brad picked up an ax that was lying next to the woodpile.

"Why do you think he did it?" Claire asked again.

Brad picked up a spike and stuck it into a piece of wood. "He didn't. I killed our father."

Then he hit the spike with the ax, and the log broke in half.

You know the witch in The Wizard of Oz—*when Dorothy throws the bucket of water on her—that's how I feel some days. Like I'm melting. My tears are the water and my sorrow is melting me. I have no substance.*

So you're saying that your sadness weakens you?

When I dissolve into it, it does.

Could it strengthen you in some way?

I know it must.

How?

I understand other people better.
I feel like sadness gives you X-ray vision. You see inside people. You see how they've been ripped apart by their own losses.

Does that help you in your line of work?

You mean being a cop?
I believe my work is about finding out the truth. This can lead to punishment. But sometimes when you discover the truth you see the guilty have already been punished.

Have you been punished enough?

That's the question.

TWENTY-ONE

CLAIRE LEFT the Spitzler place in much worse shape than she had been in when she arrived. It was rare that she felt so disheartened when her police work turned up such dramatic results. She leaned on the hood of her car and radioed in that she was bringing Brad Spitzler in. Give the sheriff advance warning.

Right before she and Brad walked out of the house, Jenny had run upstairs, crying. Mrs. Gunderson was wiping the kitchen counter, trying to hold her tears back. Nora was sitting at the kitchen table, drawing a picture of a windmill that looked like it was spiking the sky.

Climbing into the patrol car, she looked back at Brad. He was sitting up straight and tall in the back of the patrol car. Claire had handcuffed him; it hadn't seemed necessary, but it was proper procedure. He had said little after his confession. As they had left the farmhouse, he had told Mrs. Gunderson that the combine was ready to go and that the sunflowers needed to be harvested in the next week, or they would lose the crop. He reminded her that they needed the money desperately.

After they had been driving for ten minutes or so, Brad finally spoke up. "What's going to happen to me?"

Claire looked back at him in the rearview mirror. He was trying so hard to keep it together. "I'm not sure. That's not really my line of work. I apprehend the criminals, the lawyers take it from there."

"Are they going to put me in jail? I can't leave my sisters like that. They won't make it on their own."

"How old are you?"

"Seventeen. I'll be eighteen right before Christmas."

"That will work to your advantage. You're technically still a juvenile, although they've been waiving that more and more in murder cases."

Brad was quiet again, his head dropped. Claire kept a close watch on the road ahead. This part of the county was hilly, and the road wound through the glens and coulees. They dropped down off the bluffland and followed a coulee down to the river flats that would take them up to Durand. When the land opened up in front of them, it was a lovely sight: farmhouses tucked into groves of trees, the low hills topped with forests, even the fields golden with ripe crops. Claire noted that she wasn't in the right mood to appreciate this vision.

It was a rare occurrence that she felt bad when she had apprehended a perp. She had gone out to the Spitzler farm hoping to learn more about what had happened to their father, but she wasn't quite ready for the case to break open, yet again, in front of her. It reminded her of following a new path through the woods—around every corner she didn't know what she would find.

"What was your father like to live with these last few years?"

Brad lifted his head and looked out the window, then answered, "Oh, he could go along fine for a while, and then he'd get in one of his moods. Then nothing we did was right."

"What would put him in a mood?"

"Often it was money, I think. Not enough money. He blamed us for everything. Staying on the farm. That the farm wasn't doing that well. But it was all his own fault. He tried too many different things. Like the sunflowers.

Although as a crop they might be fine. They have certainly produced.''

''What would he do when he was in a mood?''

''Pick on one of us. Usually Jenny. Often me. Never Nora. At least not yet.''

''What does that mean? Pick on you?''

''Rag us, ride us. Slap us. Nothing we could do would be right. He didn't hit us too often, and hardly ever so's it would show. But he would swear at us and tell us how stupid we were.''

''That sounds awful.''

Brad nodded, his head dropping again. After a minute or so, he said, ''But you know what was the worst?''

''What?''

''When he would say he was going to kill us.''

Claire couldn't imagine a parent telling a child such a horrible thing. She decided it was time she did something she had never done before. ''Brad, I have some advice for you.''

He looked at her in the mirror.

''When we get to the sheriff's office, I want you to lawyer up.''

''What does that mean?''

''I want you to ask for a lawyer and then not say anything until you get one.''

WHEN RUTH SNYDER opened the door and saw her husband standing there, she dropped the broom she had in her hand and jumped on him, wrapping her legs around his sturdy belly and her arms around his neck. He walked into their house carrying her, then unwrapped her legs so she was standing and held her tight. She sobbed.

He said her name softly: ''Ruthie.''

She couldn't stop crying.

He held her against him and rocked her.

Finally, when she was able to stop crying, she started talking. "The house is the cleanest it's ever been. I had to do something with myself. So I cleaned and baked and sewed. But mainly I cleaned."

He looked around. The house was incredibly clean. "It looks nice."

Then she lifted her arms up, balled her fists, and pounded him on the chest as hard as she could. "I am so mad at you. How could you do that to me? Do you know what I've been going through?"

He grabbed her wrists and gently held them in his strong grip. "I'm sorry."

She stood apart from him and said, "I was afraid I would never get to be with you again. Ever. My whole life. I couldn't bear it."

She started to cry and walked back into his arms.

"I'm home," he whispered in her ear. "I'm not going anyplace for a while. You'll even get tired of having me around."

She gave a hiccup laugh, and he knew that she would get over it.

CLAIRE STOPPED AT the bottom of his driveway. Looking up through the trees, she could see that the lights were on in the kitchen. She should go home. It was after eight o'clock. Meg was probably waiting for her with Ramah, her baby-sitter. She would have her pajamas on, and they might be reading a book together. Now that Claire worked the regular day shift, it didn't happen very often that Ramah had to get Meg ready for bed.

But, she thought, this would take only a minute or two. She felt like she owed it to Rich. Not that she might not have gone out to talk to the Spitzlers again on her own, but he had certainly helped point her in the right direction.

She could call him when she got home, after Meg was in bed, but since his house was right on her way, she thought she would stop. Admit it, she said to herself; you want to see him. It was as simple as that.

Claire drove up the driveway and parked the car in front of the barn. By the time she was out of the car, he was standing in the doorway.

She waved at him. "Hi."

"Hi yourself. What brings you out this time of night?"

"Actually, I'm on my way home." She walked up his steps.

"Come on in." He motioned her through the door.

"I can only stay a minute. Meg's waiting with Ramah. I got tied up at the office. That's what I wanted to tell you about."

"Do you want to sit down?"

"Sure.

"Can I give you something to drink—beer, coffee, water?"

"Just water, thanks. I'm pretty keyed up."

He got her some water from the tap and sat down opposite her at the table. She noticed that he was being careful not to get too close to her.

"I went out to the Spitzler farm today, and Jenny and Brad showed me the sorghum press. That's what killed their mom."

Rich nodded his head.

"Have you ever seen a sorghum press?"

"Probably. I don't know for sure, but I have an idea what they look like."

"They're huge. Much bigger than I thought it would be." Claire paused and then said, "The kids told me that their father had pushed their mother into the press while they were doing the sorghum.''

Rich closed his eyes and shook his head. ''Shit.''

''Yes, and then he threatened them. That's why they never told anyone. He said he'd kill them.'' Claire put her hand up to her mouth to keep from crying. ''They have had to live with him for all these years. He was a monster.''

''Sounds like it.''

''Brad killed him. He told me today. I had to bring him in.''

''That's your job.''

''I don't blame him.''

''I don't imagine many people will.''

They both sat there. Claire took a sip of her water. ''I had to tell someone before I went home to see Meg. It's hard going home, and there's no adult I can talk to. I don't want her to know such things.''

''That's fine. I'm always here. How's your therapy going?''

''Good, I guess. I don't know how you know when you're done or if you're making progress. I still am having panic attacks, but I don't feel like they scare me as much as they did at first. Maybe I'm getting used to them, or maybe I simply understand them better.''

''Probably both.''

Claire stood up and handed him her glass. ''I should go. I haven't even had dinner yet.''

''Glad you stopped by. I'm sorry to hear about Brad. I hope they give him a break.''

''I do too. They've gotten so hard on juvenile offenders lately, it scares me.''

He walked her to the door, and she stepped outside on the stoop.

She turned to him and asked, ''Would you kiss me?''

Rich gave her an odd look.

"I think I need it. I'm starting to feel like I don't exist anymore. I'm thinking too much, I guess."

He didn't say anything. He reached for her, and she walked into his arms. He kissed her full on the lips and held her tight, then let her go.

She walked down the steps to her car and felt ready to go home.

BRAD COUNTED THE BLOCKS that made up the wall of his cell: 213. Then he counted the bars that went around the room: 47. Then he counted the flies stuck to the overhead bulb: 6. It all added up to nothing.

His food plate sat on the small table that he had pulled up to the cot. Thin slices of rubbery roast beef covered with a thick, dark gravy. Mashed potatoes that came from a box, and a small pile of yellow corn, the only dot of color on his plate. No dessert. Maybe that was the difference between a jail meal and a school meal. With a school lunch you always got dessert, even if it was only a piece of solid red Jell-O. He had drunk the milk, but that was all he could get down.

It had been a big mistake to start talking about his dad with the deputy. Once he had started, he hadn't been able to stop. He had always known no one would understand what his life had been like, and he had been proven right about that. He was in jail. Fat lot of good that would do his sisters.

He put his head in his hands. He had promised his mother he would take care of Jenny and Nora. He had told her that no matter what happened, he would watch over them. He hadn't done a very good job. The one time he had tried to stop his father, his arm had been broken in the fight.

How would he ever get to sleep in this place? He could

hear other inmates down the hallway, but at least no one was very close to him. He had been told he wouldn't be held long here. Within a day or two, he would be transferred to some kind of juvenile detention center.

His lawyer had talked it all over with him. Brad had done what the woman deputy had told him. When they arrived at the sheriff's office, he had said he wouldn't talk until he had seen his lawyer. It took them a few hours to drum up a lawyer, because Brad didn't have one and couldn't afford to pay for one. But as he suspected, his lawyer—a public defender—did not inspire great confidence. Sandy Burnet was his name, and he looked like a ferret with a wispy little mustache. He had talked to Brad in private, and then he told the police that Brad would make no statements until he knew how the case was going to be handled. He wanted to talk to the prosecuting attorney. They had set up a meeting for tomorrow morning.

Brad lay down on his cot and wrapped the blanket over his legs. What about a shower? He always took a shower before he went to bed. He was conscious of all the other bodies that had slept on this cot. He closed his eyes so he wouldn't start counting blocks again.

Suddenly he heard the jangle of keys. Assuming they had come for his plate, he sat up and was all ready to apologize for not eating much of it when he saw a tall, thin man in a suit entering his cell. The deputy behind him was carrying a chair.

"Hi—Kent Byron," the man said and put out his hand.

Brad shook his hand and said, "Hi. You probaby know that I'm Brad Spitzler."

The deputy put the chair down, and the tall man sat in it. He loosened his tie and set down his briefcase. "Sorry it took me so long to get over here."

"I wasn't expecting you."

"How are you doing?"

Brad stopped to think how he should answer that question. It felt like a trick to him. If he said fine, then they would think he had no remorse for killing his father. He gave up trying to work it out and just shrugged and said, "Not bad."

"Not good, though. Am I right?"

"Yes. Why are you here?"

"It was Pit's idea."

"Who are you?"

"I'm your new lawyer."

TWENTY-TWO

WHEN SHE WAS LITTLE, her mother read her fairy tales when she was sick: "The Tinder Box," "The Wild Swans," "Hansel and Gretel." In these tales, the heroine always overcame evil. The daunting tasks were accomplished. Her mother would sit on the bed next to Jenny and read stories that would help her grow up strong.

Jenny wanted to do the impossible.

She had set her alarm and risen with the sun. She had put on a T-shirt and overalls so she could work in the field. She had borrowed Brad's big straw hat and put on her mother's old Red Wing boots.

Her father would have never let her do this. Even though he was dead, she still wanted to show him that she could do anything she wanted to better than he would ever imagine.

She sat on the seat of the tractor and tipped her head back to the sky. It was early in the morning, and the sun was peeking over the roof of the far barn.

Jenny loved riding on the tractor. She sat up so high, and she could feel the power of the engine under her seat and in her hands as she worked the gears. Brad had taught her how to drive it when her father hadn't been around. He told her if she could drive the tractor, a car would be a piece of cake. Now that he was gone, she might need to drive the car if an emergency came up.

After Brad had been taken away last night, Jenny had decided she needed to do something to help keep their family together. She knew that the sunflower harvest was critical; Brad had planned on harvesting the crop this weekend. So as she lay awake in bed last night, jittery from taking no sweet little pills to get her to sleep, she decided she would have to take on the harvesting herself.

Maybe if she could do it, it would change everything. With the money, she could hire a lawyer and get Brad out of jail. She could prove that she was good at something. Mrs. Gunderson would believe in her again and not just see her as a stupid druggie. She would save the farm, and they all would still have a place to live. She would accomplish happily-ever-after.

She knew that Brad had worked on the combine all yesterday before he had been taken away. He had oiled it and checked it over. Then he had attached it to the tractor. Most of the new combines were tractor and harvester in one, but theirs was an old model, 1966. Same year as their tractor. Their father could never afford to buy anything new. It was a faded red color with big cutting blades. As long as the tractor, it was actually bigger, and she was always amazed that the tractor could pull it along through the fields.

Jenny had tried to call Brad yesterday at the jail, but they wouldn't let her call go through to him. She'd wanted to ask him some questions about the combine, but she would just have to wing it. She had sat up reading the combine manual last night and thought she knew what she needed to try to set the adjustments for harvesting sunflower seeds.

First thing to do was to drive the tractor and combine down to the field.

She started up the tractor and put it in a low gear to get ready to pull the combine. When she tried to move forward, the engine cut out on her. Easy, she thought, give it the gas easy. She tried again, and this time it chugged a couple of times, but caught and moved forward. Once she had it moving, it was a straight shot from the barn to the field.

After driving alongside a fallow field, she came to the beginning of the sunflowers. They spread out in front of her like a roomful of thoughtful children, their heads bending down over their work.

She sat in the sun at the edge of the field and readied herself. It would all be trial and error. It would have been even if it had been their dad doing it. He had never harvested sunflowers before. He would be swearing up a blue streak. At least she didn't have to listen to that. It was so quiet out in the fields. She could hear a bird trilling its early morning song. If Brad were here, he would know what it was. He knew all the nature stuff. If he were here, the fields would be as good as harvested.

She looked down at the manual. Written inside was the quote: "A good thrasherman wasn't made in a day." Nor a good thrasherwoman, she was afraid.

Like the heroine in Rumpelstiltskin, she would try to turn these fields of sunflowers into gold. If she did, she would save the firstborn—Brad—from being taken away. And she would save Nora, too. Because she knew if Brad went to jail for good, she and Nora would be removed from the farm and sent to foster homes.

She tied Brad's old straw hat to her head with leather shoelaces. She climbed up into the seat and started up the tractor. She moved slowly toward the golden heads. She felt like she was sneaking up on them as they were all facing away from her. She got the tractor right up next to the first row. That would be her marker. Just keep the wheels right next to the row of sunflowers.

She nosed the edge of the sunflowers with the side of the tractor. Then she moved forward and pulled the combine into the field.

She was combining a field. For better or worse, the sunflowers were being mowed down behind her. She turned around once to look, but pulled the tractor too far to the side. After that she kept facing forward and just kept the tractor moving along steadily.

When she came to the end of the field, she knew she had to stop everything and check how she was doing, but she didn't really want to stop. After she had pulled the combine completely out of the sunflowers, she turned off everything.

She walked back and looked at the seeds in the side bin. Some were crushed. That was no good. She could make an adjustment so they wouldn't be handled as roughly. Walking back along her first pass, she saw that she was not scattering too much seed out with the chaff. That was good. Not bad for a first try.

Her heart lifted for a moment, and she thought she might be able to do it. If she could keep moving, she might finish this field by lunch. She was worried about the turns. She knew that she had to do them just right to keep the combine moving smoothly behind the tractor. If she cut it too tight, the combine might jackknife on her. If she took the turns too wide, she wouldn't get back in position to harvest the next row.

Jenny wiped her face, then climbed back on the tractor. It was a perfect day—quite warm, not much of a breeze, the insects thrumming in the weeds alongside the fields. The sun was nearly overhead, and she needed to keep moving.

By shortly before noon, she had half the field done. Her back was aching from keeping the tractor steady. The sun beat a blazing hole in the back of her T-shirt. Her arms and wrists were starting to burn. She hadn't put any sunscreen on, but she didn't feel like she could stop. She wanted to finish the field before she went into the house.

As she was heading back toward the house, on one of her last passes, she saw Mrs. Gunderson walk out to the field, holding Nora's hand. They waved at her. She was surprised it had taken them so long to come looking for her. But then Mrs. Gunderson probably just figured she was sleeping in and had let her be.

She slowed the tractor down to get ready for her final turn and stood up to wave at them. The tractor hit a bump and jolted her, and she lost hold of the throttle. The tractor popped again, the engine cut out, and she fell back, one hand hanging on to the seat.

She was going to fall, and if she did she would be eaten up by the combine. She needed to get out of its way. She made a quick decision to jump free of the tractor.

With the tractor moving faster, rolling downhill, she flung herself off the vehicle and fell into the last remaining row of sunflowers. She landed on her side. Brad's hat had come off her head and fallen into the combine's path. It would be chewed up by now. The tractor kept careening ahead, the combine slowing it slightly. Mrs. Gunderson and Nora ran out of its way.

The tractor ran into the side of the barn with a thud and then died, then the combine piled up behind it. Jenny righted herself and ran to shut down the combine. She turned it off, but saw the damage that had been done. The tractor had torn a hole into the barn and bent the front axle. The attachment between the tractor and combine was also damaged, and Jenny wondered whether the tractor would even work anymore.

"What happened?" Nora came running up.

"I fell off the tractor."

"What were you doing, Jenny?" Nora asked.

Jenny shook her head.

Mrs. Gunderson came walking up. "What's going on here?"

"I harvested most of this field."

"My goodness," Mrs. Gunderson said in amazement.

"And I think I ruined the tractor."

CLAIRE GOT CALLED OFF her investigation to come in and talk to the prosecuting attorney, Wendall Thompson, about Brad Spitzler's arrest. She had been checking on a burglary that had been called in the night before and had told the dispatcher that she would come in as soon as she finished talking to the owner of the sporting goods store. All that had been taken were fishing rods. She thought it might be kids, she told the owner. They had climbed in through a window in the bathroom and left their footprints on the toilet seat.

Sheriff Talbert had Thompson in his office, and both men were looking at a golf club that the sheriff had just bought. Claire stood by the door until they were done discussing the pros and cons of steel-shaft versus graphite shaft clubs.

"What's going to happen to Brad?" she asked Thompson as they all sat down.

"His lawyer, Kent Byron, is advising him to plead self-defense."

"Really?" Claire had thought his attorney was a public defender. She wondered what had happened to change that.

"Self-defense, since his father was always threatening to kill him. Since he feared for his life and his sisters' lives."

"What do you think of that?"

"Not a bad idea."

"Are you just going to plea-bargain him out?"

Wendall Thompson pursed his lips. "I hope so. I don't think this case should go to trial. What good will it do? But before we go any further, I'd like to get the sister in here and talk to her about the past history and the stabbing itself."

Claire agreed. "I've been thinking we need that corroboration, no matter how the case is handled. I don't know how well you'll do with her on the crime itself. She was drinking and on drugs that night, from what I could tell. Out of it. She's admitted as much.''

"Can you bring her in tomorrow morning? I've got to go to court this afternoon, or I'd say we should do it sooner.''

"Will do.'' Claire stood up to leave.

"Brad Spitzler is lucky to have Kent Byron as his lawyer,'' Thompson remarked.

Claire nodded. "As far as I knew, that was not who was assigned him.''

"How did this happen?''

"You know more than I know.''

Thompson looked Claire in the eyes. "I know that Pit Snyder got him the lawyer. Did anyone suggest that to him?''

"Not that I'm aware of.''

ELLA HEARD A NOISE down in the kitchen and turned on the light by her bed. One of the girls, she thought, but she decided to go down and see. She slipped into her chenille bathrobe and put on the blue slip-on socks she had taken home from the hospital when she went in for eye surgery.

She kept a good grip on the railing as she went down the stairs and wasn't surprised to see Jenny, her golden head on the kitchen table, staring at a bottle of beer. The girl had slept most of the afternoon after her harvesting attempt and then had moped around and not eaten much of her dinner.

"You having a little nightcap?'' Mrs. Gunderson asked, but one look in the girl's eyes, and she could see that Jenny had resorted to drugs again. Her eyes were wandering, and she seemed to be having trouble focusing them.

"I can't get to sleep. I need something to help me wind down.''

"I bet you do. I think I could use one too." Mrs. Gunderson went to the refrigerator and pulled one out of the bottom shelf in the back, where Jenny had stashed them. She had noticed them hidden behind a Tupperware container when she was looking for some leftover stew.

Mrs. Gunderson pried the cap off and sat down at the table opposite Jenny. She took a big swig of beer right out of the bottle.

"You drink beer?" Jenny asked.

"Sure. I don't drink too much of it. But my late husband often liked a beer at the end of the day. I joined him as often as not."

"You had a husband?"

Mrs. Gunderson laughed. Young people never think the old people have had any kind of life. How do they imagine that they have come to exist, if their elders didn't drink and love and have sex? "Certainly. Why do you think people call me Mrs. Gunderson?"

"What happened to him?"

"He was killed in Korea, during the conflict." How easily she could say that now. So long ago, and yet some days she could still weep if she thought about it.

"What conflict?"

"In the early 1950s America sent troops over to Korea. They fought there, but they didn't call it a war, just a conflict. As if that made a difference. But men still died. Herbert went over for what he thought would be a short stint, and it was short, but he didn't come back alive."

"How old were you?"

"Not a lot older than you are now. I was twenty-two when he died. I'll never forget the day I got the phone call. I felt like the earth had just opened up and swallowed me."

Jenny went to the refrigerator and got out another bottle of beer and opened it. She sat back down at the table and rolled the bottle back and forth between her hands. "I know that feeling."

"Everyone has bad things happen to them, Jenny. You live through them, believe it or not."

"Does everyone have their mom die, her arms torn off, then their dad die, stabbed in the guts, then their brother put in jail and then maybe lose their farm?"

"No, the stories are not the same. But whole families are wiped out in Africa or India when there's a drought or a monsoon. It's a hard and terrible world sometimes. We all have our problems."

"Does that mean I don't get to feel bad?" Jenny's voice was rising, and Mrs. Gunderson could tell she was getting hysterical.

"No, quite the opposite. You should feel bad. Feel as bad as you can feel. But what you are trying to do is escape your feelings by drinking and by drugging." There. She had said it. She might as well ask another question. "Did anything ever happen between you and your father that you would like to talk about?"

Jenny's head jerked up. "Like what? What are you suggesting—that my dad was a pervert? Well, he wasn't."

"I'm just trying to understand what you're going through."

"You don't understand. You can't. It's all my fault. And now Brad's going to go to prison forever."

"I tend to be an optimist. Things might turn out better than you think. When you go into the sheriff's department tomorrow, tell them everything you know. That's what will help him the most."

Jenny slouched lower over the table. She wouldn't look at Mrs. Gunderson. She covered her head with her hands.

"Things will get better," Mrs. Gunderson assured her.

Jenny raised her head, and the look in her eyes was wild.

She took her beer bottle and threw it in the garbage can. Then she screamed, "Stop saying that! They will never get better. There's no way they can."

After forty years of teaching children how to grow up, Mrs. Gunderson knew enough not to argue. She finished her beer while Jenny put her head down on the table and wailed. What would happen would come to pass, whether Jenny believed in it or not.

"You're nothing but an old woman, what do you know?" Jenny said in a quiet and mean voice, lifting her tearstained face.

Mrs. Gunderson stood and put her beer bottle in the recycling bag under the sink. She retied her bathrobe around her and turned and spoke to Jenny. "I am an old woman. But I know many things. And one thing I know is when I'm not wanted anymore. I will stay another few days until we can get you and Nora settled with a foster family or someone else can come to stay here. It's time for me to go back home."

She turned and walked carefully back up the stairs, her heart heavy. She had hoped she would get through to Jenny.

TWENTY-THREE

CLAIRE PARKED HER CAR by the courthouse, sat for a moment, trying to remember all she had to do today, and then clambered out of the vehicle. As she reached back in to pull out her purse and a couple of files she had taken home, she was tapped on the back. When she turned around, Pit Snyder was standing next to her car.

"Hello, Mr. Snyder," she said in a friendly tone—but her first thought was that he was going to yell at her for how he had been handled in the Spitzler case.

Instead he asked pleasantly, "Do you want to go get a cup of coffee?"

"Nothing I'd like better. You want to go to the Prairie Pie?" Claire had been planning on getting in touch with Pit Snyder sometime today.

A new espresso bar with wonderful baked goods had opened up a few months ago in Durand. Claire liked to give them her business when she could. She hoped they would make a go of it, although they might have a hard time selling their espresso coffee for a dollar and a half when people around the town still expected a bottomless cup for twenty-five cents.

"Sure. I haven't tried that place." As they walked along, he told her, "I've been waiting for you. I wanted to catch you before you went in to work. I wasn't ready to go anywhere near the jail for a while."

"I don't blame you."

When they got to the restaurant, Pit ordered regular coffee and Claire a café au lait. After they had been served,

Snyder stared at her large, foamy cup of coffee. "That sure looks nice."

"Would you like a taste?"

"Don't mind if I do." He took the cup in both hands and took a sip. "Creamy. Tastes like the hot chocolate my mom used to make when she brewed it in the old coffeemaker. I didn't like it when I was a kid, but that tastes pretty good to me now." He seemed so much more relaxed than the last time she had seen him.

"What can I do for you, Mr. Snyder?"

"Pit, call me Pit. Everybody does." He took a gulp of his own coffee, then leaned forward and said in a half-whisper, "I'm sick about Brad Spitzler."

"Is that why you got him a lawyer?"

"Yes, it's the least I can do."

"Pit, what did you see that night?"

"That's the problem. I didn't see anything. When I came walking up, the two kids were standing over their father, and the knife was on the ground. Both their hands were bloody. I told them to go wash up and I grabbed the knife."

"Why? Why did you cover up for them?"

"Jed Spitzler was an evil man. He made their lives hell. I knew how mean he could be to Rainey. If I'd stepped in sooner, maybe none of this would have happened."

"So you didn't see Brad stab his father?"

"No."

"Do you think he did it?"

"I really can't say."

"Why do you think he would do it now?"

"Maybe Jed did something that Brad couldn't tolerate. I don't know. In some ways, I'm surprised he didn't do it sooner. That's all I can figure. What does Brad say?"

"Since he's got a lawyer, he's not saying much. But I

think they're going to try to plea-bargain with him so he'll have to make some kind of confession."

"Do you have any sense of what kind of time they'll give him for this?"

"No court looks kindly at patricide. But with the extenuating circumstances—his mother's death, his father's continuing brutality—I think they'll go easy. And, fortunately, he's a juvenile. I have a feeling he'll be sentenced to the juvenile center until he's eighteen, then let go. He'll serve less than six months."

Pit bent his head. "He's such a good kid. I hope this won't ruin him. What about Jenny and Nora?"

"I don't know. I don't have anything to do with that. Mrs. Gunderson is still staying with them—but who knows how long she'll last?"

JENNY SLID HER FEET forward and then followed them. It was easy, this thing called walking that she did to move around the world. She followed the deputy sheriff out of the patrol car and into the police station. She had worn her new red tennis shoes. They were the last thing Dad ever bought for her. That made them special. And they made the walking even easier.

Everyone was staring at her, but she didn't care. They couldn't touch her. She was sliding along on her feet, walking carefully so that no one could tell how high she was.

She had doubled her dosage, being careful not to take too much. She didn't need another fainting episode with the deputy. But she was concerned because she was reaching the bottom of her pill bottle. After carefully counting them three times, she saw that she had only seven pills left. She wasn't sure if her connection in school had any more, and she didn't know if she could fake another toothache.

"Jenny." The woman deputy was talking to her. She

needed to tune in again. The deputy's name was Watkins, Claire Watkins. That's right. And another deputy was sitting next to her, a cute deputy named Billy. He looked a little like Ricky Martin, who she actually thought was pretty dopey.

"Yes." Jenny made her lips slope upward in a smile.

"We're going to be taping this. Is that all right?"

"I guess."

"I'll be asking you the questions." Claire turned on the tape. "Billy will be here, and he might ask you some questions too. Are you ready?"

"I think so."

Claire said the date and time and who was present in the room. Jenny looked up at the window. It was so high you couldn't see out of it. All it did was let some light in. The room they were sitting in reminded her of a jail cell. Maybe Brad was close by. She wanted to see him before she left. She had to remember that.

"Jenny, some of these questions are going to be difficult, but I want you to answer them the best you can. We are trying to understand what led up to your brother Brad stabbing your father. Let's start with your mother's death."

"It was like Brad said." Jenny didn't want to have to talk about her mother's death. Everything had started then. Everything had ended then. It had been the worst day of her life.

"Can you elaborate?"

"Mom was putting the sorghum in the press, and Dad pushed her. You know the rest."

"Why did he do that?"

"Beats me. You never knew with Dad, how he'd take something, what would make him mad. Mom had been saying she was going to leave him. I don't think she meant to, maybe she was just bugging him, but I think that made him mad. He liked to have power over everyone in the family.''

"I think your mother *was* trying to leave, Jenny. She had called Pit Snyder and had asked him to help her.''

Jenny felt her heart break open. What if they could have gotten away from Dad? What if Mom had just piled them in the car that morning and gone away? She would still be alive. Dad would still be alive. Brad wouldn't be in jail. Oh, what could have been. Jenny felt as if what had not come to pass was freezing her up. She didn't know what to say.

"Jenny?"

She spit out: "Well, it didn't happen."

Claire looked at her with sadness in her eyes. "I know. I'm sorry."

Billy jumped in with some questions. "What happened after your mother died? Did your father change in his behavior toward you?''

"Well, like we told you, he threatened to kill us. But then it was like that never happened. Right around the funeral, he was pretty nice to us. There were other people around and all. The grieving family. That routine. But when it was just us and him again, he got meaner. We never pleased him. He yelled at us.'' Jenny looked at Billy to see if he'd understand. "Mom wasn't around anymore to take it for us, so he took all his anger out on us.''

Billy nodded as if he knew what she was talking about and kept up the questions. "Did he ever hit you or hurt you in any way?''

Jenny felt the hurts welling up in her, all the things that he had done over the years pushing to get out and be told. But she kept them in. "Not me. But he and Brad got into a fight, and he broke Brad's arm.''

Claire made a note on a pad of paper in front of her. Then she asked, "He did? When was this?"

"About a year ago."

"Did Brad go to the doctor?"

"Oh, yeah. Dad took him in. Brad wasn't much use to Dad with a broken arm."

"Good. There'll be a record of that." Claire leaned toward Jenny and put a hand out to her, but didn't touch her. "Jenny, is there anything else you want to tell us that happened with your father?"

"Not much more. He'd yell at us, threaten us, but that was about it. Sometimes he could be all right. He was always pretty nice to Nora. But she saw what went on. It was hard on her too."

Claire asked the next question, because it was something she had been wondering about. "Did your father ever do anything sexually inappropriate with you?"

Jenny felt words push into her head, into her mouth, but she managed to avoid them. She shook her head and kept her answer short. "He was a creep, not a pervert."

"Now, Jenny, can you tell us what happened the night your father was killed?"

And so Jenny went over it again. She had already told much of it before. How they had all gone together in the car, how Nora had stayed home, how it was Lola's idea, how they went their separate ways at the dance, then how she and Brad ran into their father.

"Jenny, before you told us that your father was already stabbed when you saw him again, but after what Brad has told us, that wasn't true, was it?"

"No."

"What happened?"

"Well, he was by the johns, and Brad had just found me, and then we ran into Dad. Brad was trying to persuade me to go home. He thought I was too out of it. Dad didn't want to leave yet. They got into a fight. Dad called Brad some names. He started yelling at Brad.''

''Was this unusual?''

''Not at all. Dad was always telling Brad he was a piece of shit. I can say that, can't I?''

''Yes.''

''Brad tried so hard to be good and not get Dad riled, but I think that's what bugged Dad the most. That Brad was kind of perfect.''

''What happened next?''

''I think Dad took a swing at Brad. Brad just ducked. But then Brad punched him in the face.''

''Hard?''

''Pretty hard, I think, because then Dad started to hold his head.'' Jenny remembered how black it had been all around them. Like they were standing in a pool of oil.

''Jenny, can you tell us what happened after that?''

''You know, that's when it gets pretty fuzzy. I don't think I even knew Brad had stabbed him. The next thing I remember is Dad lying on the ground, and my hands were covered with blood. I was trying to stop it from bleeding. Brad pulled me away. We went and washed our hands.''

''Did Brad say anything?''

''Not really.''

''Did you and Brad talk about what had happened to your father after that?''

''No. I don't think we wanted to. After we left the hospital and we were driving home in the car, we didn't even talk about him.'' Jenny smiled, thinking about that night. ''I don't know about Brad, but I was so happy I could have died.''

THIS TIME OF NIGHT was hard. Ten-thirty. Meg was sleeping. The dishes were done, the kitchen straightened. Claire had checked that the doors were locked, the windows shut and latched. Left the new night-light burning in the hallway. It was time for her to go to bed and try to sleep.

Claire stood next to the window in her bedroom and looked out over the town. She had started hating going to sleep, which was an odd feeling, since it had always been a refuge for her. But the dreams. She never knew when the dreams would come. The one of the woman with no hands haunted her during the day as no other dream had.

Even now, with Brad Spitzler ready to plea-bargain his case, she felt unsettled by the Spitzler ordeal. What had triggered Brad Spitzler's stabbing? What had Jed finally done that Brad could no longer tolerate? Claire wondered if it had something to do with Brad being in his last year of high school and not wanting to leave the two girls alone with Jed. What had gone on there? Claire had asked about sexual abuse, and Jenny had said there had been none, but still it niggled at Claire, the possibility of it.

Jenny hadn't been much help. But Claire had been glad to hear about the broken arm and had called before she left work and requested that the medical record be sent over to her tomorrow. She would pass it on to Brad's attorney.

Claire was actually pleased they had gotten as much out of Jenny as they had. When she had gone to pick the girl up, she had seen that Jenny was pretty wasted again.

After they had finished the interview, Jenny had asked to see Brad. Claire had called down to the jail and asked the guard to bring him up. But the guard had called back a few minutes later and said that Brad didn't want to see her.

Jenny had taken it pretty hard. She looked like the air had been knocked out of her. Then she recovered, and Claire drove her home. She didn't say much of anything for the whole drive. Poor kid.

The phone rang. Claire let it ring twice, hoping it wasn't

work, and then grabbed it on the third ring. "Hello," she said, sitting down on her bed.

"Did I wake you?" Rich's deep voice came over the line.

Just the voice she wanted to hear. She put her head on her pillow and stretched out on the bed. "No. I was just contemplating my pillow. It's a new meditative mantra my therapist has me doing."

"I know I'm not supposed to be calling, but I wanted to see how you were doing. If you still existed and all."

Claire chuckled. He had such a good memory. "Rich, there are no rules for this. I'm sorry if I made it sound that way. You can't really do anything wrong, because I don't know what I'm doing myself. I'm glad you called. After all, I was the one who stopped over the other night."

"Yes. I remember that."

"I do exist."

"Good."

"I interviewed Jenny Spitzler today. We brought her into the station and grilled her for an hour or so. Just needed corroboration for Brad's story."

"How did that go?"

"It's such a sad story, Rich. Those poor kids with that awful man. Still, after I was done talking to her, I couldn't help feeling that I hadn't gotten it all. I don't blame her for not wanting to talk about it, but we need it as background for this case. However, I don't understand why Brad killed his father. Why that night? What made it different from any other night? I feel like Jed must have done something to trigger it."

"Well, we know it wasn't for money. Jed didn't have any."

"Right."

"How about to protect someone?"

The answer struck all too close to Claire's own dilemma,

why she had shot and killed her partner. She killed him to protect her sister and her daughter. "Yes, that would be a good reason. A very good reason."

There was silence on the line. Claire didn't want to say good night. Even listening to Rich breathe made her feel safer. "Okay, I'll let you go now," he said, "but first I will tell you what the French say to one another when they go to sleep. My mother used to say it to me. *Fais des beaux rêves, rêves de moi.*"

"I didn't know you spoke French."

"I don't—that's about all I know how to say."

"What does it mean?"

"Have beautiful dreams, dream of me."

You don't know all of it.

I never imagined I did.

It didn't happen the way I told you. I've told that story so many times it's become nearly the truth. But it's not the way it happened.

Would you like to try again?

I should tell you something about myself. I'm an unusual law enforcement person, if you will. I don't believe in the death penalty.

I don't talk about this very much. It's not a popular point of view among my fellow workers. It isn't that I'm religious about it. I'm not very religious. But now that I think about it, maybe I am religious about this. If there is a God, then that force, that power, should make such decisions.

I just don't think we have the right, we humans have the right, to take away a human life. To kill someone because they've killed someone seems contradictory to me. Do you agree?

My sentiments are similar to yours.

Good. That might help you understand the rest of this. Understand how I've been feeling about what I've done. First, let me go over the particulars.

My husband was killed. We thought it was a drug gang hit. I later found out it was a hit.

My daughter saw the killer. He tried to kidnap her. He did kidnap my sister, but she got away.

I found out who had masterminded all of this. This is the part you don't know. It was Bruce, my partner.

He was behind it all. He was the leader of the drug gang. He had my husband killed. He lied and lied to me. He wanted me all to himself. He said he loved me. But I found out. I found out who he really was. He did kill the drug dealer named Red. That part's true. But Red didn't kill Bruce.

I did. I killed Bruce.

After he shot Red, he turned toward me with the gun still in his hands. I don't know what he would have done. Maybe he wasn't going to shoot me. Maybe he would have put his gun down. Maybe he would even have surrendered to me. I don't know for sure. I'll never know.

But I couldn't take the chance. I was afraid for my daughter, I was afraid for my sister. If he killed me, I was afraid he would kill them. I wouldn't be able to protect them. I felt like I had no choice.

So I shot him.

I killed him.

Then I lied about it. To save his reputation. To save myself. It was as if there were two Bruces, and I had to protect the one I had loved.

But you shot him in self-defense, didn't you?

It could be seen that way. But I felt like I went into the situation, which I had set up, gunning for him.

Have you told anyone?

No.

It's time to start talking about it. It will make you sick if you don't. It already has made you sick.

Who should I tell?

Well, you've started already. You've told me. And I'm a safe person to tell. Find one or two other people who are safe and tell them. Then be quiet for a while. That might be enough.

Telling the true story will begin to set your life back in order. I think you will feel better.

But I killed him.

Yes, but he didn't kill you. You saved yourself. What a brave woman you are.

TWENTY-FOUR

"SHE'S DISAPPEARED, and I'm afraid something awful might happen to her." Ella Gunderson was so glad to get the woman deputy on the line. Claire Watkins would know what to do.

"Who is this?" Claire's voice sounded puzzled.

"I'm sorry. This is Ella Gunderson. The school just called. She didn't go to school. Jenny. She's gone." Mrs. Gunderson knew she should slow down, but she was so upset. The last week had been a very hard one, and now she was so afraid for Jenny.

"When did you last see her?"

Mrs. Gunderson thought about the morning rush, getting the girls fed. She hadn't said much to Jenny, wishing she would dress a little nicer. She was happy to see that she was even ready to go to school. "She got up this morning like usual. She looked awful, but she was dressed and even ate some breakfast. She left when it was time to catch the school bus. That was two hours ago. Then the school called about five minutes ago. She never made it there. They're not even sure she was on the bus."

"Where do you think she is?"

"I don't know. I wonder if she even got on the bus. She might be hiding out somewhere around here. She has been very upset about her brother being in jail and all the goings-on."

"I'll ask everyone to keep a lookout here in town. I'll check in with the school. Call me if she shows up. Hang tight."

When Mrs. Gunderson put down the phone, she wondered how one did that—hang tight. Keep a hold of oneself. She always did the best when she was busy. But as she looked around the kitchen, she didn't see much else to do. She had already finished the breakfast dishes.

The horror of what Jenny might be doing to herself kept flashing into Mrs. Gunderson's mind. Maybe gone off someplace and taking those pills to kill herself—it was almost more than Mrs. Gunderson could bear to think of.

She remembered how she had felt after receiving the news that her husband had been killed in Korea. They had only been married two months when he had left to fight. She had not wanted him to go, but he had teased her and said he would be back so soon she wouldn't even miss him. He was wrong. She had gone on missing him for forty-six long years, and her time was not over.

She didn't want Jenny to die. And what was worse was that she felt responsible. She had said she would leave them. How could she have done that when the losses that Jenny had suffered were so great?

She didn't think she could quietly sit and wait. She felt too anxious. She decided to go upstairs and check Jenny's room. Was it possible that Jenny could have snuck back in the house and gone back to bed? Wouldn't that be a relief?

Mrs. Gunderson went to the bottom of the stairs and grabbed the handrail and stepped carefully up the stairs. She walked down the hallway and pushed open the door to Jenny's room. The room was a mess. She had straightened in here once, but Jenny hadn't appreciated it, so she had left it alone ever since. There were clothes strewn across the floor, and the bed was in disarray.

When Mrs. Gunderson walked up to straighten out the bedclothes, she saw the note, a piece of paper resting on the pillow. She picked it up and held it close in front of her face, but couldn't make out the words. Maybe it was some homework that Jenny had forgotten. But she had a bad feeling about it.

She walked hurriedly down to her room and found her magnifying glass, then went and stood in the flood of sunlight from the window and was able to make out the note:

Dear Brad and Nora and Mrs. Gunderson,
  I'm sorry. I can't do it anymore. It's all my fault.
Dad's death is all my fault.

Jenny

Mrs. Gunderson felt her knees start to shake. She had to find Jenny before she did something bad to herself. The note sounded so final. How could she find her in time? Where might she have gone?

She set down the note and her magnifying glass and ran to the stairs. She started down them, and then what she had always feared would happen, did. Halfway down the stairs, she missed a step and tumbled.

"BRAD, YOU HAVE to help me," Claire said to the boy as she opened up the door to his cell and let herself in.

Brad was stretched out on his cot, reading a car magazine. He looked up at her. He had a short growth of peach fuzz on his cheeks, and his hair was dark with grease and messed up. He didn't look as pulled together as he usually did. But jail often did that to people—brought out the worst in them.

Claire perched on the edge of the table in his cell. "Jenny's disappeared. Mrs. Gunderson just called. Jenny never made it to school."

He tilted his head back to look at the ceiling, then stretched down an arm and set the magazine on the floor.

He groaned and sat up. "Not Jenny. I need to be home to make sure she doesn't go off the deep end. I don't think Mrs. Gunderson can handle her."

"Do you know where she might go? Is there any place that you can think of that she might have gone to? A favorite hangout?"

Brad lifted his head up and said, "I know one place she might be. A place she'd run off to when things got too rough with Dad. Kind of a retreat for her."

"Is it on your farm?"

"Yes, she would walk out to the edge of the coulee."

"Can you tell me how to get there?"

"I'll draw you a map."

Claire handed him her notebook and a pen. Brad talked as he sketched out the map. "Here's our mailbox down by the road. You walk straight out into the field from there and head toward the trees. When you get to the treeline, you'll find a path, it's pretty winding, but follow it until you can't go any farther. You'll be at the coulee. She should be somewhere near there."

"Is that where your land drops down?"

"Yeah, the drop right under the ledge she likes to hang out at is pretty steep. I'd say a hundred feet at least."

"Okay. I'll keep you posted. Thanks."

"Would you tell her if she wants to come in and see me, I'll talk to her now? Tell her I'm sorry about before."

"Sure, I'll pass that along." Claire stopped and asked him what she'd been wondering since she got the call from Mrs. Gunderson. "Brad, do you think Jenny would hurt herself?"

"You mean like suicide?" he asked.

"Yeah."

Brad held his head in his hands and shook it wearily. "She drinks, she takes drugs. I think she'd step off a cliff."

IT WAS TIME to put an end to it.

Jenny lay on the ledge above the coulee and watched the clouds slide by overhead. If she was in a plane, she could jump onto them, through them. What a feeling that would be to fall through a cloud. She could imagine the droplets of water surrounding her as she plummeted. When she thought of jumping, she felt her stomach grab hold of the rest of her body, she felt power. For once, she would decide something and act on it. She would be in control.

She was going to go on her maiden voyage today. She laughed at her own sick joke. Maiden rock, lover's leap. But the real joke was that she wasn't a maiden. Her own sick dad had seen to that. He had come sniffing up to her not long after her mother had died. He had spoiled her, ruined her.

But she wasn't going to think about that now. She was lying on the cold ledge, trying to purify her mind. She believed if she could empty it of all thoughts, like in meditation, she might go straight to nirvana.

She didn't want to think too much about where she was going. All she knew was that where she had been, she couldn't be anymore. It was too hard. Especially without Brad. And now he wouldn't even talk to her anymore. He had cut her off. She had no one.

Last night, she had yelled at Mrs. Gunderson, and now she was leaving too. There would be no place to be anymore. The farm would be sold. Nora would be taken away. She would have nothing left. Life like that was too hard.

Nora would be okay. She was so cute and sweet, she might even get adopted by some loving couple. Maybe the Snyders would adopt her. They didn't have any kids, and they had always been so nice to her.

Her mom had told her once that Pit Snyder had been her boyfriend. Her mom had said, "I should never have left him for your father. Even though he's short, he's twice the man your father will ever be.''

Jenny hoped she would be with her mother. That would be the greatest blessing in the universe. She missed her mom sometimes so much that she couldn't breathe. She had stopped thinking about her mother so that she could get on with her life and the world, as it was, wouldn't seem so bad. When she thought of her mother, she felt like someone had stabbed her in the guts. The pain of missing her mother would tear her right open.

One day, a year after her mother had died, she had bled into the toilet. She had known she was going to die, and part of her had been glad. She would see her mother again. She had been so afraid she hadn't been able to stand up. When she tried to wipe the blood away, it came again. And again. Finally Brad had yelled at her and, without opening the door, she had told him what was happening. He had gone and gotten her some paper towels and explained it to her. She had heard about menstruation in school, but had never thought it would actually happen to her.

Shortly after that, her father had found out that she was having her period and called her a real woman.

She knew Brad wouldn't understand what she was about to do. He was a real fighter. He had believed they could outsmart their father. But had they? She gave up.

Who knows? Maybe she would see him soon.

The clouds were filling her eyes.

She closed them.

The clouds were filling her mind. Her mother's face floated among them.

She couldn't remember how many pills she had taken.

TWENTY-FIVE

THE STILLNESS of the farmhouse disquieted her. Claire knocked on the kitchen door, and there was no answer. Chickens pecked and clucked out in the yard. The tractor was parked right next to the side of the barn. It almost looked as if it had run into the side of the old building.

Claire could see no one in the farmyard or out in the fields. She knocked again. Mrs. Gunderson must be around. Claire knew Mrs. Gunderson, with her failing eyesight, would not have driven off anyplace. Maybe she had called a neighbor and gone off to pick up Jenny.

When Claire tried to open the kitchen door, she found it locked. Unusual for around these parts—most people always left their doors unlocked, except at night. Which made her think that Mrs. Gunderson had gone off with someone. Possibly Jenny had called and wanted to come home. That would make sense. But then why hadn't Mrs. Gunderson left her a note?

Claire stepped back from the door and was just about to leave when she heard a faint sound, a soft mewling. She looked around to see if there was a kitten hiding in the weeds or in one of the outbuildings. She saw nothing but the chickens stalking and fluttering over the yard.

Claire stood quietly, hardly breathing, and heard it again. From the house. Something inside the house had made that noise. She needed to get in there.

She hollered, "Hello. Can you hear me?"

No response. That wasn't good.

Walking up to the window next to the door, she looked

it over. The inside window was open, but there was a screen over it. A screen was a lot easier to repair than a door. She looked inside but couldn't see anyone.

Then she heard the sound again, this time recognizable as a human voice in pain. Claire worked all the nails loose and pried off the screen. The old wood snapped, and the whole thing came loose at once. She caught it as it fell toward her and set it under the window. Then she reached in and pushed the window up. She hoisted herself up onto the window ledge and climbed through.

"Hello," she shouted.

"Help," a faint voice bleated.

Claire went toward the voice and found Mrs. Gunderson sprawled out on the floor. She was lying on her back with a leg skewed awkwardly in front of her. Her soft white hair framed a bruised face.

Claire bent down next to her and asked, "Are you okay?"

"I hurt. In my head, in my ankle." The old woman spoke softly, as if she hadn't much air in her lungs.

"You'll be okay," Claire told her.

Mrs. Gunderson licked her lips and gave a faint smile. She took a few deep breaths and then spoke again, stronger this time. "I think I got the air knocked out of me pretty good. That hasn't happened since I was a child playing on a slide."

"Let me check you over." Claire took the old woman's head in her hands and looked closely at the bruise on her face. Then she felt her arms and legs and finally touched the ankle that looked like it had been hurt. Mrs. Gunderson gulped in a quick intake of air.

"That hurts?"

"Yes, I think I twisted it."

"What happened to you?"

"I missed a blasted step. I'm usually so careful, but I'm so worried about Jenny." As soon as those words came out of her mouth, she grabbed Claire's hand. "You must go find her. I found an awful note. I think she might harm herself. You have to find her and stop her."

"Let me call someone for you."

When Claire walked over to get the phone, Mrs. Gunderson managed to sit up. Claire dialed emergency and told them to send an ambulance. "What note?" Claire asked Mrs. Gunderson when she got off the phone.

"It's upstairs. In my room."

Claire ran up the stairs and went into the first bedroom she saw. It was all straightened, the bed neatly dressed. Lying on top of the blanket was the note. Claire read it and frowned. This could mean many things, she thought, but we can't take any chances. She grabbed a pillow and the blanket off the bed and raced downstairs.

"Let's see if we can't make you more comfortable until the ambulance gets here. I don't feel that I should try to move you, but you can rest on this pillow and let me put the blanket over you."

"The note? Did you read the note?"

"Yes. Don't worry—I'll find her."

"You must go and try to find her. I'll be fine here. Leave the door open, and they'll come and help me."

"Are you sure?"

"Yes, I couldn't stand it if you stayed with me while you could have helped Jenny. I'm fine. Get me a glass of water and an ibuprofen. There's some in the drawer right next to the sink."

Claire brought her the water and pills. "Brad told me where Jenny might be. It isn't far. Out past the field. I'll go and see if Jenny is there."

MY FEET ARE DANGLING over the edge, Jenny thought as she watched her feet move below her in the dank air of the coulee. She swung them slowly back and forth, and they looked like fish swimming in the water of the air. She would soon be a fish moving through that same water.

She just had to stand up. And she didn't seem to have enough energy to do that yet. Her whole body felt heavy and wobbly, like a bowl of spaghetti noodles. The image amused her.

What she liked about taking the pills is that they let her have really cool thoughts; she saw everything in a different light. But what she didn't like about the pills is that they slowed her down—nothing seemed urgent. Sleepy. She had fallen asleep. But now she was awake, and it was time.

The sun was straight up above her. She could just make it out between the web of tree branches. It would help guide her out of the world. She would follow its beams up into the heavens.

She lifted her feet up onto the limestone ledge and slid back on her seat.

She wondered where her mother was, if she had her hands with her wherever she was.

Jenny shivered and wondered where her father was.

Time to stand.

Time to say good-bye.

Time to jump.

THE COOLNESS of the forest hit her face like a slap when Claire stepped out of the bright sunshine of the sunflower fields and into the woods that surrounded them. She knew the coulee was ahead of her—she could tell from the way the land sloped near the road—but she wasn't sure she was on the path that Brad had told her about. A faint trail was marked through the woods, and she followed it, but thought it might have been made by deer. She was thankful for the trail, even as narrow as it was, for the brambles and branches caught on her uniform, and she would have had trouble bushwhacking through the underbrush.

After following it for a few minutes, she found herself suddenly at the edge of the coulee—a drop-off in front of her that fell a good distance down before it landed in the rock-littered bottom of the coulee, the dried riverbed that held water only when it rushed off the land in the spring or after a heavy thunderstorm. The sides of the coulee were overgrown with spindly trees that could barely reach up to the light, vines that covered them and curled around fallen limbs, and towering above them all, the oak and maple and cedar that made the woods so dark.

When Claire looked down into that damp darkness, she felt her fears well up in her as if she were looking into one of her own nightmares. The coulee could be the dreamworld she inhabited at night, the place of her own horrors, the edge of reality. She started to shake and thought of running back out into the sun.

But then she saw Jenny and knew she had to get to her fast.

Jenny was standing close to the edge of a rock ledge that hung out over the coulee. Claire thought Brad's estimate of the fall from the ledge to the bottom of the coulee was about right—a good hundred-foot drop. Jenny was about twenty yards away from Claire. Her arms were stretched up into the air in a form of salutation, and Claire was afraid that any sound or movement from her would send the girl into the void.

She started to sneak up on her. A silent prayer—Let me get to her and pull her back from the edge. Don't let another person die in this family.

Jenny had her eyes closed, and she was facing away from

the coulee. She seemed to be singing or chanting something. Claire couldn't hear what she was saying.

Claire had to watch where she was putting her feet down so she didn't step on a twig or walk into a branch. As a child, she had practiced moving silently through the forest around her house. Then she had walked in tennis shoes. Her heavy black shoes didn't make it very easy to move silently, but she tried to be as quiet as she could.

Claire reached the beginning of the limestone outcropping that formed the ledge, about ten feet away from Jenny. She decided that if she had a chance she would grab the black belt that was buckled around Jenny's waist and pull her back to safety. She didn't know how she would have a chance to grab it, though, as any movement toward Jenny would automatically cause her to pull back, and that would send her plummeting over the edge.

Jenny looked younger than fifteen years old. Her sandy blond hair was parted in the middle and hung below her shoulders in a style reminiscent of Alice in Wonderland. She was wearing a plain white T-shirt and baggy jeans, loose clothes that made her look thinner than Claire remembered. On her feet a pair of boots stuck out from under the jeans. A typical teenager—one who deserved to live.

She could hear what Jenny was saying now. She was chanting one word: "Away, away, away, away, away, away…"

Then Jenny opened her eyes and saw Claire. Claire took a step backward so she wouldn't feel threatened.

Jenny stood her ground and smiled at her, seemingly not surprised to see Claire. "You've come to watch me jump?"

"No, I've come to talk to you."

"There's not much to talk about anymore. It's all been decided. The son has put his head upon the altar and is the sacrificial lamb, so to speak."

"That's what Brad has done?"

"Yes." Jenny nodded her head slowly. "He's such a good boy, isn't he? Always takes care of everything. Mom loved him. She loved me too."

Claire thought she could work with this statement. "I bet she did. And she wouldn't want you to jump. She'd want you to live."

Jenny cocked her head. "You didn't know our mother, did you?"

"No."

"That's too bad. It wasn't her fault."

Claire realized that Jenny was using her as a witness. That the dialogue was one that was already written in Jenny's mind, and Claire might as well hear it out. She hoped there would be an opening for her, a way to reach Jenny, to rewrite this script into one where she could also hear what Claire had to say. "What wasn't her fault?"

"What Dad did."

"What did your father do?"

Jenny hunched her shoulders and pulled her arms in close to her body, wrapping them over her thin chest. "He decided that I could be the mom after he killed her. He started coming to my bed."

Claire's heart sunk. "He shouldn't have done that."

"No one could stop him. He told me it was the way it was supposed to be. It was my turn."

"I'm so sorry."

"Yes, I'm not a maiden any longer."

"It wasn't your fault. Your father was an evil man."

Jenny thought about it for a moment. "I think it was my fault. If I hadn't been a pretty girl—my dad said I was pretty, when he did it to me he told me how pretty I was—then he would have left me alone. Nora's quite pretty too, isn't she?"

"Yes, Nora's a pretty girl."

"So you see, it was my fault. He said he would kill Brad if I told anyone. He even told me how he would kill him. He said it would look like an accident. He would run over him with the tractor. He never let me drive the tractor, but Brad did. Brad taught me how to drive it. But then I crashed the tractor. I couldn't even do that right."

"Jenny, come over here and sit down and tell me what happened."

Jenny shuffled in place. "Don't say that to me. Don't tell me what to do. I shouldn't even be talking to you."

"Why?"

"Because I'm bad."

"Why?"

Jenny's face cleared. "Don't you know? It's because of me my father died. That was my knife. I had started carrying it with me. I wasn't going to let Dad touch me anymore. When Dad and Brad started fighting, I pulled out the knife."

"You killed your father? Not Brad?"

"Brad didn't do it. He just said that to take care of me. He always has to take care of me. Mom told him to. But he couldn't stop Dad from coming to my room. He tried once. That's when Dad broke his arm. He said that would show us. That would teach us a lesson. Brad never tried to stop him again."

"Why did you kill him, Jenny? Did you kill your father because he was molesting you?"

"No. I was used to that. That isn't why. Why we were fighting was because he said that it was just about time to try out Nora. He told Brad and me that he was going to sleep with Nora."

"Nora? Your little sister?"

"Yes. She's too little. He shouldn't do that to her."

"You are right, Jenny. You are absolutely right. You stopped your father from hurting Nora."

Jenny's face crumpled. "But you don't understand. I loved my father. I loved him, and now he's dead. How could that happen?"

"I do understand."

"No, you don't." Without looking behind her, Jenny took a step back toward the edge. Another foot or so, and she would fall. "Nobody will ever understand me. You haven't tried to kill anyone."

Claire felt her heart being wrenched out of her body. She had to stop Jenny. She had to break through to her. Maybe this was the way to get through to Jenny—her own confession. Let her know she wasn't alone. "I do understand. I killed someone too. I killed someone I loved."

Jenny stopped moving backward and looked straight at Claire for the first time. "You did?"

"Yes, it was in a fight, like you. I shot him."

Jenny took another step away from the edge. "You shot him? Did you know he would die?"

"Yes, I was pretty sure he would."

Jenny crumpled onto the limestone ledge, wailing out her plaintive words. "I wasn't sure Dad would die, but he did. I wanted to teach him a lesson. I loved him. He's dead. I loved him."

Claire leaned over Jenny, took a firm hold of the black belt that circled her waist, and comforted her.

TWENTY-SIX

WHEN ONE OF the supervisors came for Jenny in her room in the juvenile detention center and told her that Pit Snyder was there to see her, Jenny was not surprised. She had been expecting him.

She had been in the center for not quite a week. They were trying to get her in to see a counselor, but she was balking. She didn't want to talk about her father and what he had done to her. Other than that, she was trying to be agreeable and fit in. She went to the gym every day and read a lot. With no Darvocet to mute the world, she was using books to escape.

The only person she liked to talk to was her lawyer. He was a tall and lanky man who treated her like she was smart, and he was on her side. Mr. Byron was pretty sure that he could get a sentence deal, factoring in that she was a juvenile, only fifteen, that her father had killed her mother, that he had molested her and threatened her younger sister, and that at the time he was killed, he was fighting with her brother. He said if they weren't lucky, she might have to spend a year in juvenile. But he thought there was a good chance that she would be released with counseling and probation. Mrs. Gunderson had decided to stay on for a while and take care of Nora, so she would have a home to go back to.

She went to the mirror in her room and checked her hair. She was wearing it pulled back from her face in a ponytail, and she liked it that way. It kept the strands of hair off her face, and it was tidy. She knew her mother would approve.

Her mother had always told her she had a pretty face, that there was no reason to hide it. But the hairstyle made her look plain and simple. Not a bad way to appear. Then people left you alone.

She had been sleeping better in the dormitory than she had slept for years at home, even though it was often noisy. At least she didn't have to lie awake wondering if her father would decide to come into her room that night.

She patted her hair and followed the guard down to the visiting room.

Pit Snyder sat at a table, and he stood up when she came in. Jenny liked that. It made her feel like an adult. She looked him over. He was wearing a denim workshirt and a clean pair of jeans. On his feet he had Red Wing workboots. She remembered her mom telling her that he was a contractor and he built houses. He dressed the part. Even though he was a short man, he carried himself well. It made him appear important.

He smiled at her, a smile that broke open his face and almost made him handsome. Jenny could see why her mother might have liked him.

"Hi, Jenny," he said.

"Hi, Mr. Snyder. I thought you might show up." She sat down opposite him at the table, and he sat down again.

"Sorry I didn't come sooner," he said.

Jenny leaned in close to him, even though they were alone in the room, and whispered, "Thanks for helping out Brad and me."

"Listen, that's what I came in to talk to you about."

"Brad and I have already talked. We're fine with everything the way it is." Jenny remembered all too clearly the fight at the street dance. She had not been that out of it at the time. Right afterward, she had taken a pill to forget it. She and Brad had run into their father. He had been pretty loaded. He started making comments about Jenny, about what he did with her in bed, then he mentioned Nora. That's when Brad went ballistic.

"I don't want you taking the blame for what happened," Mr. Snyder said.

Jenny was prepared for this. "My father is to blame for what happened. Don't worry about it."

Brad had slugged his father, and then Jed turned on him. Jenny was afraid her father would pound Brad until there was nothing left. She pulled out the knife, slashed at her father, but she couldn't do it. She couldn't stab him with it. She was too afraid.

"I'm going to turn myself in," he said.

Jenny looked at Mr. Snyder and shook her head. "No, you're not."

Then Mr. Snyder had appeared. He had heard what her father had said about sleeping with her and Nora. She knew this because he told her father to keep his hands off his girls. Jed called him a little prick who couldn't keep a woman, then turned toward Jenny and grabbed her. Mr. Snyder took the knife from her hands and stabbed her father. Her father had let go of her and dropped to the ground. It had happened so fast. A few seconds of time, and everything had changed. No, she would never forget it.

"Don't even think about it. Brad and I have decided that we won't let you. We both agreed that I will say I did it. After all, it was my knife. If I hadn't been trying to kill him, you would never have done it."

"It doesn't feel right to me."

"Have you talked to the lawyer, Mr. Byron? You hired him; I assume you talk to him. He thinks I'm going to get off easy. So don't sweat it. Just tell me why you did it. Why did you step in like that?"

Pit tilted back in his chair. "Because of what he was

saying to you. I couldn't stand it. The idea of him molesting you."

"But why do you care so much?" Jenny wanted to know. She felt like this man had a connection to her life that she had never understood.

"Where to start? Did you know that your mom and I went out together in high school?"

"Yes, she told me."

Pit's face lit up. "She did?"

"Oh, yeah. She would kind of brag about you."

"Really? Oh, that's nice. Then you probably know that after I went off to Vietnam, she married your father."

Jenny nodded. She wondered where he was going with this story.

"After Brad was born, your parents had some problems. Your father could be cruel to your mother sometimes. And I wasn't married at the time. Rainey came to me and told me how bad things were. And, well, we started seeing each other again for a while."

"You did?" Jenny was surprised by this information. Her mother hadn't mentioned this. "You mean like you were sleeping together?"

"Yeah—it was all my fault. Your mother was in a vulnerable position, and I took advantage of her. I should have tried to help her out more, but I loved her."

"I'm glad. I'm glad Mom got some more time with you. It probably was good for her. My dad could be a real prick."

"Yeah, well, I hope it was good for her. But then she went back to your father. And you were born not too long after."

Jenny didn't say anything. She was watching Mr. Snyder. He seemed very uncomfortable. He wouldn't look at her, and he was twisting a piece of paper in his hands. She felt like grabbing it away from him.

"Then I met Ruth and married her. Your mother and I didn't see each other, except in passing. Until four years ago. Right before your mother died. She called me and asked me to help her. She wanted to get away from your father and take all you kids. And she told me something else."

Pit stopped again. He was sweating. Obviously, this was hard for him. Jenny was getting very puzzled. What was he talking about?

"She told me something that I didn't know what to do with, but I feel I need to tell you."

"What?" Jenny felt like screaming at him, but she asked it as quietly and politely as she could.

"It looks like I'm your father."

Jenny stood up. Her chair fell over backward. She turned away from Pit Snyder. She had to think. Her father wasn't her father. The world was spinning around in a way she had never thought it would. What had been up was down. Left danced with right. Brad and Nora's father was not her father. She felt released. She could take more steps away from that man. It would be okay to hate him. She could love him a little less and hate him a little more.

Jenny turned around. "My father?"

Snyder nodded. His eyes were squinted into thin lines. "What do you think?" he asked, his voice breaking.

Jenny couldn't help it. She had to ask him. "What do you think?"

He spoke without taking a moment to think about it. "I'm absolutely thrilled. I've always wanted a daughter."

Jenny looked at this short, pudgy man and wondered what they might find to talk about or what they might do together.

"What about you?" he asked.

"I always believed I had a real father somewhere."

THE QUILT HUNG ON the wall in the living room. Ruth said that her grandmother had done it. Claire couldn't believe how lovely it was—a creamy white with the smallest stitches imaginable, a floral design all around the edges and a checkerboard in the middle. Some parts of the quilt looked padded. She reached out a finger and touched it. What a treasure.

"I'll never be able to make a quilt like that."

"Well, certainly not right away. It's good to start small," Ruth said as she showed Claire another quilt. "This is the first quilt I ever did. That was about fifteen years ago. Even though it's small, it was fairly ambitious with the appliqués."

Claire held up the quilt. A white background with two kittens in the middle and pussy willows sewn around the border. "It's so sweet."

"I thought I might use it as a crib blanket. Then, after I married Pit, I found out I couldn't have children."

"I'm so sorry."

"Yeah, me too."

Claire looked at the stitches on the quilt. "Your stitches are so even."

"Thanks—on that piece they weren't very small. There's about five stitches an inch. Now I can do closer to ten. I do all of my piecing on the machine, but I hand-stitch all the parts that will show. Have you done anything like this before?"

"I embroidered when I was in high school, especially my last year, when I was doing a lot of baby-sitting. It was in style. Workshirts with embroidered collars. I like to hand sew." Claire remembered that year well; she had given everyone in her family embroidered shirts for Christmas.

Ruth led her back to the sewing room. "Would you like to try to do some stitching on the piece I'm working on?"

Claire loved the room they walked into: three large windows looking out over the backyard and a small pond, one whole wall of shelves full of material in all colors and patterns, a large table to work on, and a sewing machine on the opposite wall. A large overstuffed chair had a quilt curled up in it. Ruth held the quilt out to Claire.

"Are you sure?"

"Why not? I can use all the help I can get."

Ruth showed her how to put the piece in a quilting hoop and how to hold it in her lap. Then she threaded the thin needle for her and gave her a demonstration of how to move the needle quickly in and out of the fabric. She would pile up about four stitches on the needle, then push it through, then do it again.

Ruth handed it to Claire, and Claire tried to follow her example. She could only get a couple stitches on the needle before she needed to push it through the fabric. Her stitches were more than twice as long as Ruth's.

"This is harder than it looks."

"You'll catch on. You have the basics down. I've taught women who have never held a needle in their hand before."

Claire tried it a little longer and then handed it back to Ruth. Ruth started stitching away on the quilt, and Claire loved watching the easy rhythm of her hands.

"What's going to happen to Jenny?" Ruth asked.

"It's not completely clear yet. But they are still working on the deal. I have a feeling that she won't do much more time at the juvenile center than she's already done. The elements of the case are all in her favor: her age, the abuse, the threats. I just hope the kid gets some help."

"Good."

"It's been really nice to Pit of hire a lawyer for her."

"Well, I think Pit feels he has a kind of responsibility to the kids, because of his relationship with their mother. There's a chance that Pit and I will become foster parents for Jenny and Nora. Brad's going to be leaving in the spring. I think he's pretty sure he's going to enlist in the army and get some training. Pit went and helped him harvest the rest of the sunflowers. They talked." Ruth put her quilt down and looked at Claire. "I think he wants to get away from here."

"Yeah, I don't blame him."

"Do you think Jenny will be able to get over what happened to her?"

Claire thought about the thin teenage girl who had stood up to her father in the most brutal of ways. "She won't get over it, but maybe she'll come through it."

A FEW WEEKS after Jenny Spitzler was arrested for murdering her father, Rich got a call from Claire. She mentioned that Meg had gone to stay with her aunt Bridget for the weekend and wondered what he was doing that night.

"Would you like to come over?" she asked.

He was surprised to find he wasn't sure. He had fallen in love with Claire, but now he wasn't sure she was someone he could trust with that love.

"Rich?"

"Yes," he said.

"Are you thinking about it?"

"I am, as a matter of fact." Questions roiled around in his head, and finally he asked, "Did you think I would just wait for you?"

"I hoped."

He softened. "I suppose I could come for a drink."

"We can see what happens, right?"

"We can see."

After he was finished with all his nightly chores, Rich showered and shaved and put on clean clothes. He decided to walk over. It was only half a mile's walk, and that way the neighbors would see no car in the driveway.

Night was falling quickly, and by the time he was close to her house, he was walking in darkness. The stars were blurred spots in the sky. The wind blew through the trees and rattled leaves.

When Claire answered the door, he saw that she had her hair down and was wearing a pretty soft blue sweater and jeans. He wanted to gather her up in his arms, but he resisted.

"Come on in," she said. "I made an apple pie, and I thought hot rum toddies might go good with that."

"You made an apple pie?"

"I got State Fair apples from the orchard on my way home. They're an early apple."

"I know."

"Oh, yes, I forgot you're mister I-know-everything-about-the-country man." She moved in close to him and poked him in the side.

"You don't get to poke me."

"Why not?"

"Because we haven't made up yet."

"Whose fault is that? I've declared a truce. Invited you over, made pie, and you won't even give me a kiss."

Accepting the challenge, he pulled her close and kissed her. He could swear he tasted nutmeg on her lips. She must have sampled the pie.

After a few more kisses, they settled down on the couch next to each other with pie and toddies and a fire going in the woodstove.

"How's your therapy going?" He figured it was time to ask.

"I'm making progress, and now I even know what that means."

"Really?"

"Yeah. Not that I don't have a lot more work to do, but I think I've got some things in place to help me. I haven't had a bad dream for over a week, and the last one I had didn't scare me that much. It's almost as if my body, my adrenaline system, is calming down."

"So have you figured out why this has been happening to you?"

"It's pretty clear that it's a direct result of Bruce Jacobs's death."

"It must have been hard to see your partner shot. Especially since you were so close to him."

"I have to tell you something, Rich." She reached toward him and took both of his hands in hers, as if she needed his strength and support to go on with what she had started. "When I called and invited you over, I didn't tell you that I had something to tell you, because that's what I said last time and I was afraid it would scare you off."

"Now you've got me good and scared."

She bent her head forward in front of him, and her hair fell down each side of her face so he couldn't see her.

"You know the night it happened, when Bruce was killed?" She lifted her head up and flung her hair back over her shoulders. She looked him straight in the eyes.

He nodded.

"Well, I suspected that he was behind my husband's death."

He stayed silent. Let her keep going.

"That night I found out for sure that he was. And that

he was also responsible for Bridget being shot and the attempted kidnapping of Meg.''

Rich couldn't keep quiet. ''That bastard.''

''Yes. So what I told you about what happened that night wasn't true. Bruce did kill Red. But Red didn't kill Bruce. I did. I shot him. He was turning toward me with the gun in his hands that had just killed Red. I had my gun in my hands. So I pulled the trigger and killed him.''

Rich was stunned. Feelings shifted in his mind like boulders being tumbled down a mountain. Claire had killed Bruce, her partner. She might have loved him at one time, but she killed him.

She squeezed his hands. ''What do you think?''

Rich didn't think he could say anything that would make sense. What a horrible burden she had been carrying around with her for the last half a year. No wonder she was having nightmares.

He gathered her up in his arms and held her tight.

When I drove here, up along the river, I felt like I could now see the bones of the land. I love this time of year when the leaves come off the trees, the underbrush sinks down, the colors mute. Dark brown trees against the graying grass. All that is gaudy and bold is stripped away. We are back to the bones.

Why are you thinking of that?

I feel like my life is like that now. I've stripped away so much. My fears, my guilt, my high emotions. I take great joy now in getting up in the morning and watching for the turkey out the kitchen window while I make coffee. I have these perfect moments of contentment. I hold my breath to keep them.

How is your quilting going?

That's part of it. The handwork. The quiet. The doing something useful.

What about your police work? Isn't that useful?

It's necessary. I don't want to change my job. But I've gotten over the thrill of it, the urgency of each case, the rush of the work. I'm beginning to like the slower pace in this border county.

Good. How are you doing with your guilt around the man you killed?

I've talked about it. With two people. And the weight of it is now shared. I feel the difference in my body. I walk more easily. *I don't expect anyone to understand what I did, or completely condone it, but I have found a kind of peace.*

And? Were you going to say something more?

I would do it again.

Camille Minichino

The Beryllium Murder

A GLORIA LAMERINO MYSTERY

Physicist-sleuth Gloria Lamerino heads back to her old stomping grounds in Berkeley, California, to look into the death of a former colleague, Gary Larkin, dead of beryllium poisoning. Though his death has been ruled accidental, Gloria is suspicious: Gary was much too aware of the hazards of this dangerous element to be so reckless in his handling of it.

The pieces of the puzzle come together like a new molecular formula for homicide: Internet pornography, hacking, extortion, jealousy and revenge—and a killer making murder into a science.

"It's a good thing the periodic table is big enough for 100 more adventures."
—Janet Evanovich, author of *Hot Six*

Available October 2001 at your favorite retail outlet.

Kathleen Anne Barrett

Milwaukee
Autumns
Can Be
LETHAL

A BETH HARTLEY MYSTERY

Lawyer turned legal researcher and amateur
sleuth, Beth Hartley is hired to do some
work for an old law school acquaintance,
Don Balstrum. But when she finds Don
murdered in his office, her meticulous
mind for details leads her immediately
on the path of a complex crime.

With her tenacity and insight into
the legal profession, she soon opens
many dark doors into Don's world: his
unforgiving father, his antagonistic twin
brother, his cagey business partners and
his ex-wife—all with secrets to hide.

Available October 2001 at your favorite retail outlet.

WORLDWIDE LIBRARY ®

WKAB399